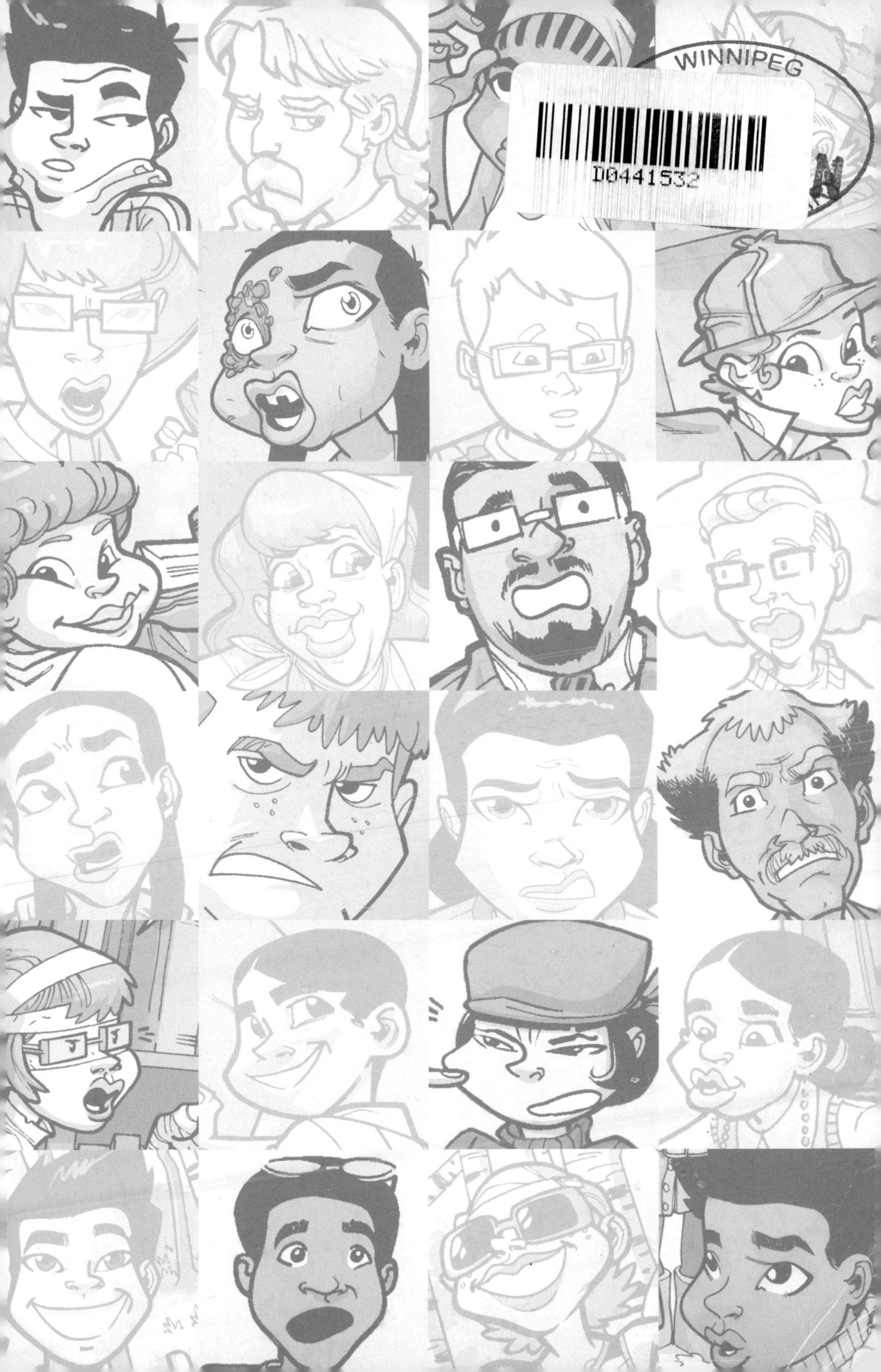

ALSO IN THE SERIES

Max Finder Mystery Collected Casebook, Volume 1
2007 Winner for Graphic Novel,
The Association of Educational Publishers'
Distinguished Achievement Award

Max Finder Mystery Collected Casebook, Volume 2
2008 Winner for Graphic Novel,
The Association of Educational Publishers'
Distinguished Achievement Award

Max Finder Mystery Collected Casebook, Volume 3
2008 Finalist for Graphic Novel,
The Association of Educational Publishers'
Distinguished Achievement Award

Max Finder Mystery Collected Casebook, Volume 4

Max Finder Mystery
Collected Casebook

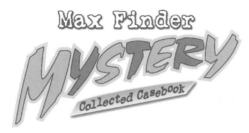

Volume 5

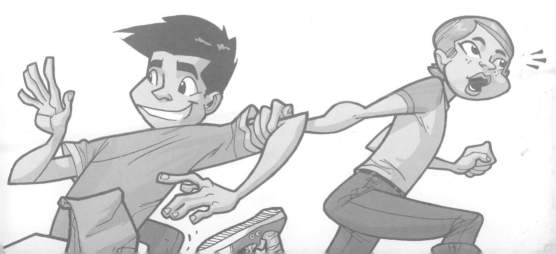

© 2011 Owlkids Books Inc.
10 Lower Spadina Avenue, Suite 400, Toronto, Ontario M5V 2Z2
www.owlkids.com

Text © 2011 Liam O'Donnell (The Case of the Bullied Bully, The Case of the Cheerleader Cheat)

Distributed in Canada by Raincoast Books
2440 Viking Way, Richmond, British Columbia V6V 1N2

Distributed in the United States by Publishers Group West
1700 Fourth Street, Berkeley, California 94710

Library and Archives Canada Cataloguing in Publication

O'Donnell, Liam, 1970-
        Max Finder mystery : collected casebook / Liam O'Donnell, Michael Cho.

Vol. 4 by Liam O'Donnell, Craig Battle, Ramón Pérez. Vol. 5. by Craig Battle,
    Liam O' Donnell, Ramón Pérez.
Vol. 5 issued also in electronic format.
ISBN 2-89579-116-3 (v. 1).--ISBN 978-2-89579-116-4 (pbk. : v. 1).--ISBN
978-1-926818-02-3 (bound : v. 1).--ISBN 978-2-89579-121-8 (pbk. : v.
2).--ISBN 978-1-926818-03-0 (bound : v. 2).--ISBN 978-2-89579-149-2 (pbk.
: v. 3).--ISBN 978-1-926818-04-7 (bound : v. 3).--ISBN 978-1-897349-80-9
(pbk. : v. 4).--ISBN 978-1-926818-05-4 (bound : v. 4).--ISBN
978-1-926818-11-5 (bound : v. 5).--ISBN 978-1-926818-12-2 (pbk. : v. 5)

        1. Detective and mystery comic books, strips, etc. 2. Mystery games.
I. Cho, Michael II. Battle, Craig, 1980- III. Pérez, Ramón IV. Title.

PN6733.O36M38 2006   j741.5'971   C2006-903300-5

Library of Congress Control Number: 2009935531

Series Design: John Lightfoot/Lightfoot Art & Design Inc.
Design and Art Direction: Susan Sinclair

Canada Council   Conseil des Arts
for the Arts   du Canada

ONTARIO ARTS COUNCIL
CONSEIL DES ARTS DE L'ONTARIO

We acknowledge the financial support of the Canada Council for the Arts, the Ontario Arts Council,
the Government of Canada through the Canada Book Fund (CBF), and the Government of Ontario
through the Ontario Media Development Corporation's Book Initiative for our publishing activities.

Manufactured by Sheck Wah Tong Printing Press Ltd.
Manufactured in Guang Dong, China in December 2010
Job #51107

A   B   C   D   E   F

 Publisher of Chirp, chickaDEE and OWL
www.owlkids.com

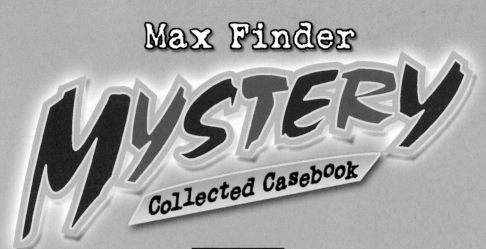

Max Finder
MYSTERY
Collected Casebook

Volume 5

Craig Battle and Ramón Pérez

Created by Liam O'Donnell

Owl
kids

Max Finder MYSTERY Collected Casebook

Contents

Comics

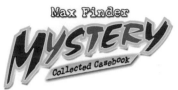

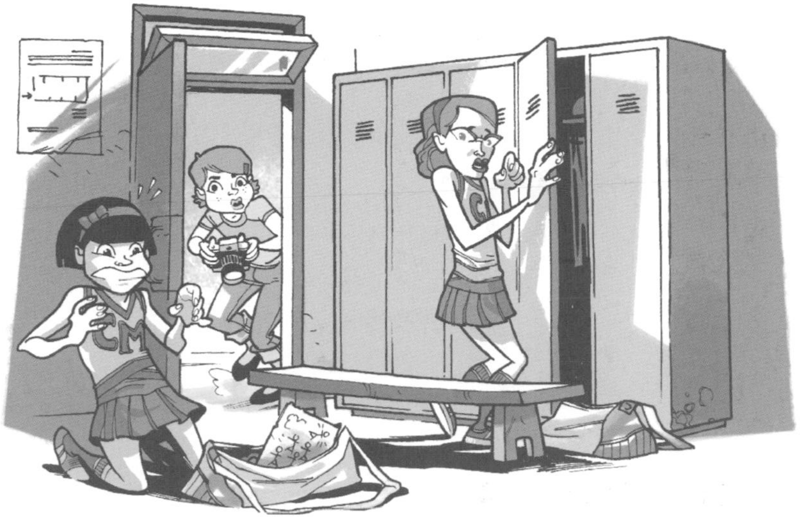
CM
CM

Stories

Extra Stuff

Collected
Casebook
Volume 5

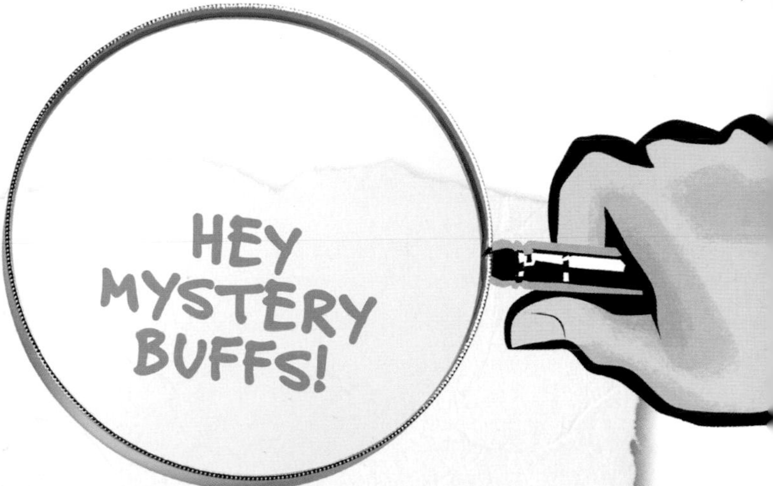

HEY MYSTERY BUFFS!

Did you know that the book in your hands features a whopping ten comics and two short stories? Max Finder here, fact collector and junior high detective. In our hometown of Whispering Meadows, my best friend Alison and I are the go-to investigators of mysteries big and small. This casebook collects some of our best moments yet.

From the **Cafeteria Crisis** all the way to the **Campsite Crime Spree**, each mystery is crammed with enough clues, suspects, and red herrings to keep you guessing until the end. We've done all the legwork, but solving the mystery is up to you! Read the mysteries, watch for clues, and try to crack the case. Solutions are at the end of each comic. But remember: real detectives never peek.

So fire up your mystery radar and get solving!

Max

P.S. Check out our school yearbook starting on page 11, and go to page 89 to sharpen your detective skills with tips from Alison and me!

CENTRAL MEADOWS Junior High YEARBOOK

Go Meteors

It tickles me and makes me laugh to think you want

My autograph crystal

Yay Summer.

Leslie Chang
Clubs/sports: Beauty Brigade
Most likely to: throw her own surprise party
Favorite movie: *Princess Protection Program, The Princess and the Frog, The Princess Diaries* (tie)

Crystal Diallo
Clubs/sports: Manga Club, Healthy-Eating Club
Most likely to: stage a protest in favor of shorter school hours
Role model: Buffy the Vampire Slayer

Max Finder
Clubs/sports: Soccer, Knowledge Bowl, Junior Detectives Society
Most likely to: work for the FBI
Favorite quote: "Once you eliminate the impossible, whatever remains... must be the truth."
– Sir Arthur Conan Doyle

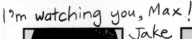

I'm watching you, Max!
Jake

Jake Granger
Clubs/sports: Magician's Society, School Newspaper
Most likely to: vanish before a big test
Role model: Harry Houdini

Nanda Kanwar
Clubs/sports: Drama, Hockey, Basketball, Beauty Brigade
Most likely to: play in the WNBA

WHO'S UP FOR SUMMER SCHOOL?
MR. REED

PUNCH YOU LATER, FINDER!!
BASHER

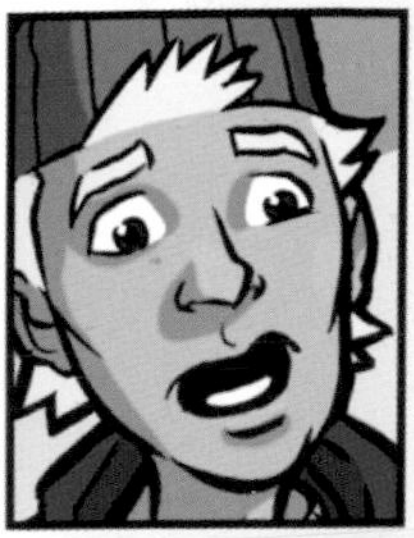

Kyle Kressman
Clubs/sports: none (but I've pranked them all!)
Most likely to: put something in Jello
Favorite quote: "Gotcha!" – Kyle Kressman, Esq.

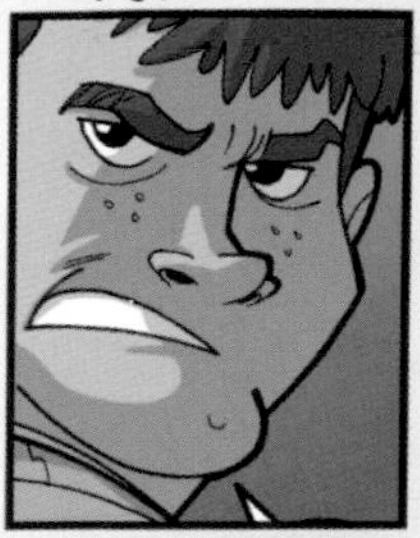

Ben McGintley
Nickname: Basher
Clubs/sports: Hockey, Soccer, Healthy-Eating Club
Most likely to: need a lawyer

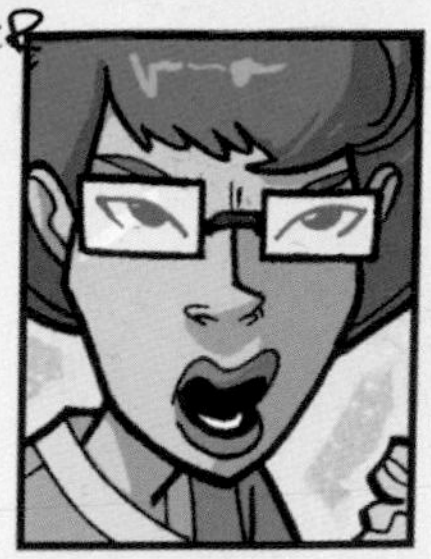

Dorothy Pafko
Clubs/sports: Chess, Drama
Most likely to: win the science fair
Favorite quote: "Nothing in life is to be feared..." – Marie Curie

What's that behind you?! Made you look!
Kyle

Have a great summer, Max!
Zoe

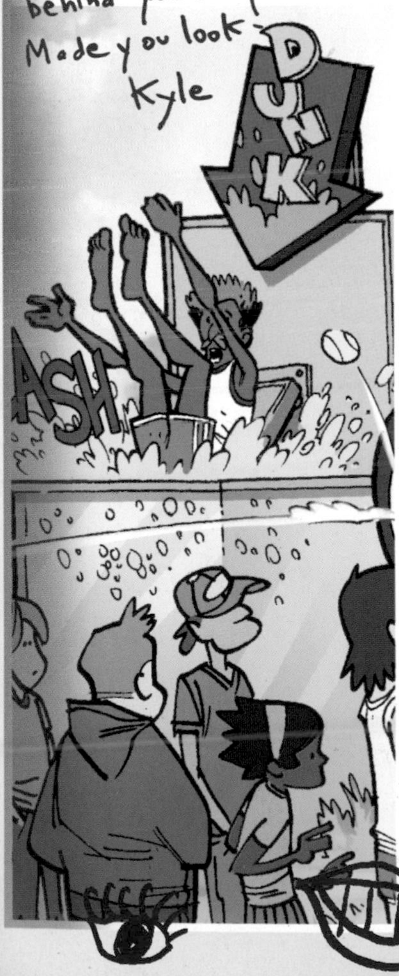
DUNK
ASH

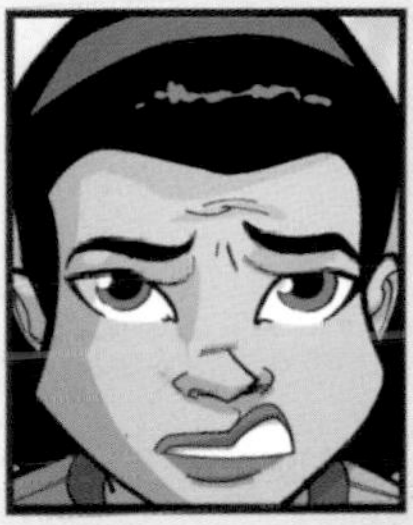

Zoe Palgrave
Clubs/sports: Junior Detectives Society
Most likely to: dig through the garbage for clues
Favorite show: *C.S.I.*

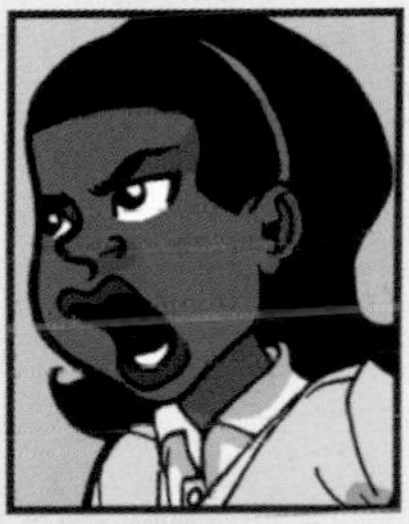

Jessica Peeves
Clubs/sports: Track
Most likely to: be Googling herself right now
Role model: Oprah

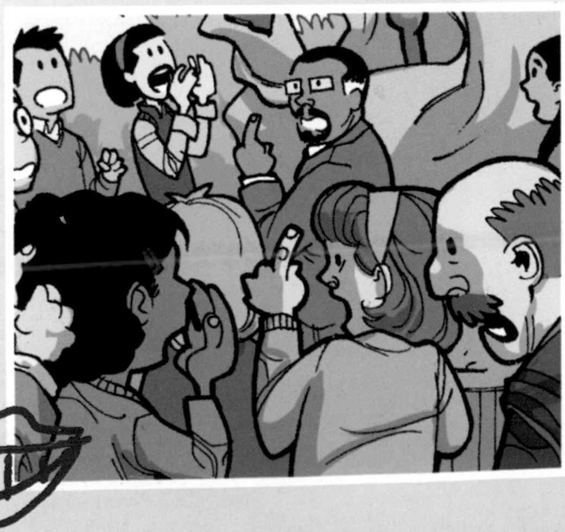

Have a great summer, Max! Alex

Sasha Price
Clubs/sports: no thanks!
Most likely to: wouldn't you like to know?
Favorite quote: "Here's your allowance, Sasha!" — my parents

Alex Rodriguez
Clubs/sports: Chess Club, Drama Club, Flying Ace Model Plane Club, Knowledge Bowl
Most likely to: become President
Favorite show: *The Apprentice*

Alison Santos
Clubs/sports: Soccer, School Newspaper, Junior Detectives Society
Most likely to: uncover a political conspiracy
Favorite saying: "Let me help you with that, Max!"

Catch you later, Max
Ethan

Josh Spodek
Nickname: Rumbler
Clubs/sports: Basketball, Baseball
Least likely to: be seen without Ethan Webster

Ethan Webster
Clubs/sports: Cross Country, Basketball, Baseball
Least likely to: be seen without Josh Spodek
Favorite quote: "There is no 'I' in 'team,' but there is in 'win.'" — Michael Jordan

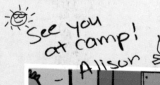

See you at camp!
Alison

From the desk of Max Finder

The Case of the...

Cafeteria Crisis

W T
MENU
DISP
HOME

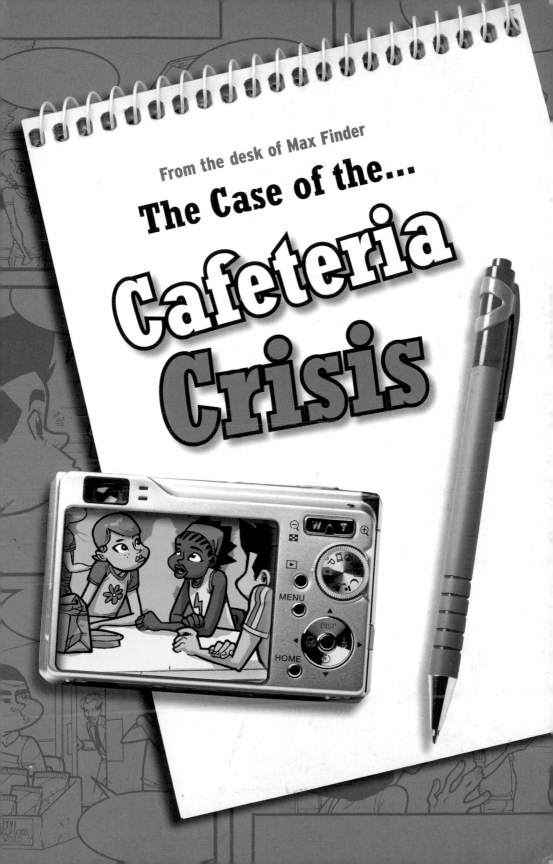

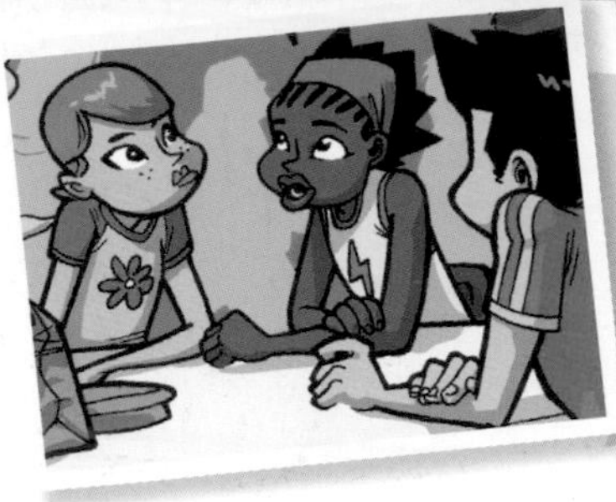

The Case of the... Cafeteria Crisis

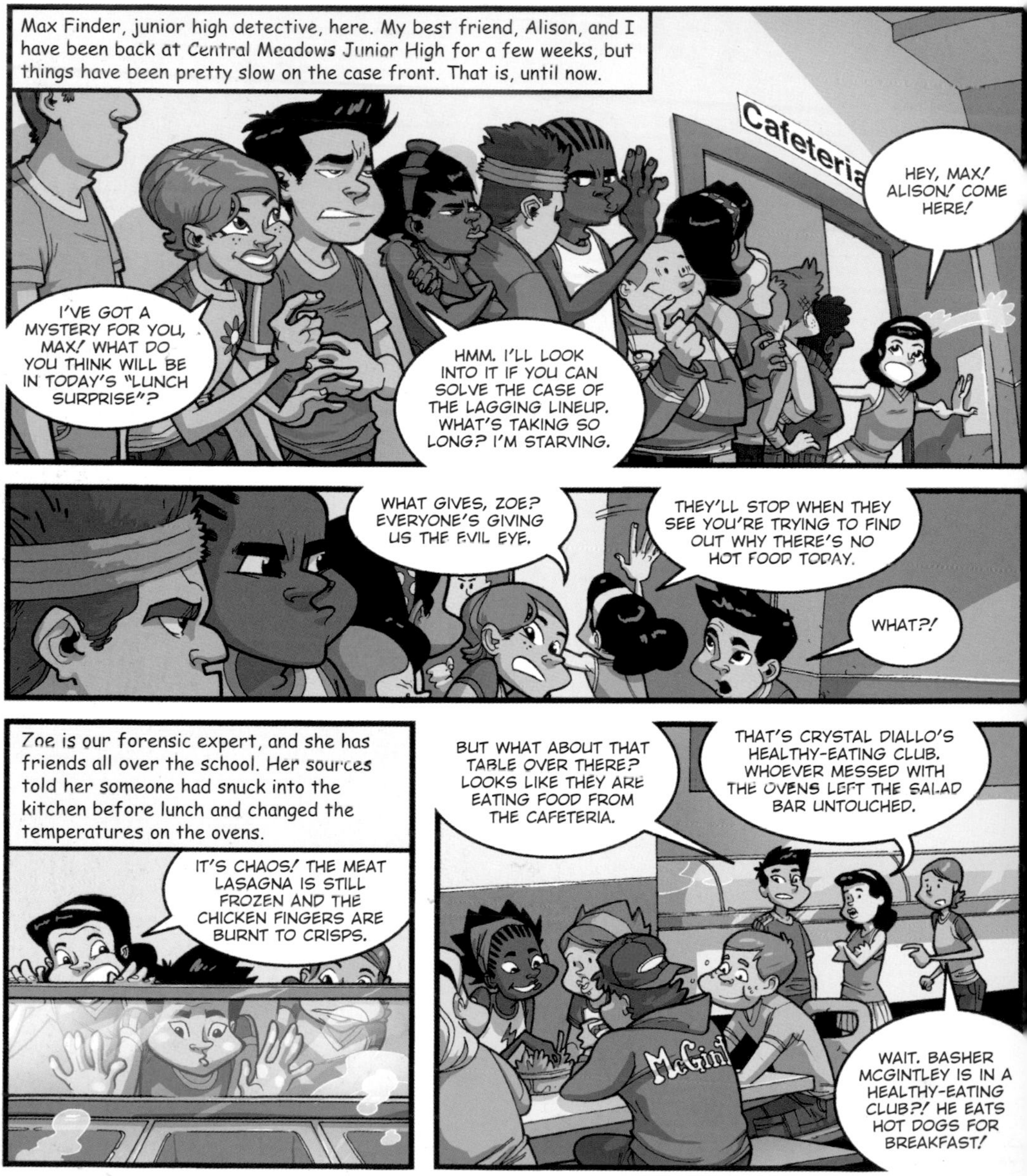

Max Finder, junior high detective, here. My best friend, Alison, and I have been back at Central Meadows Junior High for a few weeks, but things have been pretty slow on the case front. That is, until now.
Cafeteria
I'VE GOT A MYSTERY FOR YOU, MAX! WHAT DO YOU THINK WILL BE IN TODAY'S "LUNCH SURPRISE"?
HMM. I'LL LOOK INTO IT IF YOU CAN SOLVE THE CASE OF THE LAGGING LINEUP. WHAT'S TAKING SO LONG? I'M STARVING.
HEY, MAX! ALISON! COME HERE!
WHAT GIVES, ZOE? EVERYONE'S GIVING US THE EVIL EYE.
THEY'LL STOP WHEN THEY SEE YOU'RE TRYING TO FIND OUT WHY THERE'S NO HOT FOOD TODAY.
WHAT?!
Zoe is our forensic expert, and she has friends all over the school. Her sources told her someone had snuck into the kitchen before lunch and changed the temperatures on the ovens.
IT'S CHAOS! THE MEAT LASAGNA IS STILL FROZEN AND THE CHICKEN FINGERS ARE BURNT TO CRISPS.
BUT WHAT ABOUT THAT TABLE OVER THERE? LOOKS LIKE THEY ARE EATING FOOD FROM THE CAFETERIA.
THAT'S CRYSTAL DIALLO'S HEALTHY-EATING CLUB. WHOEVER MESSED WITH THE OVENS LEFT THE SALAD BAR UNTOUCHED.
WAIT. BASHER MCGINTLEY IS IN A HEALTHY-EATING CLUB?! HE EATS HOT DOGS FOR BREAKFAST!

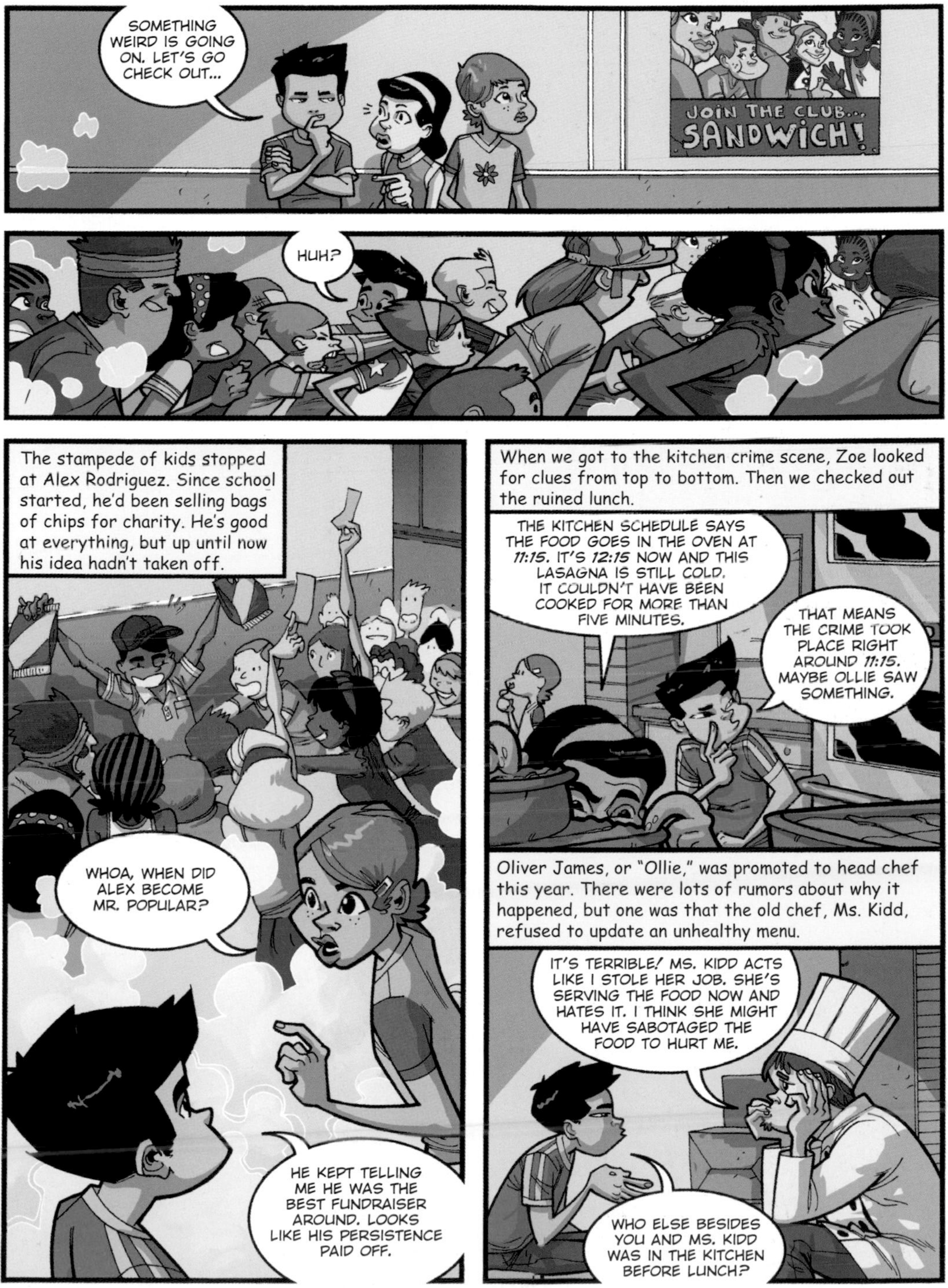
SOMETHING WEIRD IS GOING ON. LET'S GO CHECK OUT...
JOIN THE CLUB... SANDWICH!
HUH?
The stampede of kids stopped at Alex Rodriguez. Since school started, he'd been selling bags of chips for charity. He's good at everything, but up until now his idea hadn't taken off.
WHOA, WHEN DID ALEX BECOME MR. POPULAR?
HE KEPT TELLING ME HE WAS THE BEST FUNDRAISER AROUND. LOOKS LIKE HIS PERSISTENCE PAID OFF.
When we got to the kitchen crime scene, Zoe looked for clues from top to bottom. Then we checked out the ruined lunch.
THE KITCHEN SCHEDULE SAYS THE FOOD GOES IN THE OVEN AT 11:15. IT'S 12:15 NOW AND THIS LASAGNA IS STILL COLD. IT COULDN'T HAVE BEEN COOKED FOR MORE THAN FIVE MINUTES.
THAT MEANS THE CRIME TOOK PLACE RIGHT AROUND 11:15. MAYBE OLLIE SAW SOMETHING.
Oliver James, or "Ollie," was promoted to head chef this year. There were lots of rumors about why it happened, but one was that the old chef, Ms. Kidd, refused to update an unhealthy menu.
IT'S TERRIBLE! MS. KIDD ACTS LIKE I STOLE HER JOB. SHE'S SERVING THE FOOD NOW AND HATES IT. I THINK SHE MIGHT HAVE SABOTAGED THE FOOD TO HURT ME.
WHO ELSE BESIDES YOU AND MS. KIDD WAS IN THE KITCHEN BEFORE LUNCH?

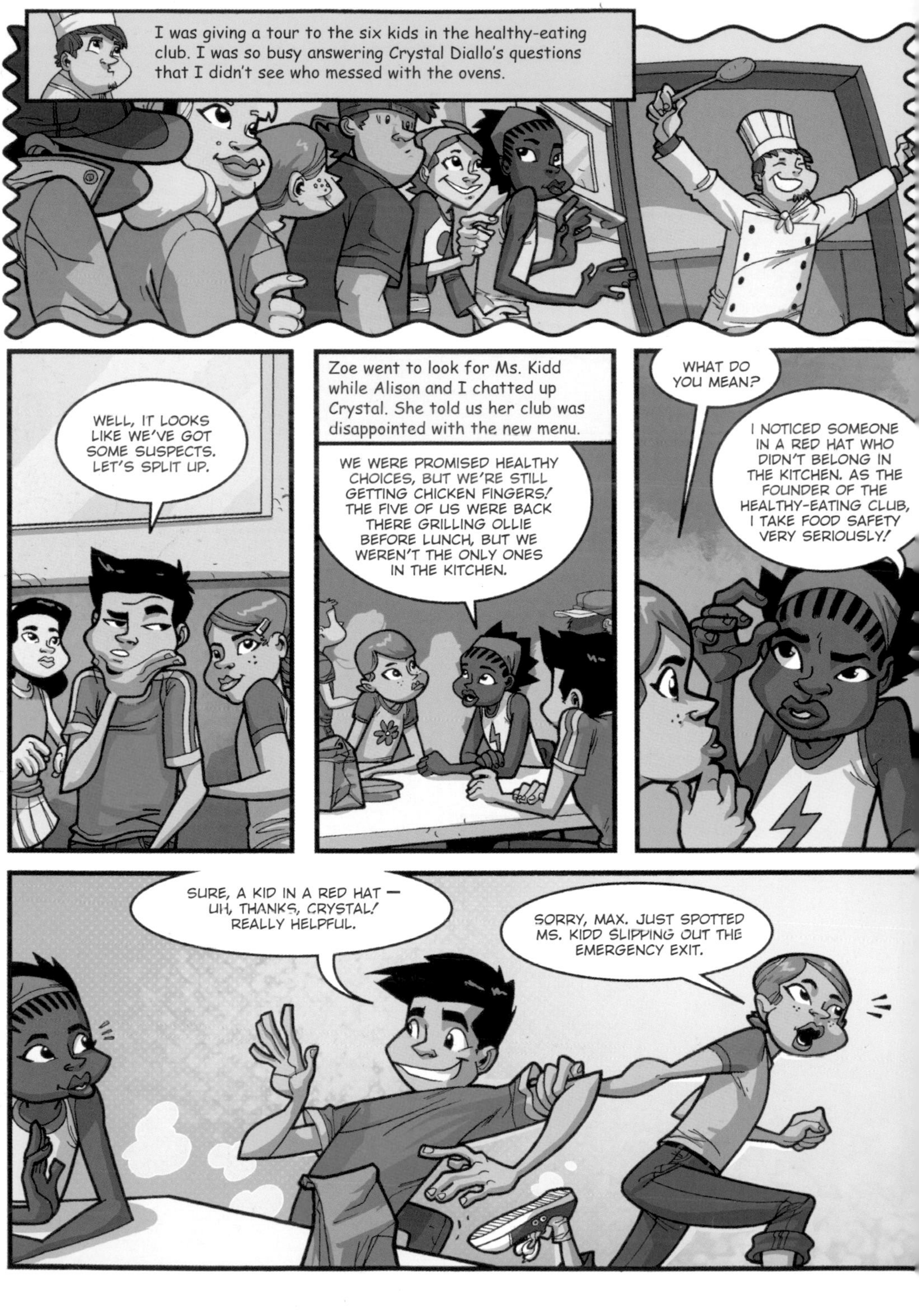
I was giving a tour to the six kids in the healthy-eating club. I was so busy answering Crystal Diallo's questions that I didn't see who messed with the ovens.
WELL, IT LOOKS LIKE WE'VE GOT SOME SUSPECTS. LET'S SPLIT UP.
Zoe went to look for Ms. Kidd while Alison and I chatted up Crystal. She told us her club was disappointed with the new menu.
WE WERE PROMISED HEALTHY CHOICES, BUT WE'RE STILL GETTING CHICKEN FINGERS! THE FIVE OF US WERE BACK THERE GRILLING OLLIE BEFORE LUNCH, BUT WE WEREN'T THE ONLY ONES IN THE KITCHEN.
WHAT DO YOU MEAN?
I NOTICED SOMEONE IN A RED HAT WHO DIDN'T BELONG IN THE KITCHEN. AS THE FOUNDER OF THE HEALTHY-EATING CLUB, I TAKE FOOD SAFETY VERY SERIOUSLY!
SURE, A KID IN A RED HAT — UH, THANKS, CRYSTAL! REALLY HELPFUL.
SORRY, MAX. JUST SPOTTED MS. KIDD SLIPPING OUT THE EMERGENCY EXIT.

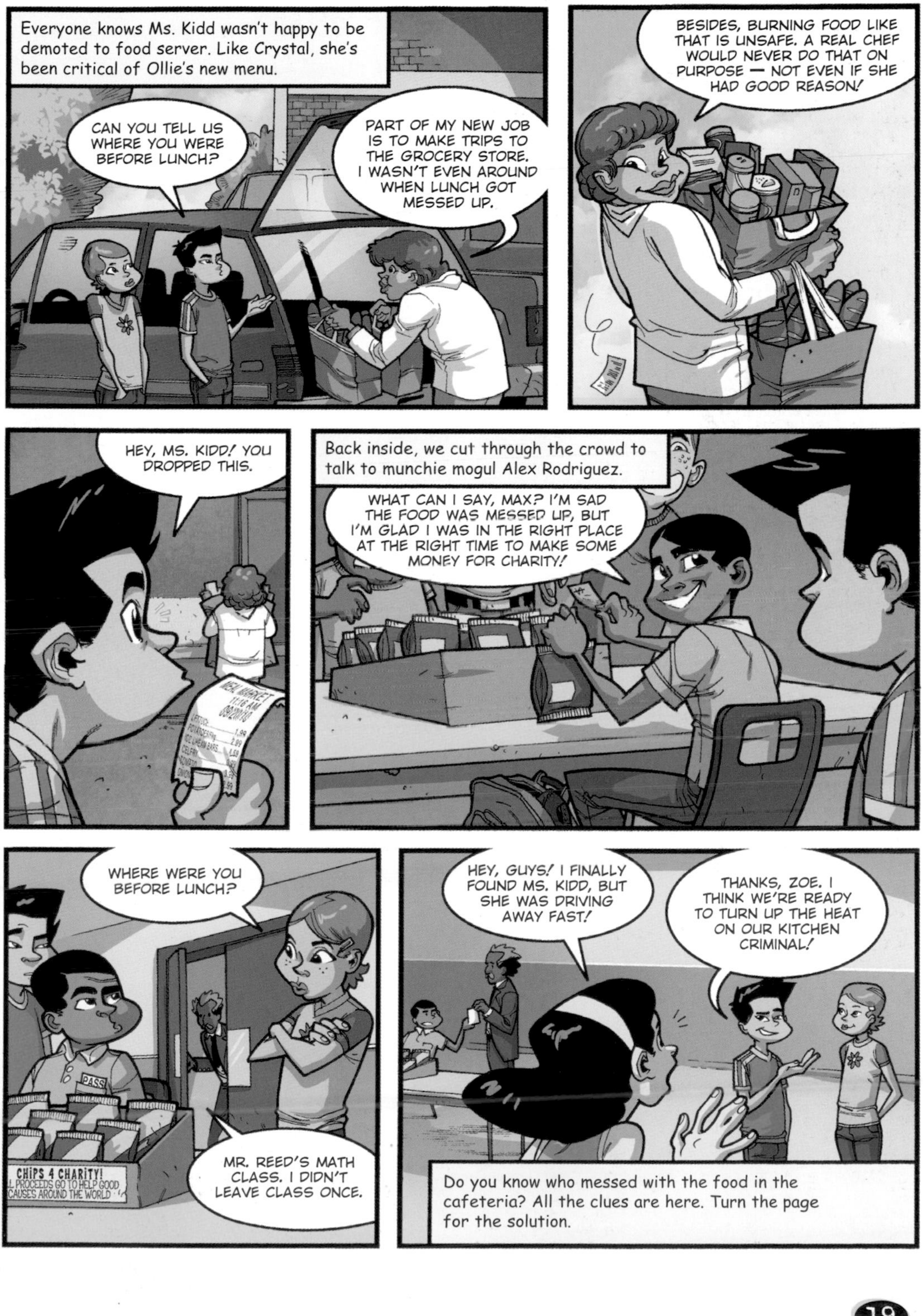
Everyone knows Ms. Kidd wasn't happy to be demoted to food server. Like Crystal, she's been critical of Ollie's new menu.
CAN YOU TELL US WHERE YOU WERE BEFORE LUNCH?
PART OF MY NEW JOB IS TO MAKE TRIPS TO THE GROCERY STORE. I WASN'T EVEN AROUND WHEN LUNCH GOT MESSED UP.
BESIDES, BURNING FOOD LIKE THAT IS UNSAFE. A REAL CHEF WOULD NEVER DO THAT ON PURPOSE — NOT EVEN IF SHE HAD GOOD REASON!
HEY, MS. KIDD! YOU DROPPED THIS.
Back inside, we cut through the crowd to talk to munchie mogul Alex Rodriguez.
WHAT CAN I SAY, MAX? I'M SAD THE FOOD WAS MESSED UP, BUT I'M GLAD I WAS IN THE RIGHT PLACE AT THE RIGHT TIME TO MAKE SOME MONEY FOR CHARITY!
WHERE WERE YOU BEFORE LUNCH?
PASS
CHIPS 4 CHARITY!
MR. REED'S MATH CLASS. I DIDN'T LEAVE CLASS ONCE.
HEY, GUYS! I FINALLY FOUND MS. KIDD, BUT SHE WAS DRIVING AWAY FAST!
THANKS, ZOE. I THINK WE'RE READY TO TURN UP THE HEAT ON OUR KITCHEN CRIMINAL!
Do you know who messed with the food in the cafeteria? All the clues are here. Turn the page for the solution.

Solution: The Case of the...

Cafeteria Crisis

Who changed the temperatures on the ovens?
Alex Rodriguez. He's good at everything and couldn't stand having one of his ideas flop.

Clues

* Ollie said he gave a tour to the six kids from the healthy-eating club. But there are only five people in the club. That means Crystal was telling the truth when she said there was another kid. Also, Ollie corroborated Crystal's story that she was asking questions the whole time she was in the kitchen.
* Alex said he was in Mr. Reed's class until lunch. But Max noticed that he had a hall pass, and that Mr. Reed came to collect it. If Alex had stayed in class until lunch he wouldn't have needed a hall pass.
* Alison noticed a red hat popping out the top of Alex's backpack. He used the hat to cover his face while he changed the oven temperatures.
* Basher may be known for eating hot dogs for breakfast, but that doesn't mean he can't change his ways. A poster in the cafeteria proves Basher is a full-fledged member of the healthy-eating club.
* Because Basher is a club member, and because Crystal said she saw "someone" in a red hat, the culprit couldn't have been Basher.
* Ms. Kidd was angry she lost her chef job, but the grocery receipt Max picked up said she checked out at 11:16 a.m.—right about the time Max estimated the crimes were committed.

Conclusion

After Max and Alison presented their evidence, Alex confessed. He apologized to everyone for ruining their lunch, and Mr. Reed hauled him off to detention. Ollie apologized to Ms. Kidd for suspecting her. The two agreed to work together on the healthiest menu possible.

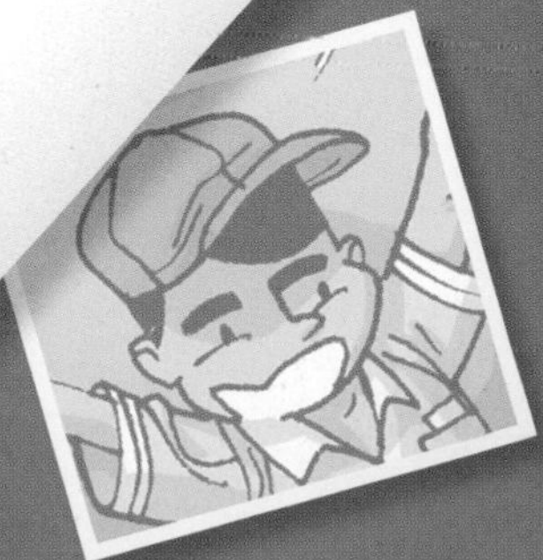

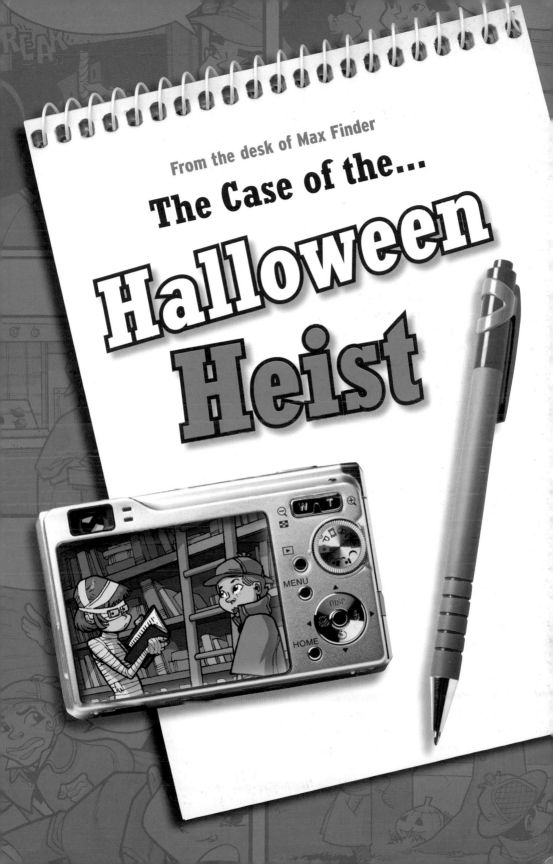

From the desk of Max Finder

The Case of the...

Halloween

Heist

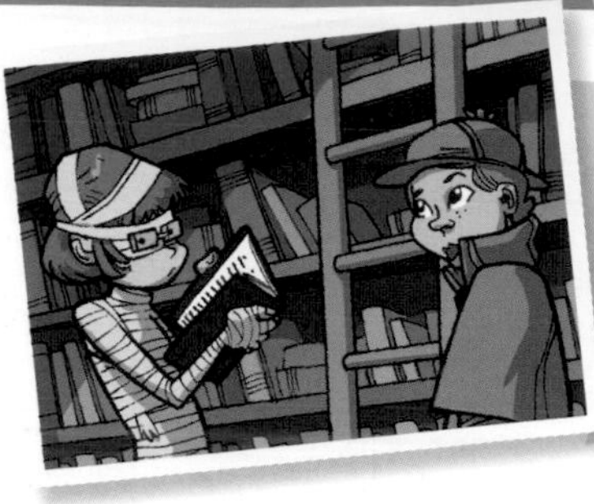

The Case of the... Halloween Heist

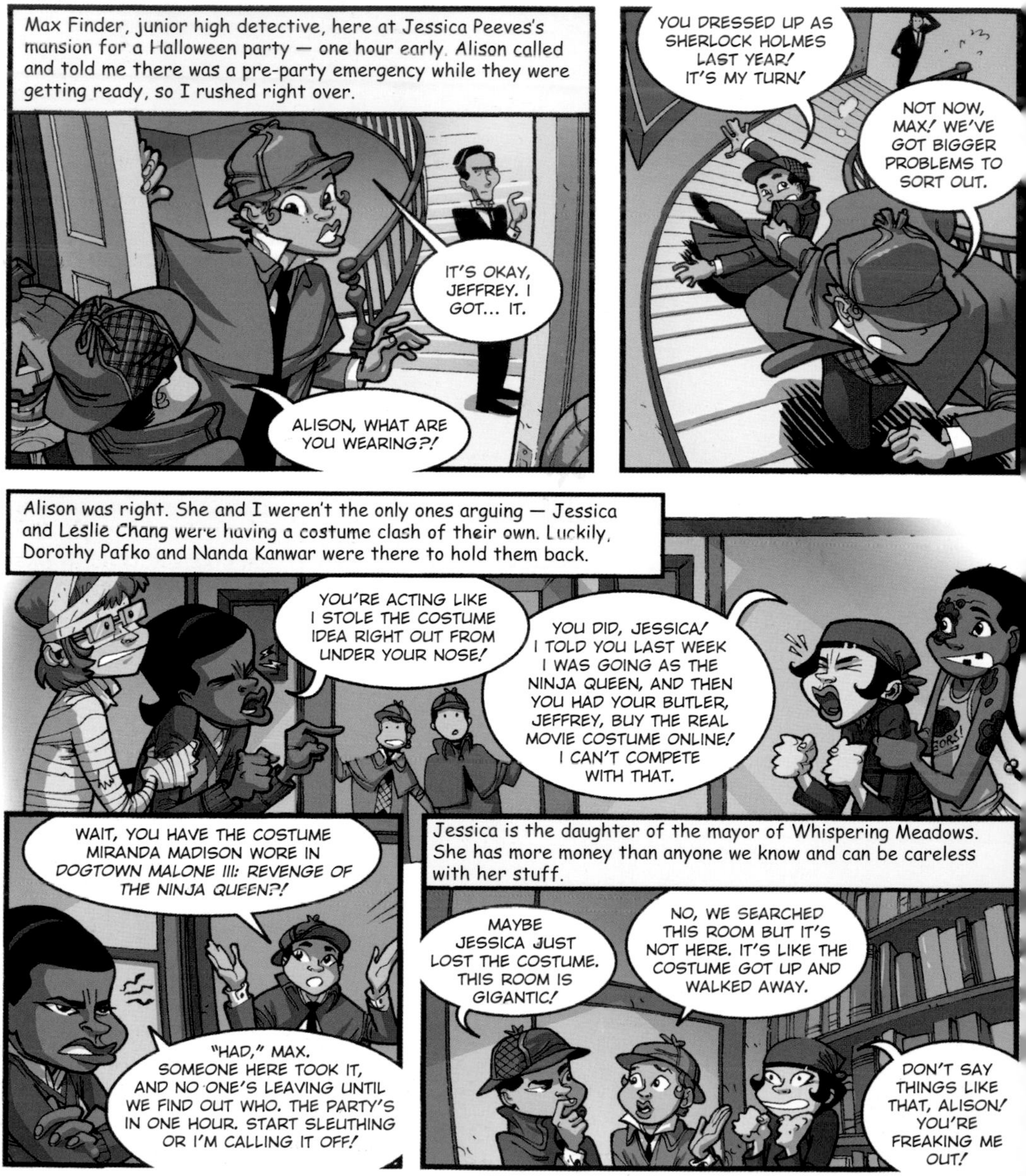

Max Finder, junior high detective, here at Jessica Peeves's mansion for a Halloween party — one hour early. Alison called and told me there was a pre-party emergency while they were getting ready, so I rushed right over.
IT'S OKAY, JEFFREY. I GOT... IT.
ALISON, WHAT ARE YOU WEARING?!
YOU DRESSED UP AS SHERLOCK HOLMES LAST YEAR! IT'S MY TURN!
NOT NOW, MAX! WE'VE GOT BIGGER PROBLEMS TO SORT OUT.
Alison was right. She and I weren't the only ones arguing — Jessica and Leslie Chang were having a costume clash of their own. Luckily, Dorothy Pafko and Nanda Kanwar were there to hold them back.
YOU'RE ACTING LIKE I STOLE THE COSTUME IDEA RIGHT OUT FROM UNDER YOUR NOSE!
YOU DID, JESSICA! I TOLD YOU LAST WEEK I WAS GOING AS THE NINJA QUEEN, AND THEN YOU HAD YOUR BUTLER, JEFFREY, BUY THE REAL MOVIE COSTUME ONLINE! I CAN'T COMPETE WITH THAT.
WAIT, YOU HAVE THE COSTUME MIRANDA MADISON WORE IN DOGTOWN MALONE III: REVENGE OF THE NINJA QUEEN?!
"HAD," MAX. SOMEONE HERE TOOK IT, AND NO ONE'S LEAVING UNTIL WE FIND OUT WHO. THE PARTY'S IN ONE HOUR. START SLEUTHING OR I'M CALLING IT OFF!
Jessica is the daughter of the mayor of Whispering Meadows. She has more money than anyone we know and can be careless with her stuff.
MAYBE JESSICA JUST LOST THE COSTUME. THIS ROOM IS GIGANTIC!
NO, WE SEARCHED THIS ROOM BUT IT'S NOT HERE. IT'S LIKE THE COSTUME GOT UP AND WALKED AWAY.
DON'T SAY THINGS LIKE THAT, ALISON! YOU'RE FREAKING ME OUT!

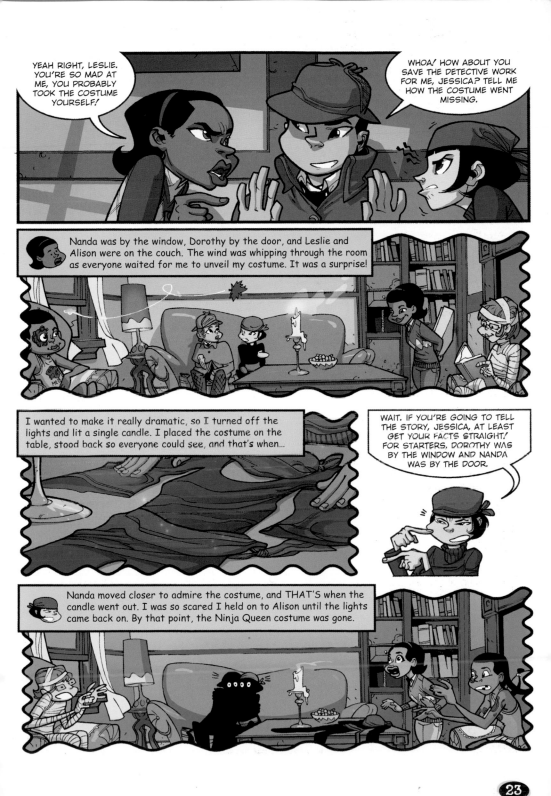

YEAH RIGHT, LESLIE. YOU'RE SO MAD AT ME, YOU PROBABLY TOOK THE COSTUME YOURSELF!

WHOA! HOW ABOUT YOU SAVE THE DETECTIVE WORK FOR ME, JESSICA? TELL ME HOW THE COSTUME WENT MISSING.

Nanda was by the window, Dorothy by the door, and Leslie and Alison were on the couch. The wind was whipping through the room as everyone waited for me to unveil my costume. It was a surprise!

I wanted to make it really dramatic, so I turned off the lights and lit a single candle. I placed the costume on the table, stood back so everyone could see, and that's when...

WAIT. IF YOU'RE GOING TO TELL THE STORY, JESSICA, AT LEAST GET YOUR FACTS STRAIGHT! FOR STARTERS, DOROTHY WAS BY THE WINDOW AND NANDA WAS BY THE DOOR.

Nanda moved closer to admire the costume, and THAT'S when the candle went out. I was so scared I held on to Alison until the lights came back on. By that point, the Ninja Queen costume was gone.

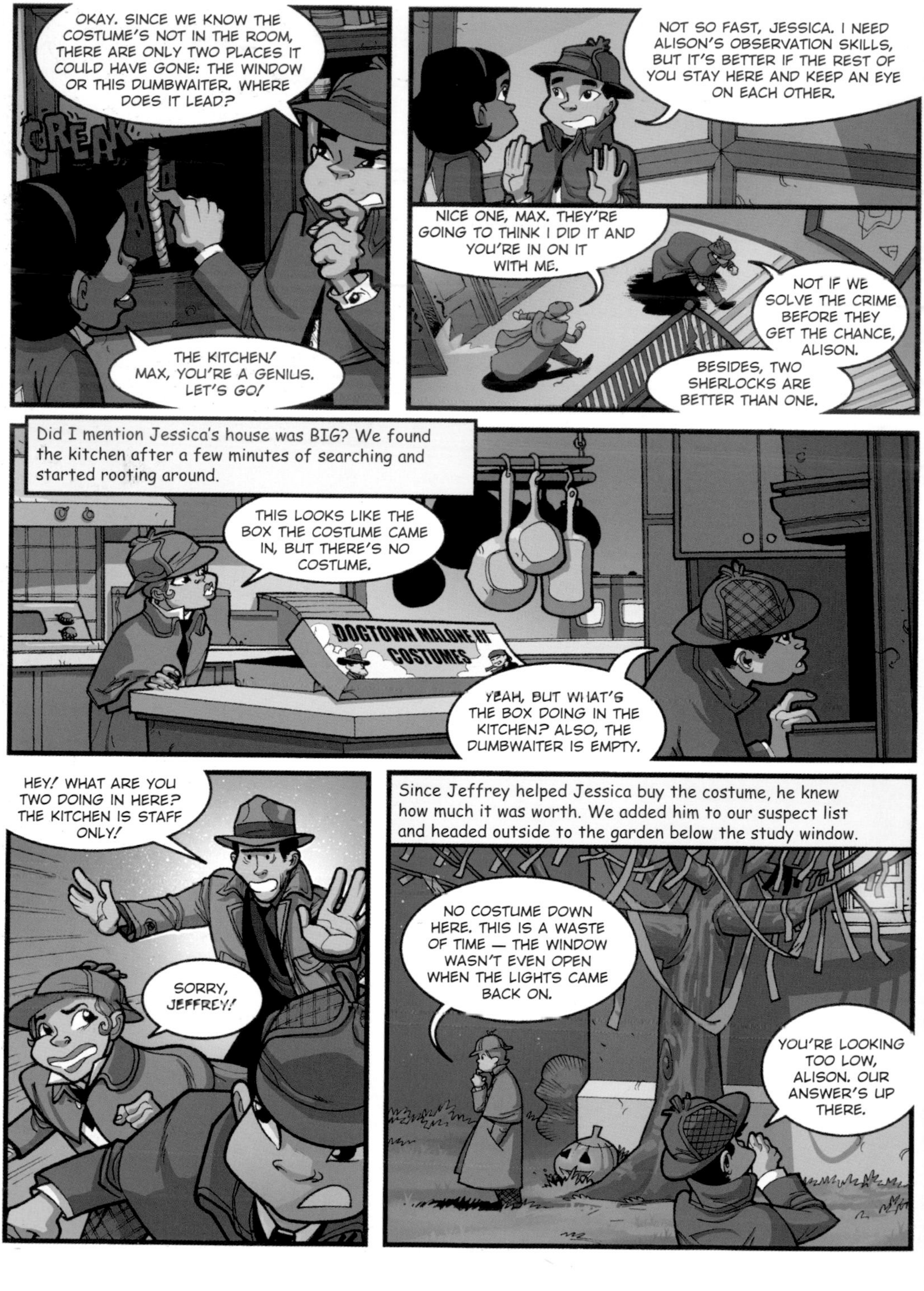
OKAY. SINCE WE KNOW THE COSTUME'S NOT IN THE ROOM, THERE ARE ONLY TWO PLACES IT COULD HAVE GONE: THE WINDOW OR THIS DUMBWAITER. WHERE DOES IT LEAD?
CREAK
THE KITCHEN! MAX, YOU'RE A GENIUS. LET'S GO!
NOT SO FAST, JESSICA. I NEED ALISON'S OBSERVATION SKILLS, BUT IT'S BETTER IF THE REST OF YOU STAY HERE AND KEEP AN EYE ON EACH OTHER.
NICE ONE, MAX. THEY'RE GOING TO THINK I DID IT AND YOU'RE IN ON IT WITH ME.
NOT IF WE SOLVE THE CRIME BEFORE THEY GET THE CHANCE, ALISON.
BESIDES, TWO SHERLOCKS ARE BETTER THAN ONE.
Did I mention Jessica's house was BIG? We found the kitchen after a few minutes of searching and started rooting around.
THIS LOOKS LIKE THE BOX THE COSTUME CAME IN, BUT THERE'S NO COSTUME.
DOGTOWN MALONE III COSTUMES
YEAH, BUT WHAT'S THE BOX DOING IN THE KITCHEN? ALSO, THE DUMBWAITER IS EMPTY.
HEY! WHAT ARE YOU TWO DOING IN HERE? THE KITCHEN IS STAFF ONLY!
SORRY, JEFFREY!
Since Jeffrey helped Jessica buy the costume, he knew how much it was worth. We added him to our suspect list and headed outside to the garden below the study window.
NO COSTUME DOWN HERE. THIS IS A WASTE OF TIME — THE WINDOW WASN'T EVEN OPEN WHEN THE LIGHTS CAME BACK ON.
YOU'RE LOOKING TOO LOW, ALISON. OUR ANSWER'S UP THERE.

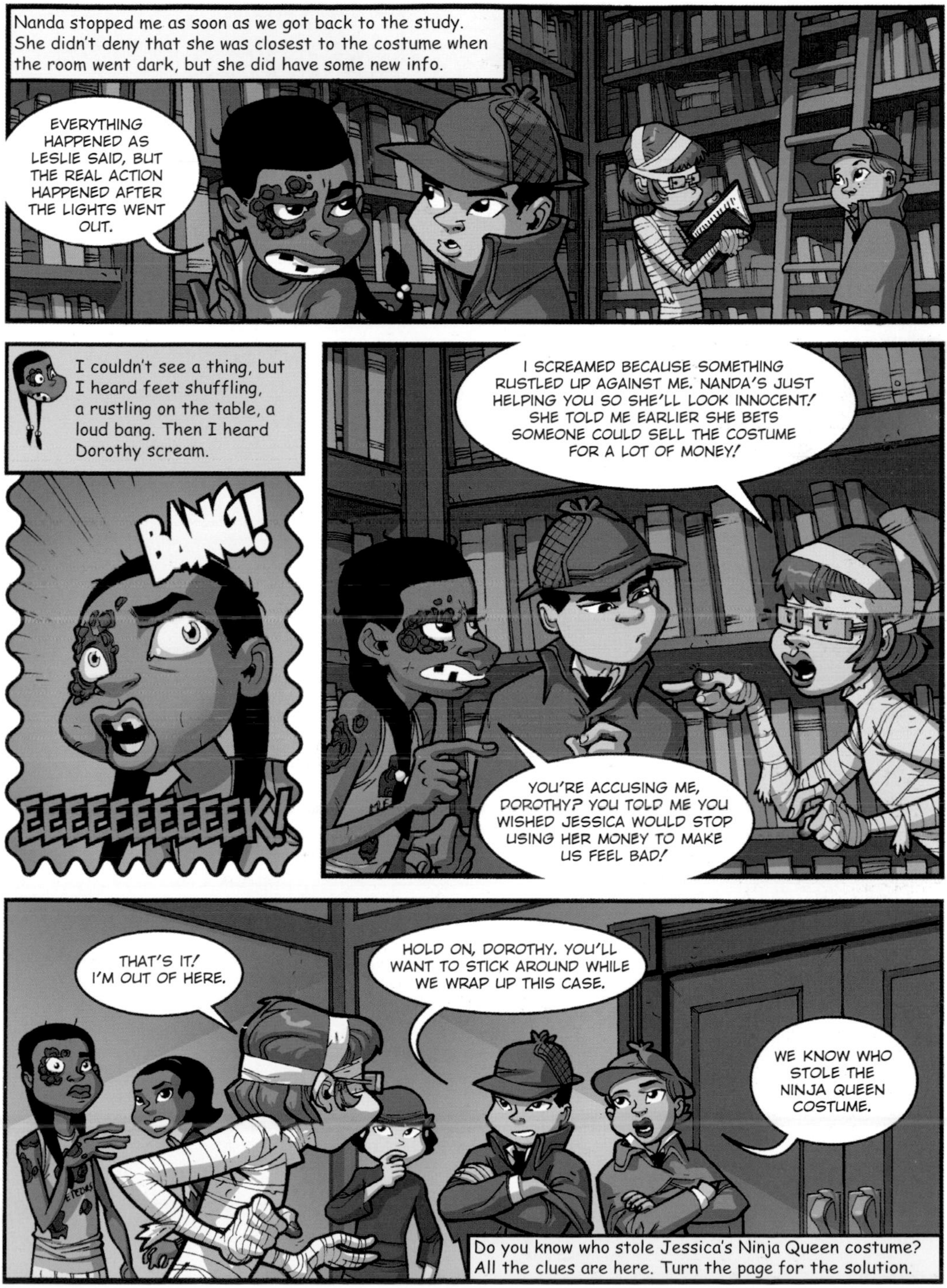

Nanda stopped me as soon as we got back to the study. She didn't deny that she was closest to the costume when the room went dark, but she did have some new info.
EVERYTHING HAPPENED AS LESLIE SAID, BUT THE REAL ACTION HAPPENED AFTER THE LIGHTS WENT OUT.
I couldn't see a thing, but I heard feet shuffling, a rustling on the table, a loud bang. Then I heard Dorothy scream.
BANG!
EEEEEEEEEEEK!
I SCREAMED BECAUSE SOMETHING RUSTLED UP AGAINST ME. NANDA'S JUST HELPING YOU SO SHE'LL LOOK INNOCENT! SHE TOLD ME EARLIER SHE BETS SOMEONE COULD SELL THE COSTUME FOR A LOT OF MONEY!
YOU'RE ACCUSING ME, DOROTHY? YOU TOLD ME YOU WISHED JESSICA WOULD STOP USING HER MONEY TO MAKE US FEEL BAD!
THAT'S IT! I'M OUT OF HERE.
HOLD ON, DOROTHY. YOU'LL WANT TO STICK AROUND WHILE WE WRAP UP THIS CASE.
WE KNOW WHO STOLE THE NINJA QUEEN COSTUME.
Do you know who stole Jessica's Ninja Queen costume? All the clues are here. Turn the page for the solution.

Solution: The Case of the...

Halloween Heist

Who stole Jessica's costume? Dorothy Pafko. She was tired of Jessica hogging the spotlight, so she took the opportunity to throw the costume out the window when the candle went out.

Clues

* When Max said "Our answer's up there" while he was outside, he meant it—literally. He noticed that the Ninja Queen costume was hanging from the branches of the tree outside the study. It had been thrown out of the study window.
* Nanda confirmed everything that Leslie said. That means that Dorothy was the one sitting closest to the window.
* Max noticed Dorothy's thumbs were red and bruised. She slammed the window on them after she threw out the costume. That explains two of the noises Nanda heard: the loud bang and Dorothy's scream. She lied about someone brushing past her to throw Max and Alison off track.
* Leslie may have been angry at Jessica, but she didn't steal the Ninja Queen outfit. Both Nanda and Alison confirmed she didn't move a muscle while the lights were out.
* Jeffrey, the Peeveses' butler, had the costume box in the kitchen because he bought the Dogtown Malone costume for himself when he bought the Ninja Queen costume for Jessica. The box clearly said "costumes" —and had a picture of the outfit that Jeffrey was wearing when he sent them out. He was embarrassed that they caught him out of uniform.

Conclusion

When Max and Alison presented their evidence, Dorothy stepped forward. She said she was sorry but wished Jessica would be more considerate to her friends. Jessica forgave her, and Jeffrey pulled the Ninja Queen costume back inside. Jessica surprised everyone by giving it to Leslie, who wore it proudly to the party and won "Best Costume."

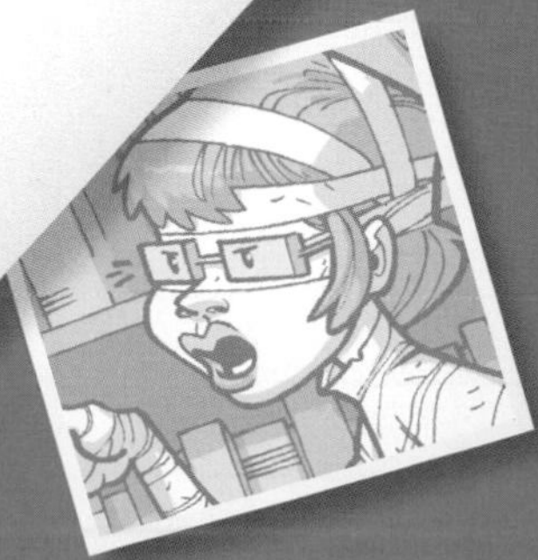

From the desk of Max Finder

The Case of the...

Dastardly Defamer

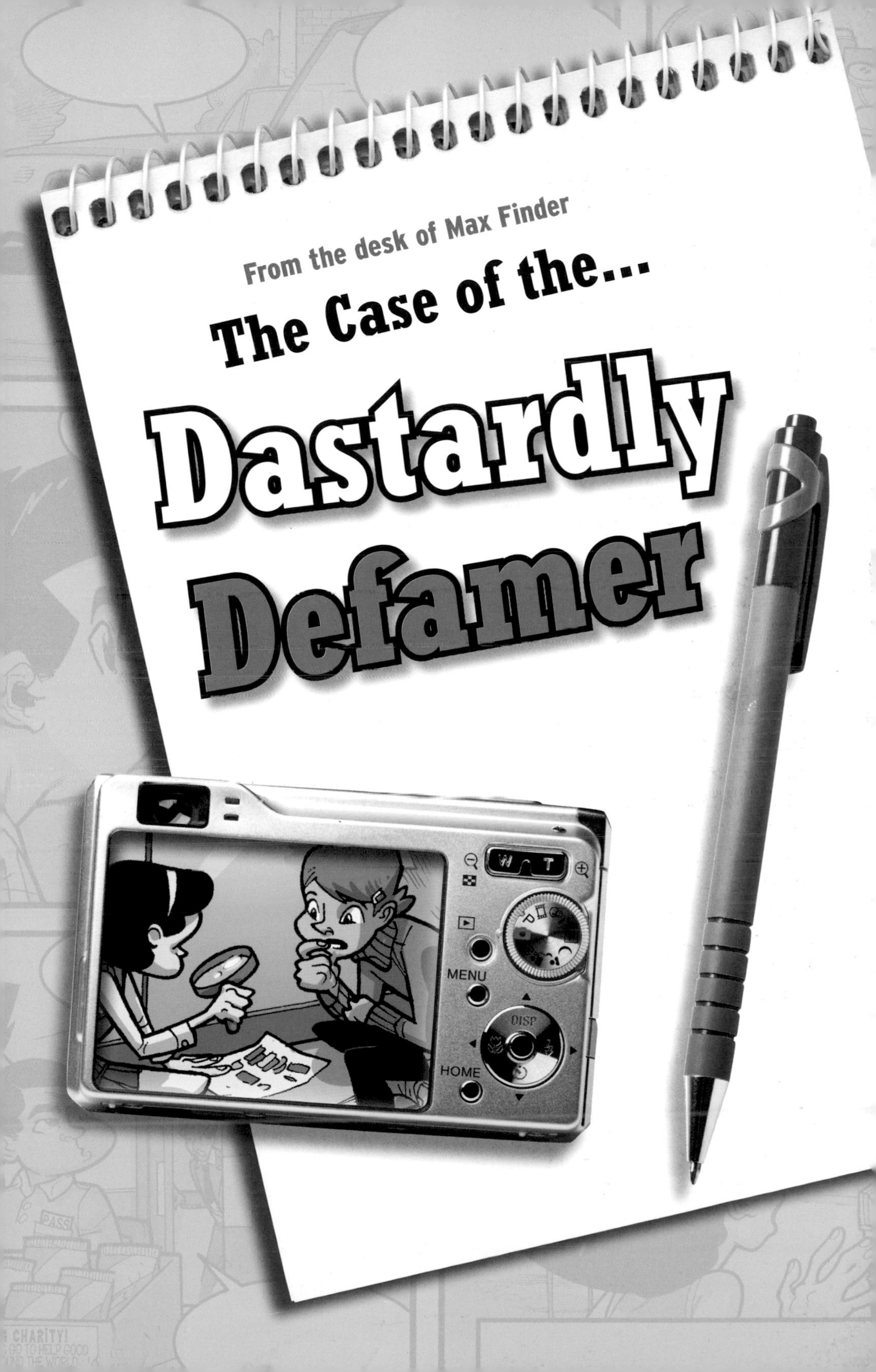

W
T
MENU
DISP
HOME

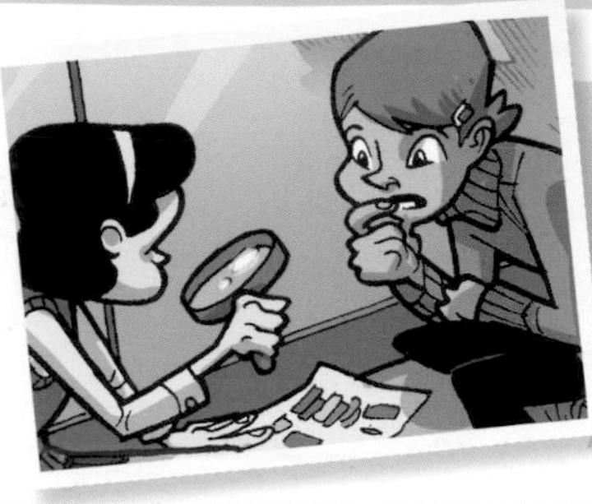

The Case of the... Dastardly Defamer

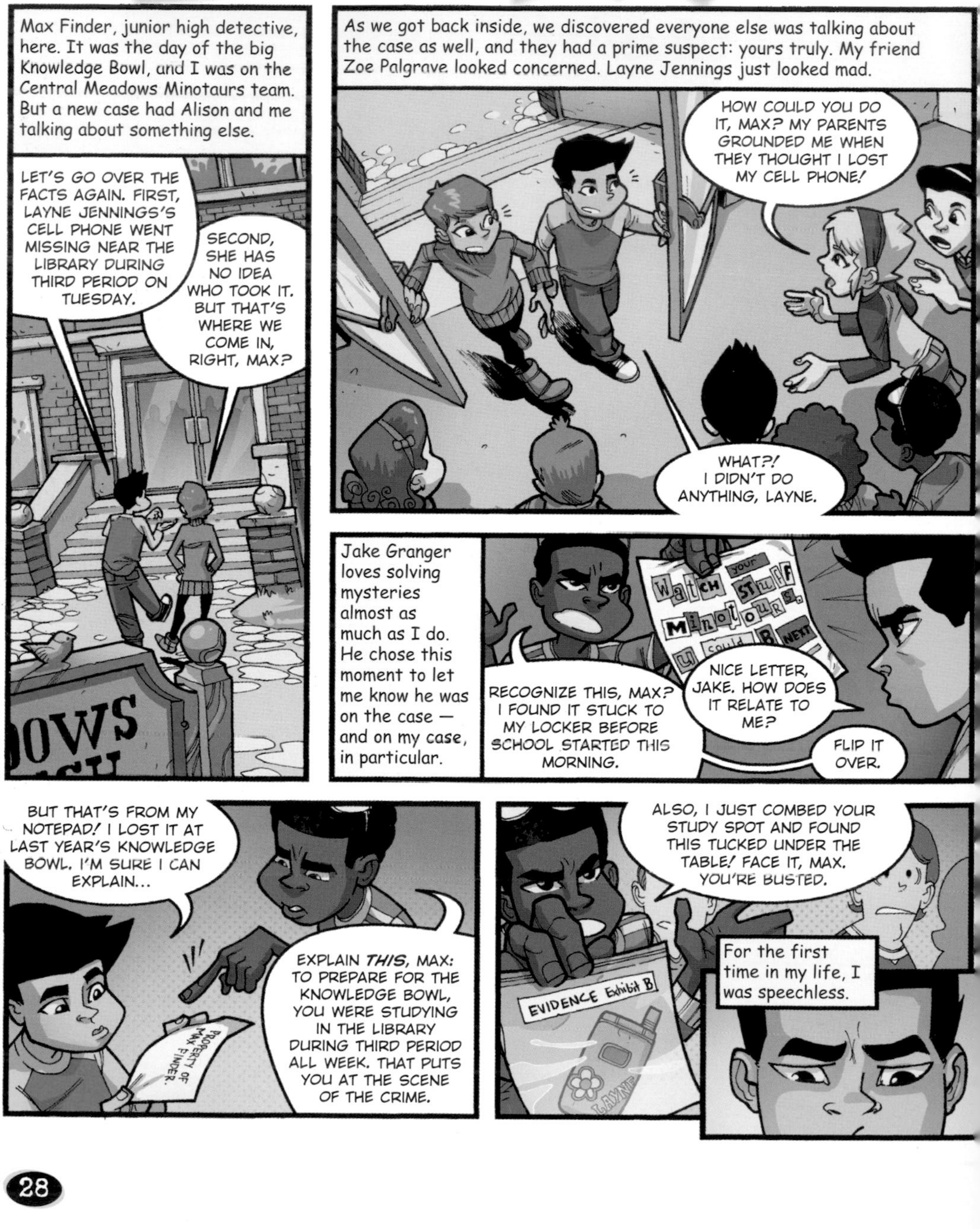
Max Finder, junior high detective, here. It was the day of the big Knowledge Bowl, and I was on the Central Meadows Minotaurs team. But a new case had Alison and me talking about something else.
LET'S GO OVER THE FACTS AGAIN. FIRST, LAYNE JENNINGS'S CELL PHONE WENT MISSING NEAR THE LIBRARY DURING THIRD PERIOD ON TUESDAY.
SECOND, SHE HAS NO IDEA WHO TOOK IT. BUT THAT'S WHERE WE COME IN, RIGHT, MAX?
As we got back inside, we discovered everyone else was talking about the case as well, and they had a prime suspect: yours truly. My friend Zoe Palgrave looked concerned. Layne Jennings just looked mad.
HOW COULD YOU DO IT, MAX? MY PARENTS GROUNDED ME WHEN THEY THOUGHT I LOST MY CELL PHONE!
WHAT?! I DIDN'T DO ANYTHING, LAYNE.
Jake Granger loves solving mysteries almost as much as I do. He chose this moment to let me know he was on the case — and on my case, in particular.
Watch your stuff Minotaurs. u could B next
RECOGNIZE THIS, MAX? I FOUND IT STUCK TO MY LOCKER BEFORE SCHOOL STARTED THIS MORNING.
NICE LETTER, JAKE. HOW DOES IT RELATE TO ME?
FLIP IT OVER.
BUT THAT'S FROM MY NOTEPAD! I LOST IT AT LAST YEAR'S KNOWLEDGE BOWL. I'M SURE I CAN EXPLAIN...
PROPERTY OF MAX FINDER.
EXPLAIN *THIS*, MAX: TO PREPARE FOR THE KNOWLEDGE BOWL, YOU WERE STUDYING IN THE LIBRARY DURING THIRD PERIOD ALL WEEK. THAT PUTS YOU AT THE SCENE OF THE CRIME.
ALSO, I JUST COMBED YOUR STUDY SPOT AND FOUND THIS TUCKED UNDER THE TABLE! FACE IT, MAX. YOU'RE BUSTED.
EVIDENCE Exhibit B
LAYNE
For the first time in my life, I was speechless.

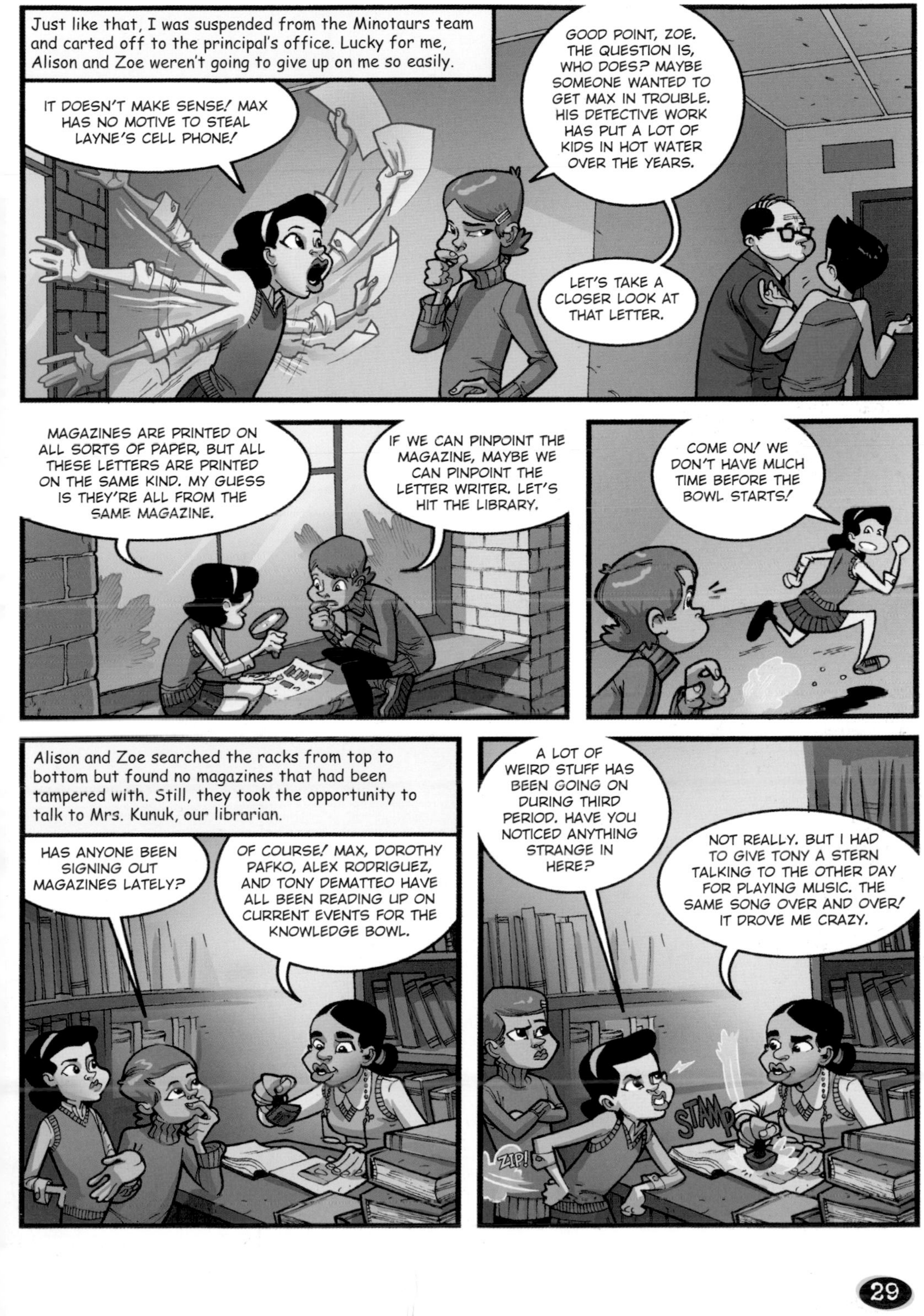
Just like that, I was suspended from the Minotaurs team and carted off to the principal's office. Lucky for me, Alison and Zoe weren't going to give up on me so easily.
IT DOESN'T MAKE SENSE! MAX HAS NO MOTIVE TO STEAL LAYNE'S CELL PHONE!
GOOD POINT, ZOE. THE QUESTION IS, WHO DOES? MAYBE SOMEONE WANTED TO GET MAX IN TROUBLE. HIS DETECTIVE WORK HAS PUT A LOT OF KIDS IN HOT WATER OVER THE YEARS.
LET'S TAKE A CLOSER LOOK AT THAT LETTER.
MAGAZINES ARE PRINTED ON ALL SORTS OF PAPER, BUT ALL THESE LETTERS ARE PRINTED ON THE SAME KIND. MY GUESS IS THEY'RE ALL FROM THE SAME MAGAZINE.
IF WE CAN PINPOINT THE MAGAZINE, MAYBE WE CAN PINPOINT THE LETTER WRITER. LET'S HIT THE LIBRARY.
COME ON! WE DON'T HAVE MUCH TIME BEFORE THE BOWL STARTS!
Alison and Zoe searched the racks from top to bottom but found no magazines that had been tampered with. Still, they took the opportunity to talk to Mrs. Kunuk, our librarian.
HAS ANYONE BEEN SIGNING OUT MAGAZINES LATELY?
OF COURSE! MAX, DOROTHY PAFKO, ALEX RODRIGUEZ, AND TONY DEMATTEO HAVE ALL BEEN READING UP ON CURRENT EVENTS FOR THE KNOWLEDGE BOWL.
A LOT OF WEIRD STUFF HAS BEEN GOING ON DURING THIRD PERIOD. HAVE YOU NOTICED ANYTHING STRANGE IN HERE?
NOT REALLY. BUT I HAD TO GIVE TONY A STERN TALKING TO THE OTHER DAY FOR PLAYING MUSIC. THE SAME SONG OVER AND OVER! IT DROVE ME CRAZY.
STAMP
ZIP!

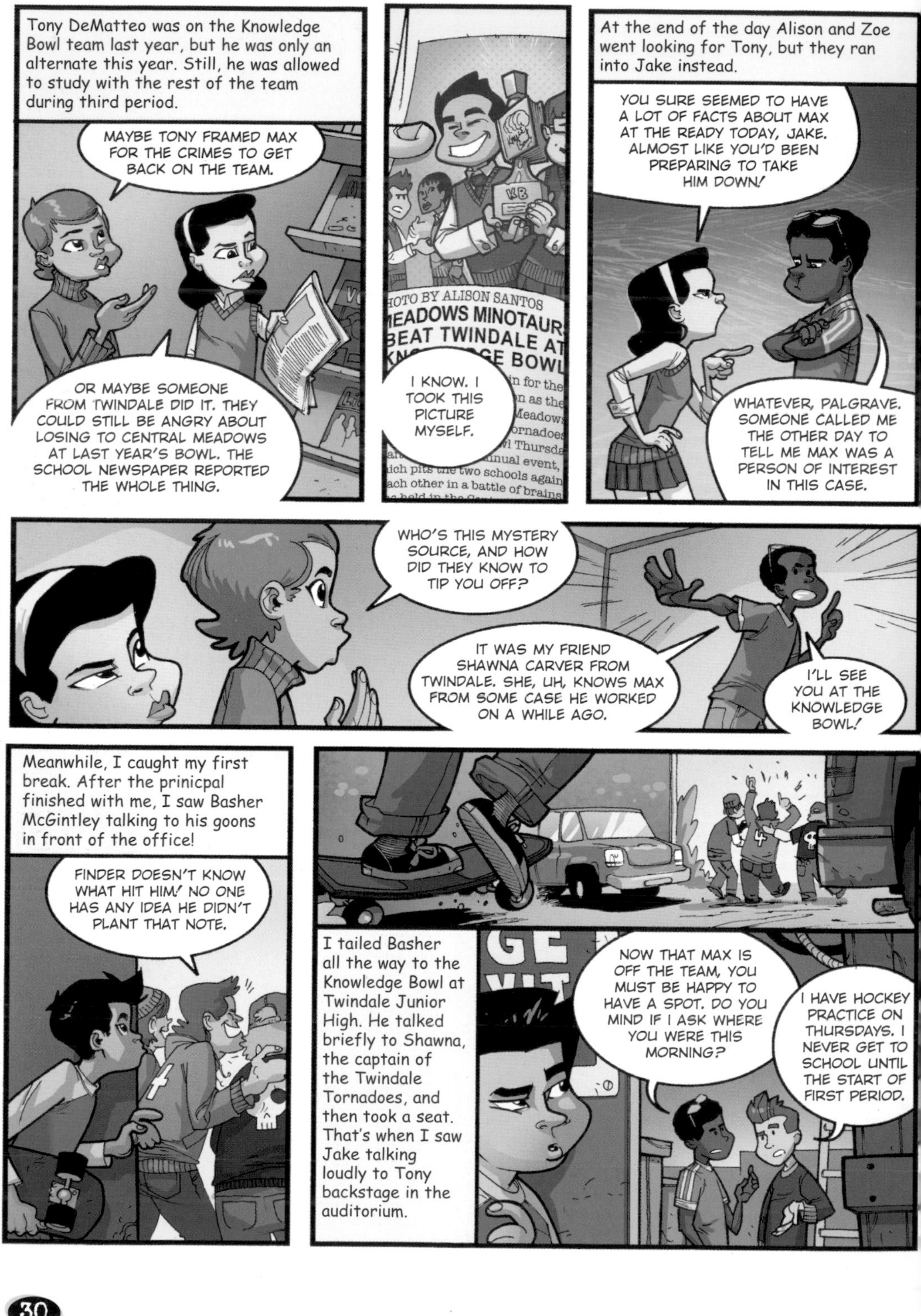

Tony DeMatteo was on the Knowledge Bowl team last year, but he was only an alternate this year. Still, he was allowed to study with the rest of the team during third period.
MAYBE TONY FRAMED MAX FOR THE CRIMES TO GET BACK ON THE TEAM.
OR MAYBE SOMEONE FROM TWINDALE DID IT. THEY COULD STILL BE ANGRY ABOUT LOSING TO CENTRAL MEADOWS AT LAST YEAR'S BOWL. THE SCHOOL NEWSPAPER REPORTED THE WHOLE THING.
HOTO BY ALISON SANTOS
EADOWS MINOTAUR
BEAT TWINDALE AT
I KNOW. I TOOK THIS PICTURE MYSELF.
At the end of the day Alison and Zoe went looking for Tony, but they ran into Jake instead.
YOU SURE SEEMED TO HAVE A LOT OF FACTS ABOUT MAX AT THE READY TODAY, JAKE. ALMOST LIKE YOU'D BEEN PREPARING TO TAKE HIM DOWN!
WHATEVER, PALGRAVE. SOMEONE CALLED ME THE OTHER DAY TO TELL ME MAX WAS A PERSON OF INTEREST IN THIS CASE.
WHO'S THIS MYSTERY SOURCE, AND HOW DID THEY KNOW TO TIP YOU OFF?
IT WAS MY FRIEND SHAWNA CARVER FROM TWINDALE. SHE, UH, KNOWS MAX FROM SOME CASE HE WORKED ON A WHILE AGO.
I'LL SEE YOU AT THE KNOWLEDGE BOWL!
Meanwhile, I caught my first break. After the prinicpal finished with me, I saw Basher McGintley talking to his goons in front of the office!
FINDER DOESN'T KNOW WHAT HIT HIM! NO ONE HAS ANY IDEA HE DIDN'T PLANT THAT NOTE.
I tailed Basher all the way to the Knowledge Bowl at Twindale Junior High. He talked briefly to Shawna, the captain of the Twindale Tornadoes, and then took a seat. That's when I saw Jake talking loudly to Tony backstage in the auditorium.
NOW THAT MAX IS OFF THE TEAM, YOU MUST BE HAPPY TO HAVE A SPOT. DO YOU MIND IF I ASK WHERE YOU WERE THIS MORNING?
I HAVE HOCKEY PRACTICE ON THURSDAYS. I NEVER GET TO SCHOOL UNTIL THE START OF FIRST PERIOD.

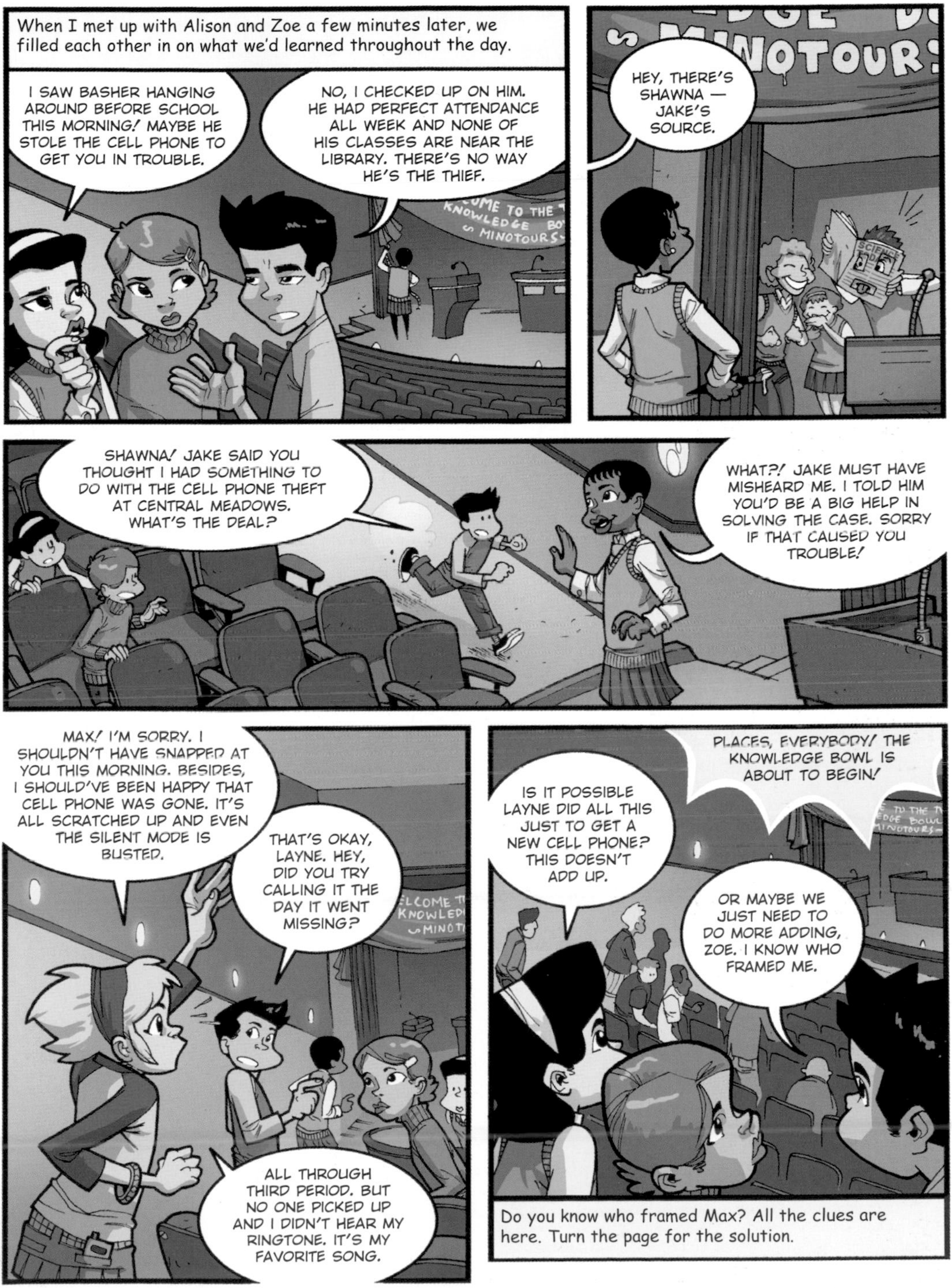
When I met up with Alison and Zoe a few minutes later, we filled each other in on what we'd learned throughout the day.
I SAW BASHER HANGING AROUND BEFORE SCHOOL THIS MORNING! MAYBE HE STOLE THE CELL PHONE TO GET YOU IN TROUBLE.
NO, I CHECKED UP ON HIM. HE HAD PERFECT ATTENDANCE ALL WEEK AND NONE OF HIS CLASSES ARE NEAR THE LIBRARY. THERE'S NO WAY HE'S THE THIEF.
HEY, THERE'S SHAWNA — JAKE'S SOURCE.
SHAWNA! JAKE SAID YOU THOUGHT I HAD SOMETHING TO DO WITH THE CELL PHONE THEFT AT CENTRAL MEADOWS. WHAT'S THE DEAL?
WHAT?! JAKE MUST HAVE MISHEARD ME. I TOLD HIM YOU'D BE A BIG HELP IN SOLVING THE CASE. SORRY IF THAT CAUSED YOU TROUBLE!
MAX! I'M SORRY. I SHOULDN'T HAVE SNAPPED AT YOU THIS MORNING. BESIDES, I SHOULD'VE BEEN HAPPY THAT CELL PHONE WAS GONE. IT'S ALL SCRATCHED UP AND EVEN THE SILENT MODE IS BUSTED.
THAT'S OKAY, LAYNE. HEY, DID YOU TRY CALLING IT THE DAY IT WENT MISSING?
ALL THROUGH THIRD PERIOD. BUT NO ONE PICKED UP AND I DIDN'T HEAR MY RINGTONE. IT'S MY FAVORITE SONG.
PLACES, EVERYBODY! THE KNOWLEDGE BOWL IS ABOUT TO BEGIN!
IS IT POSSIBLE LAYNE DID ALL THIS JUST TO GET A NEW CELL PHONE? THIS DOESN'T ADD UP.
OR MAYBE WE JUST NEED TO DO MORE ADDING, ZOE. I KNOW WHO FRAMED ME.
Do you know who framed Max? All the clues are here. Turn the page for the solution.

Solution: The Case of the...

Dastardly Defamer

Who framed Max?
Shawna Carver, Basher McGintley, and Tony DeMatteo. Shawna wrote the letter, Basher planted it at Jake's locker, and Tony stole the cell phone.

Clues

* In the newspaper photo of last year's Knowledge Bowl, Tony is talking to Shawna instead of celebrating his team's victory. Max also saw Basher talking to Shawna. That connects all three.
* The letter on Max's notepad said "Minotours." That's a misspelling of Minotaurs, the name of the Central Meadows Knowledge Bowl team. Max noticed the same misspelling on the banner that Shawna was hanging up.
* Max lost his notepad at last year's Knowledge Bowl, which is how Shawna got a hold of it.
* Alison saw one of Shawna's Knowledge Bowl teammates holding a magazine with holes in it. It was the same magazine Shawna used to write the letter.
* The song Mrs. Kunuk heard over and over again in the library was actually Layne Jennings's ringtone. Tony couldn't keep the cell phone quiet because the silent mode was broken.
* Basher told his friends that Max didn't plant the note. That's because Basher did it himself. Zoe saw him hanging around just before school.
* Jake Granger was guilty only of jumping to conclusions. Shawna, Tony, and Basher knew he was an amateur detective and would jump at the opportunity to help solve a big case. That's why they planted the note at his locker. Max knew Jake wasn't involved in the frame job when he saw him questioning Tony about where he was before school.

Conclusion

When Max and Alison presented their evidence, the three confessed and apologized. Max regained his position on the team and helped Central Meadows to a second consecutive Knowledge Bowl victory.

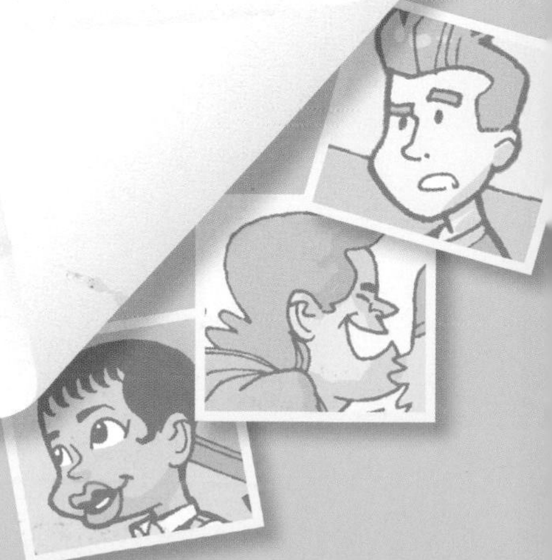

The Case of the...

Bullied Bully

As told by Max Finder

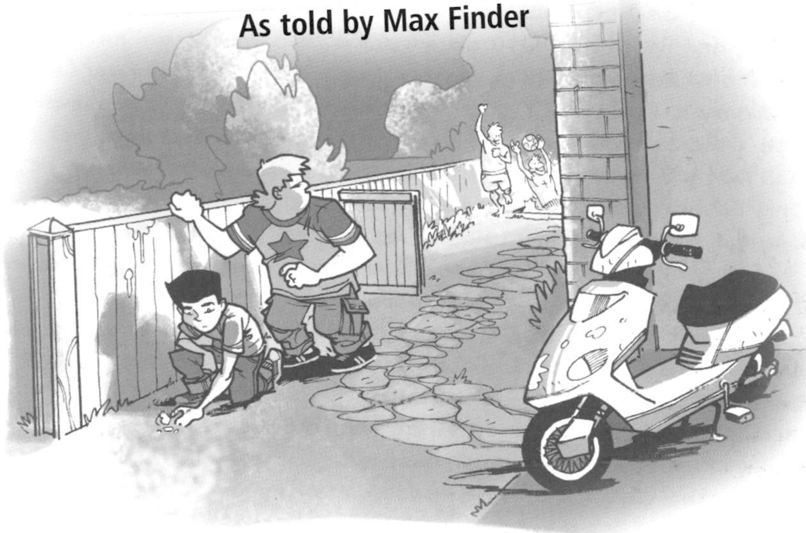

I was coming out of Slurp King when Basher nabbed me.

"Finder!" He growled and yanked me by the collar around the corner. "Get over here."

I followed. I didn't have much choice.

"Basher, whatever it is I didn't do it."

"Relax. I don't want to hit you. I want to hire you."

In all his years of picking on little kids and stealing lunch money, I had never seen Basher McGintley look so pale.

"You're scared," I said.

His freckled face tightened for half a second, then his toughness slipped away.

"Max, I need your help."

From our hiding spot in the bushes across the street, it was easy to see Rex Taggart was mad. The sixteen-year-old stomped around his brand new, cherry red electric motorbike. Sticky, yellow egg yolk and powdery flour covered the bike and much of the driveway.

I didn't know Rex, but I knew his e-bike and so did half of Whispering Meadows. Last month, Rex and his pals all bought electric motorbikes. Since then, they've been terrorizing the neighborhood, chasing pets, kids, and anyone else foolish enough to get in their way.

Basher's eyes darted from side to side. "I didn't want to tell you because you'd think I was guilty, but I'm not. Honest."

And there it was again. Basher's face with all his toughness melted away. For a moment, he wasn't the bully who tormented you all recess or cornered you in the bathroom at school. He was just a kid accused of something he didn't do. A kid just like me.

"That would explain why the footprints go in two directions," I said, trying to picture the crime scene. For the millionth time today, I wished Alison was here with her brains and her camera. She would know if I could trust Basher.

As I tried to work things out, a yellow car with a cracked windscreen pulled into the driveway next door to Rex's house. The driver dragged himself out of the car. Alex Rodriguez, a kid from our class, opened the door as the man shuffled up the driveway.

I didn't even know Alex lived around here.

"Hey Dad," Alex called. "Mom left dinner in the fridge. Want me to heat it up?"

"All I want is sleep," his dad called back in a weary voice and practically fell into the house.

"Dinner?" Basher chuckled. "Who eats dinner at ten in the morning?"

"Exactly." I smiled. "This case just got more interesting."

"You'll still help me?" Basher actually sounded like he appreciated my help.

"For now." I walked back toward Rex's house. All his buddies had disappeared into the backyard. "Time for a closer look at the crime scene."

From the music, shouts, and splashes coming from Rex's backyard, he was having too much fun to hear Basher and me sneaking up his driveway. We kept to the fence running along the side of the driveway, moving slowly and carefully. I moved around a pile of pizza boxes when something cracked under my feet. Flecks of white covered the ground at the base of the fence.

"Egg shells," I whispered.

Basher pointed to dried yolk sticking to the top of the fence. "You got to be a bad shot to get egg yolk up there."

The fence gate creaked open.

"Someone's coming!" I hissed and dragged Basher behind the stack of pizza boxes.

Two of Rex's pals came through the gate: a tall girl with eyes like a bug, and a small boy with more zits than freckles.

"I know who egged the e-bike and it wasn't that Basher kid," Bug-eyes whispered. "Think about it. Who was going to buy the very

"Dinner?" Basher chuckled. "Who **eats dinner** at ten in the morning?"

same bike but Rex beat them to it?"

"Stacy!" the boy said a little too loudly.

"And Stacy always gets super-jealous when she's not the first to have something cool."

From behind the pizza boxes Basher jabbed me with his elbow. "You see!"

Basher's jabs are more like shoves. I toppled into the stack of pizza boxes.

The teens glared at me as I tumbled from the shadows on a pile of pepperoni-plastered cardboard boxes.

"Get Rex!" Bug-eyes growled. "Tell him the snoop is still here."

I hurried back to the fence. Basher was one step ahead of me. A flash of sneaker and he was over the top of the fence. I scrambled up after him.

I landed with a thump in the next yard. I got to my feet, wiped the dirt from my hands, and came face to face with Alex and his dad. The two teens popped their heads over the fence. They got one look at Mr. Rodriguez, dropped back down, and disappeared.

"That's right!" Alex's dad yelled at them. "Go back to your party!"

"Easy, Dad," Alex put his hand on his father's arm.

"I'm working the night shift and need to sleep during the day." Mr. Rodriguez sighed. He looked exhausted. "Ever since Rex's folks went away on vacation, he's been playing music and making noise with his pals. I haven't slept in days."

The music coming from Rex's backyard was pretty loud. I peered over the fence. The teens were gone and the e-bike stood close by in the driveway. A path of white flour ran from the fence to the bike.

"Do you know who egged Rex's e-bike?" I asked.

Alex glanced at his dad, then answered. "I saw Basher around the e-bike this morning."

"I didn't do it!" Basher moaned.

"It's okay, Basher." I gave my client a reassuring smile. "I know who egged the e-bike."

Do you know who egged Rex's e-bike?
Turn the page for the solution.

Solution: The Case of the...
Bullied Bully

Who egged Rex's e-bike?
Alex Rodriguez.

Clues

* Max noticed there was egg
on only the side facing Rex's
neighbor, Mr. Rodriguez.
Basher couldn't have thrown
the eggs from the street, as
Rex had said.
* The cracked eggshells
and yolk on the top of the
fence told Max that the egg
thrower must have climbed up
the fence and thrown down to
get a good shot at the bike.
* The footprints in the flour
pointed both toward and away
from the e-bike, which meant
that Basher had walked
through the flour after it
was thrown and from the
direction of the street. If
Basher had thrown the flour,
only footprints leaving
the scene would be on
the driveway.

Conclusion

Alex admitted to egging the
e-bike. He was so frustrated
with Rex's noise keeping
his dad awake, that he
decided to damage Rex's
prize possession: his e-bike.
Alex apologized and Rex
promised to keep the noise
down. Basher thanked Max for
clearing his name and vowed
to stop bullying other kids
(for the rest of the day).

From the desk of Max Finder

The Case of the... Cracked Sled

MENU
HOME
DISP

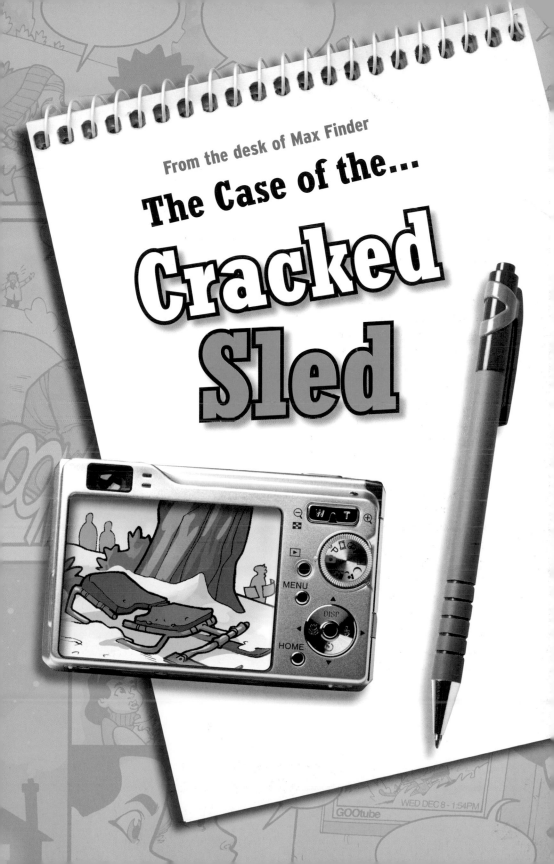

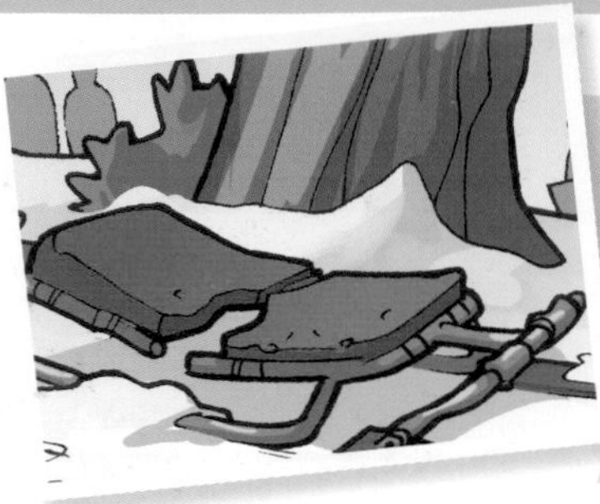

The Case of the... Cracked Sled

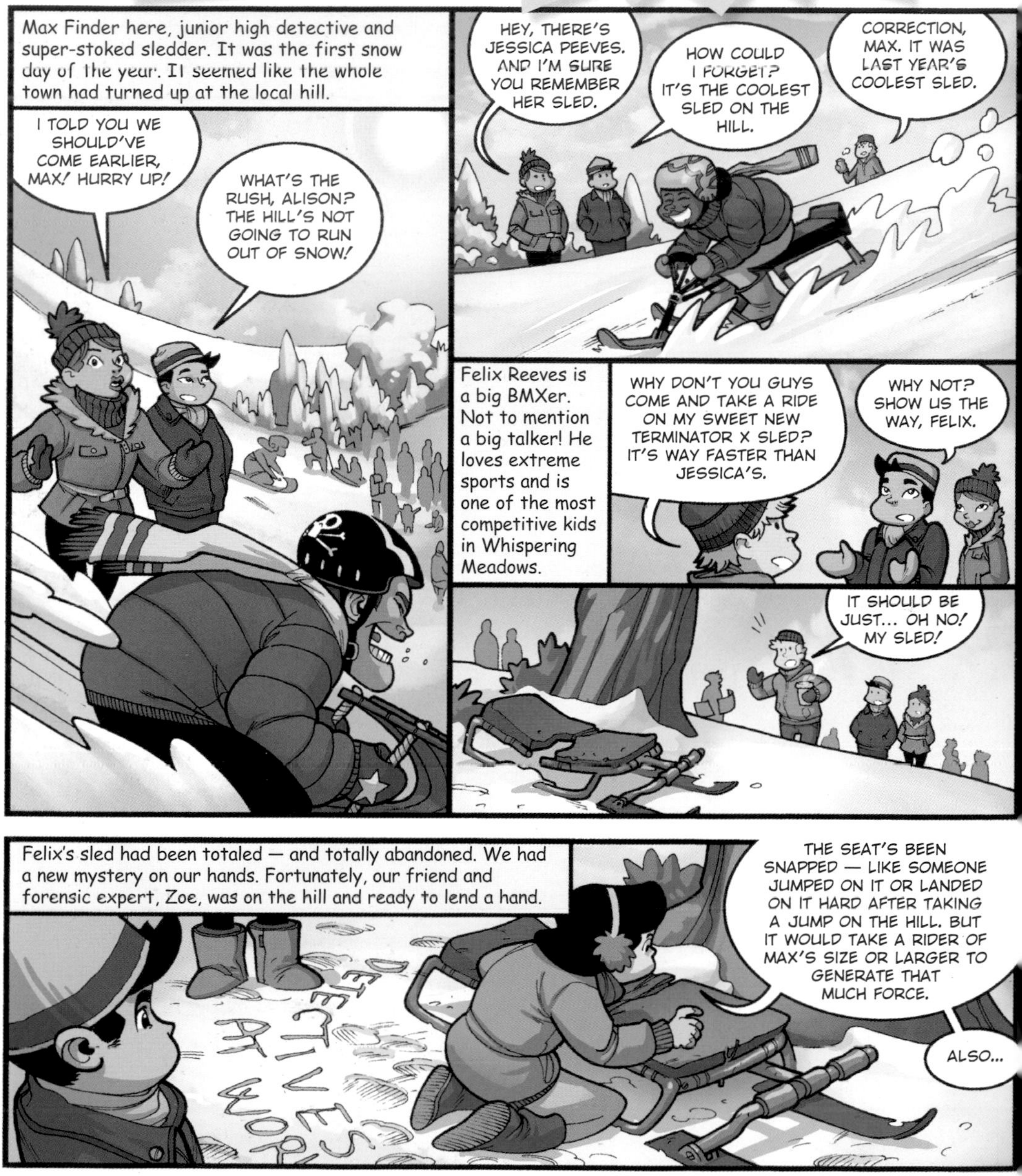

Max Finder here, junior high detective and super-stoked sledder. It was the first snow day of the year. It seemed like the whole town had turned up at the local hill.
I TOLD YOU WE SHOULD'VE COME EARLIER, MAX! HURRY UP!
WHAT'S THE RUSH, ALISON? THE HILL'S NOT GOING TO RUN OUT OF SNOW!
HEY, THERE'S JESSICA PEEVES. AND I'M SURE YOU REMEMBER HER SLED.
HOW COULD I FORGET? IT'S THE COOLEST SLED ON THE HILL.
CORRECTION, MAX. IT WAS LAST YEAR'S COOLEST SLED.
Felix Reeves is a big BMXer. Not to mention a big talker! He loves extreme sports and is one of the most competitive kids in Whispering Meadows.
WHY DON'T YOU GUYS COME AND TAKE A RIDE ON MY SWEET NEW TERMINATOR X SLED? IT'S WAY FASTER THAN JESSICA'S.
WHY NOT? SHOW US THE WAY, FELIX.
IT SHOULD BE JUST... OH NO! MY SLED!
Felix's sled had been totaled — and totally abandoned. We had a new mystery on our hands. Fortunately, our friend and forensic expert, Zoe, was on the hill and ready to lend a hand.
THE SEAT'S BEEN SNAPPED — LIKE SOMEONE JUMPED ON IT OR LANDED ON IT HARD AFTER TAKING A JUMP ON THE HILL. BUT IT WOULD TAKE A RIDER OF MAX'S SIZE OR LARGER TO GENERATE THAT MUCH FORCE.
ALSO...

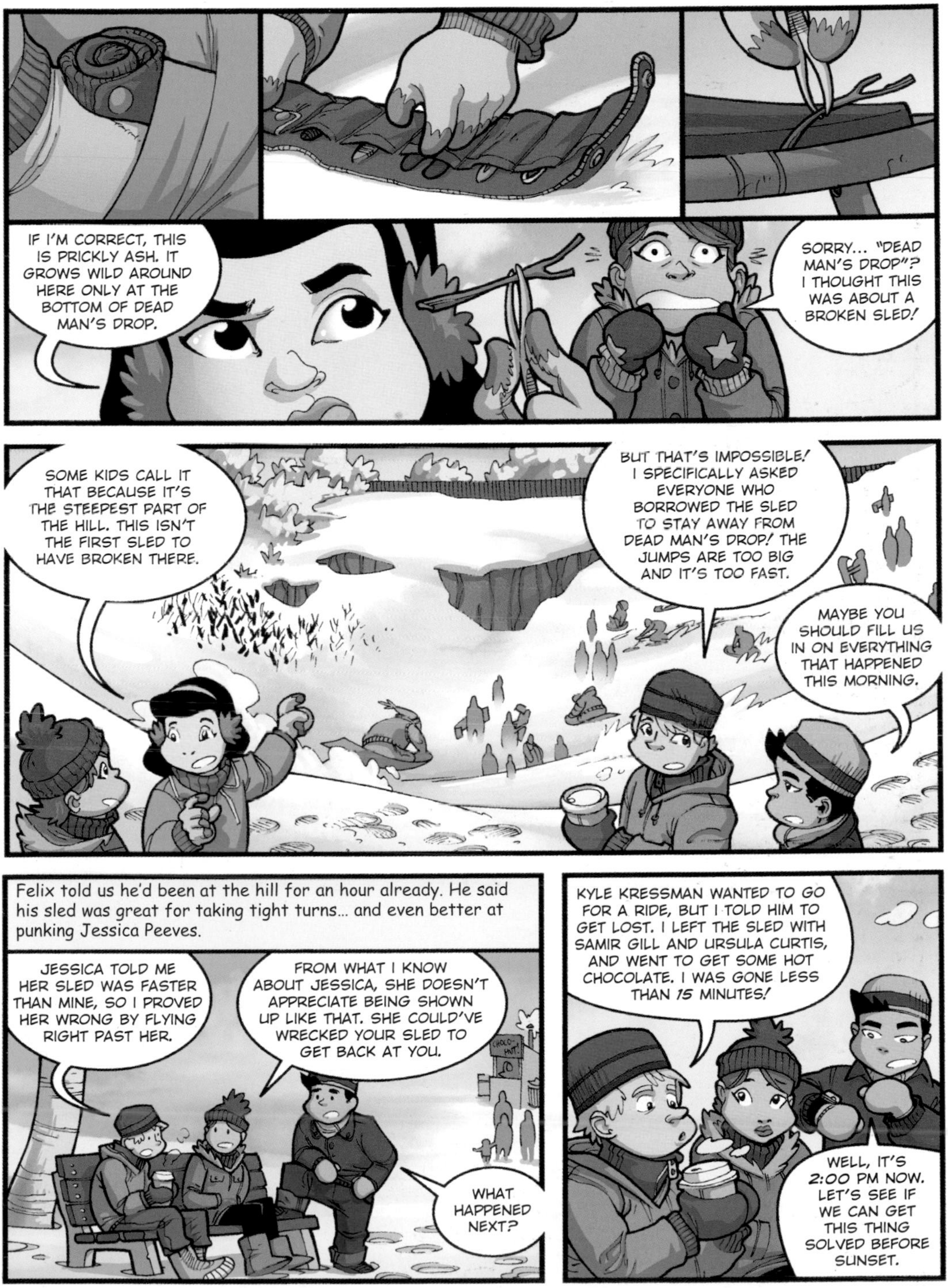

IF I'M CORRECT, THIS IS PRICKLY ASH. IT GROWS WILD AROUND HERE ONLY AT THE BOTTOM OF DEAD MAN'S DROP.
SORRY... "DEAD MAN'S DROP"? I THOUGHT THIS WAS ABOUT A BROKEN SLED!
SOME KIDS CALL IT THAT BECAUSE IT'S THE STEEPEST PART OF THE HILL. THIS ISN'T THE FIRST SLED TO HAVE BROKEN THERE.
BUT THAT'S IMPOSSIBLE! I SPECIFICALLY ASKED EVERYONE WHO BORROWED THE SLED TO STAY AWAY FROM DEAD MAN'S DROP! THE JUMPS ARE TOO BIG AND IT'S TOO FAST.
MAYBE YOU SHOULD FILL US IN ON EVERYTHING THAT HAPPENED THIS MORNING.
Felix told us he'd been at the hill for an hour already. He said his sled was great for taking tight turns... and even better at punking Jessica Peeves.
JESSICA TOLD ME HER SLED WAS FASTER THAN MINE, SO I PROVED HER WRONG BY FLYING RIGHT PAST HER.
FROM WHAT I KNOW ABOUT JESSICA, SHE DOESN'T APPRECIATE BEING SHOWN UP LIKE THAT. SHE COULD'VE WRECKED YOUR SLED TO GET BACK AT YOU.
WHAT HAPPENED NEXT?
KYLE KRESSMAN WANTED TO GO FOR A RIDE, BUT I TOLD HIM TO GET LOST. I LEFT THE SLED WITH SAMIR GILL AND URSULA CURTIS, AND WENT TO GET SOME HOT CHOCOLATE. I WAS GONE LESS THAN 15 MINUTES!
WELL, IT'S 2:00 PM NOW. LET'S SEE IF WE CAN GET THIS THING SOLVED BEFORE SUNSET.

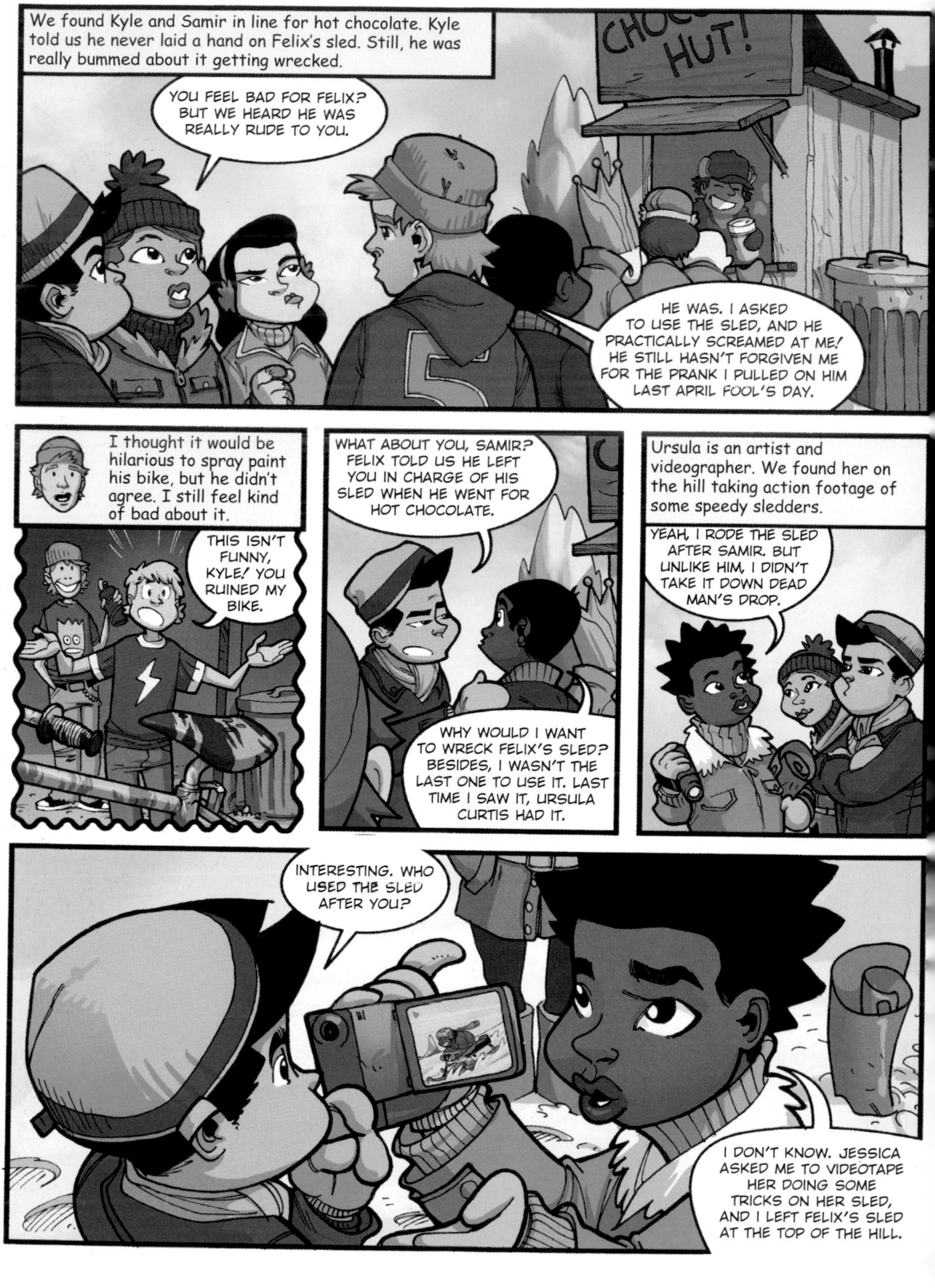

We found Kyle and Samir in line for hot chocolate. Kyle told us he never laid a hand on Felix's sled. Still, he was really bummed about it getting wrecked.
CHOCO HUT!
YOU FEEL BAD FOR FELIX? BUT WE HEARD HE WAS REALLY RUDE TO YOU.
HE WAS. I ASKED TO USE THE SLED, AND HE PRACTICALLY SCREAMED AT ME! HE STILL HASN'T FORGIVEN ME FOR THE PRANK I PULLED ON HIM LAST APRIL FOOL'S DAY.
I thought it would be hilarious to spray paint his bike, but he didn't agree. I still feel kind of bad about it.
THIS ISN'T FUNNY, KYLE! YOU RUINED MY BIKE.
WHAT ABOUT YOU, SAMIR? FELIX TOLD US HE LEFT YOU IN CHARGE OF HIS SLED WHEN HE WENT FOR HOT CHOCOLATE.
WHY WOULD I WANT TO WRECK FELIX'S SLED? BESIDES, I WASN'T THE LAST ONE TO USE IT. LAST TIME I SAW IT, URSULA CURTIS HAD IT.
Ursula is an artist and videographer. We found her on the hill taking action footage of some speedy sledders.
YEAH, I RODE THE SLED AFTER SAMIR. BUT UNLIKE HIM, I DIDN'T TAKE IT DOWN DEAD MAN'S DROP.
INTERESTING. WHO USED THE SLED AFTER YOU?
I DON'T KNOW. JESSICA ASKED ME TO VIDEOTAPE HER DOING SOME TRICKS ON HER SLED, AND I LEFT FELIX'S SLED AT THE TOP OF THE HILL.

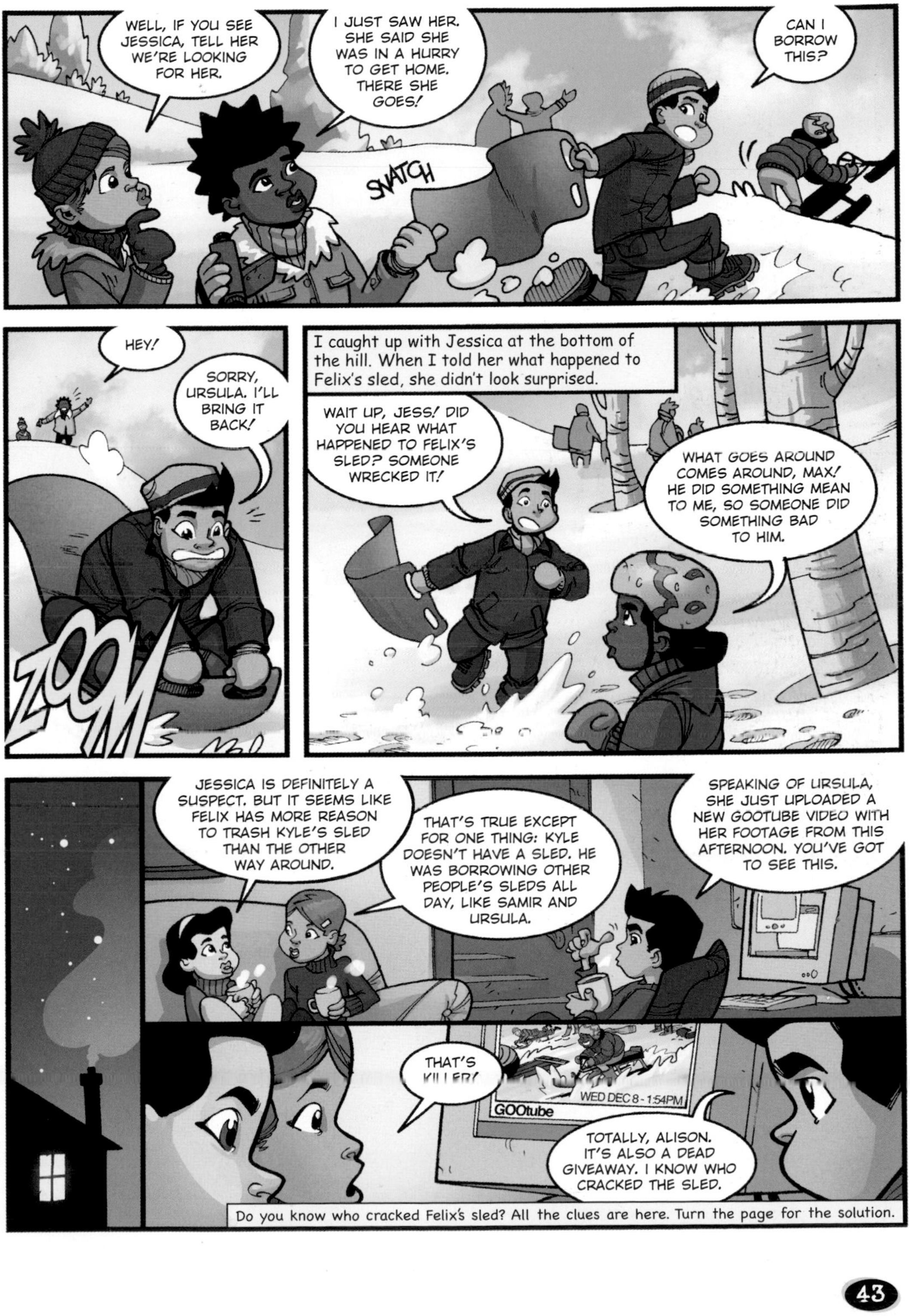
WELL, IF YOU SEE JESSICA, TELL HER WE'RE LOOKING FOR HER.
I JUST SAW HER. SHE SAID SHE WAS IN A HURRY TO GET HOME. THERE SHE GOES!
SNATCH
CAN I BORROW THIS?
HEY!
SORRY, URSULA. I'LL BRING IT BACK!
ZOOM
I caught up with Jessica at the bottom of the hill. When I told her what happened to Felix's sled, she didn't look surprised.
WAIT UP, JESS! DID YOU HEAR WHAT HAPPENED TO FELIX'S SLED? SOMEONE WRECKED IT!
WHAT GOES AROUND COMES AROUND, MAX! HE DID SOMETHING MEAN TO ME, SO SOMEONE DID SOMETHING BAD TO HIM.
JESSICA IS DEFINITELY A SUSPECT. BUT IT SEEMS LIKE FELIX HAS MORE REASON TO TRASH KYLE'S SLED THAN THE OTHER WAY AROUND.
THAT'S TRUE EXCEPT FOR ONE THING: KYLE DOESN'T HAVE A SLED. HE WAS BORROWING OTHER PEOPLE'S SLEDS ALL DAY, LIKE SAMIR AND URSULA.
SPEAKING OF URSULA, SHE JUST UPLOADED A NEW GOOTUBE VIDEO WITH HER FOOTAGE FROM THIS AFTERNOON. YOU'VE GOT TO SEE THIS.
THAT'S KILLER!
WED DEC 8 - 1:54PM
GOOtube
TOTALLY, ALISON. IT'S ALSO A DEAD GIVEAWAY. I KNOW WHO CRACKED THE SLED.
Do you know who cracked Felix's sled? All the clues are here. Turn the page for the solution.

Solution: The Case of the...
Cracked Sled

Who cracked Felix's sled?
Kyle Kressman. When Ursula left the sled alone, Kyle took it for a test drive down Dead Man's Drop, but it broke under his weight.

Clues

* In the video Ursula sent Max, Kyle can be seen riding Felix's sled. Kyle lied about not laying a finger on the sled.
* The time stamp on the video says 1:54 PM. And because Max noted that it was 2:00 PM when they were talking to Felix, that means Kyle was the last person who had a chance to ride the sled before they found it at the top of the hill.
* Zoe noticed a small branch in Kyle's toque. It was prickly ash, the same plant that Zoe said grows only at the bottom of Dead Man's Drop. That means Kyle rode the sled down the forbidden slope.
* Alison noticed that Kyle was bigger than Max when the two stood next to each other. According to Zoe's quick calculations, that means he's large enough to generate the amount of force necessary to crack the sled.
* Felix said he warned everyone who used the sled not to go down Dead Man's Drop. But because he didn't allow Kyle to use the sled, he wouldn't have given him the same warning.
* Samir may have been guilty of taking the sled down Dead Man's Drop, but he wasn't the one who wrecked it. First, he's smaller than Max, which means he wouldn't generate enough force to break the sled. Second, the sled was still intact when Ursula used it after him.

Conclusion

Kyle admitted to wrecking the sled, but he said it was an accident. He was jealous he couldn't ride the sled and figured one little run couldn't hurt. He apologized to Felix and offered to pay for a new sled with his allowance.

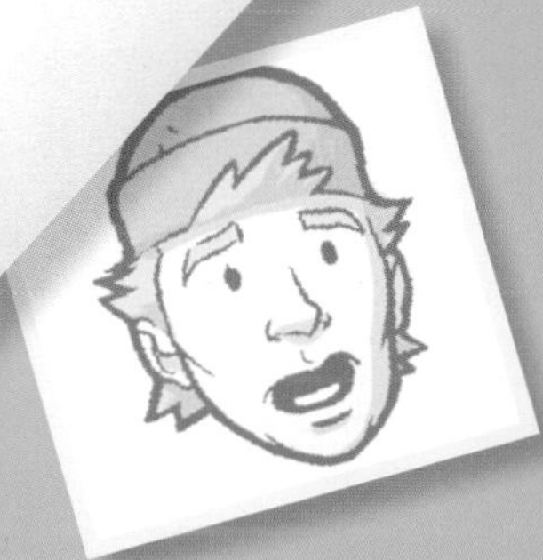

From the desk of Max Finder

The Case of the...

Stopped Presses

MENU
HOME

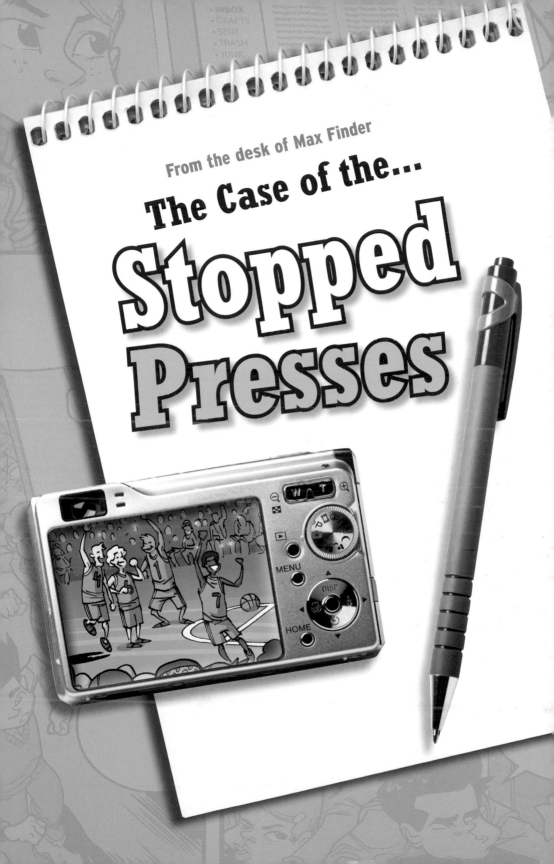

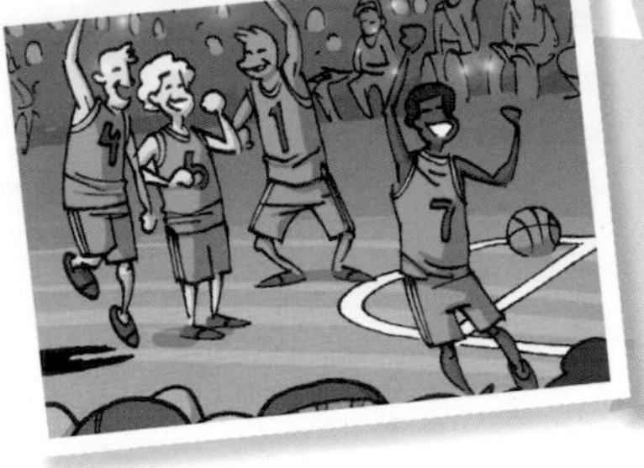

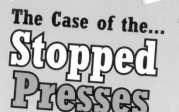

The Case of the... Stopped Presses

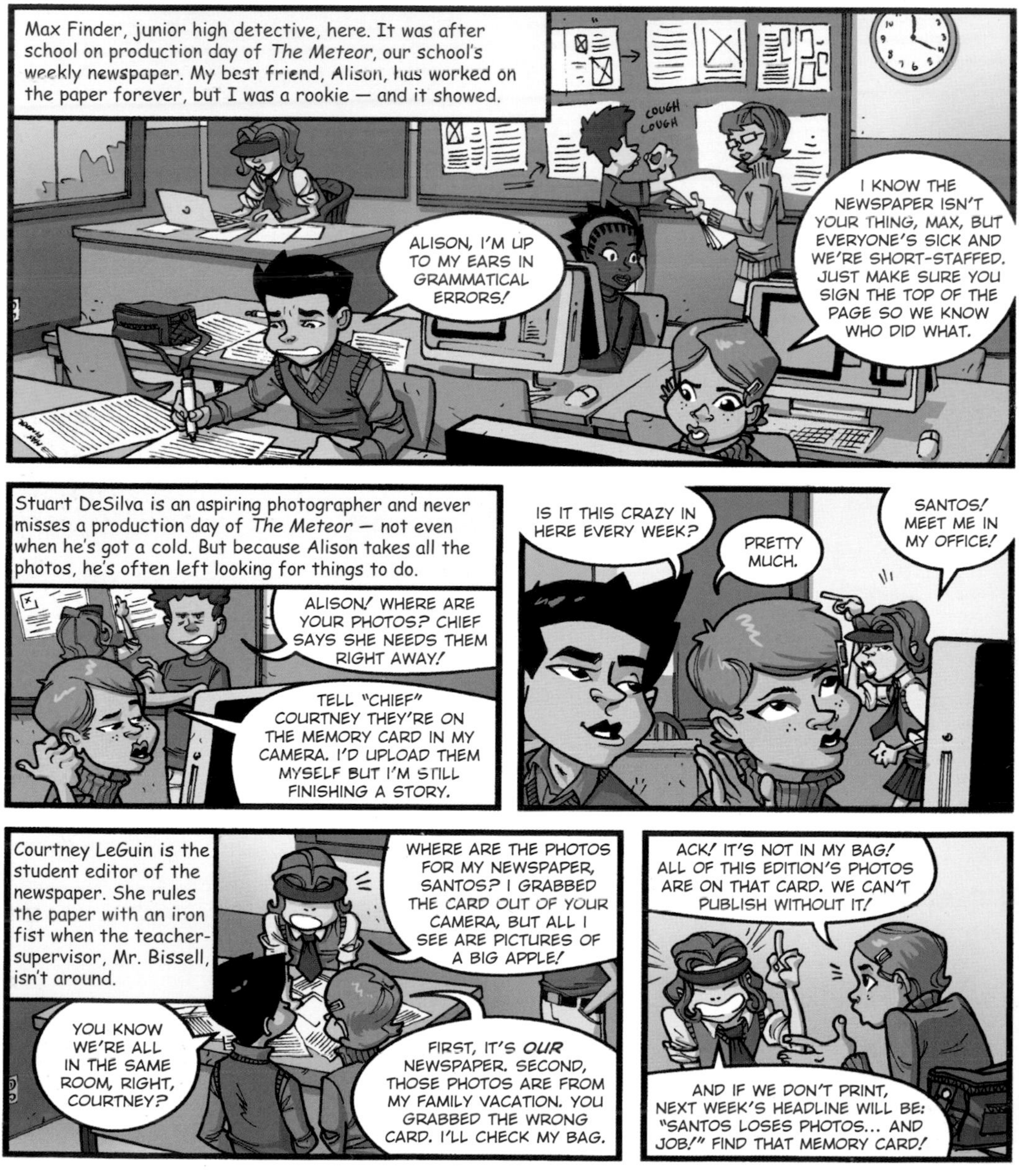
Max Finder, junior high detective, here. It was after school on production day of *The Meteor*, our school's weekly newspaper. My best friend, Alison, has worked on the paper forever, but I was a rookie — and it showed.
COUGH COUGH
ALISON, I'M UP TO MY EARS IN GRAMMATICAL ERRORS!
I KNOW THE NEWSPAPER ISN'T YOUR THING, MAX, BUT EVERYONE'S SICK AND WE'RE SHORT-STAFFED. JUST MAKE SURE YOU SIGN THE TOP OF THE PAGE SO WE KNOW WHO DID WHAT.
Stuart DeSilva is an aspiring photographer and never misses a production day of *The Meteor* — not even when he's got a cold. But because Alison takes all the photos, he's often left looking for things to do.
ALISON! WHERE ARE YOUR PHOTOS? CHIEF SAYS SHE NEEDS THEM RIGHT AWAY!
TELL "CHIEF" COURTNEY THEY'RE ON THE MEMORY CARD IN MY CAMERA. I'D UPLOAD THEM MYSELF BUT I'M STILL FINISHING A STORY.
IS IT THIS CRAZY IN HERE EVERY WEEK?
PRETTY MUCH.
SANTOS! MEET ME IN MY OFFICE!
Courtney LeGuin is the student editor of the newspaper. She rules the paper with an iron fist when the teacher-supervisor, Mr. Bissell, isn't around.
WHERE ARE THE PHOTOS FOR MY NEWSPAPER, SANTOS? I GRABBED THE CARD OUT OF YOUR CAMERA, BUT ALL I SEE ARE PICTURES OF A BIG APPLE!
YOU KNOW WE'RE ALL IN THE SAME ROOM, RIGHT, COURTNEY?
FIRST, IT'S *OUR* NEWSPAPER. SECOND, THOSE PHOTOS ARE FROM MY FAMILY VACATION. YOU GRABBED THE WRONG CARD. I'LL CHECK MY BAG.
ACK! IT'S NOT IN MY BAG! ALL OF THIS EDITION'S PHOTOS ARE ON THAT CARD. WE CAN'T PUBLISH WITHOUT IT!
AND IF WE DON'T PRINT, NEXT WEEK'S HEADLINE WILL BE: "SANTOS LOSES PHOTOS... AND JOB!" FIND THAT MEMORY CARD!

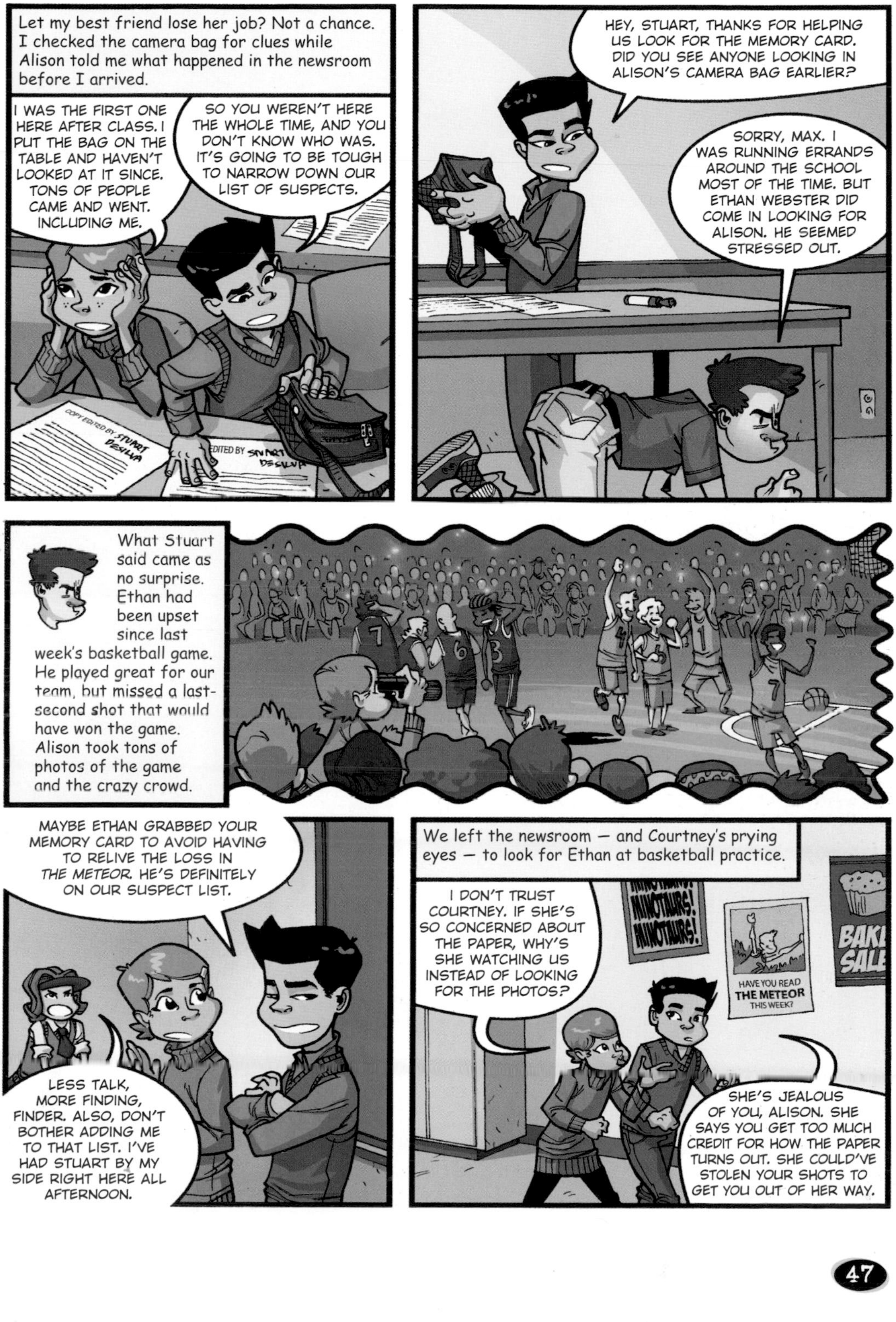
Let my best friend lose her job? Not a chance. I checked the camera bag for clues while Alison told me what happened in the newsroom before I arrived.
I WAS THE FIRST ONE HERE AFTER CLASS. I PUT THE BAG ON THE TABLE AND HAVEN'T LOOKED AT IT SINCE. TONS OF PEOPLE CAME AND WENT. INCLUDING ME.
SO YOU WEREN'T HERE THE WHOLE TIME, AND YOU DON'T KNOW WHO WAS. IT'S GOING TO BE TOUGH TO NARROW DOWN OUR LIST OF SUSPECTS.
COPY EDITED BY: STUART DESILVA
EDITED BY STUART DESILVA
HEY, STUART, THANKS FOR HELPING US LOOK FOR THE MEMORY CARD. DID YOU SEE ANYONE LOOKING IN ALISON'S CAMERA BAG EARLIER?
SORRY, MAX. I WAS RUNNING ERRANDS AROUND THE SCHOOL MOST OF THE TIME. BUT ETHAN WEBSTER DID COME IN LOOKING FOR ALISON. HE SEEMED STRESSED OUT.
What Stuart said came as no surprise. Ethan had been upset since last week's basketball game. He played great for our team, but missed a last-second shot that would have won the game. Alison took tons of photos of the game and the crazy crowd.
MAYBE ETHAN GRABBED YOUR MEMORY CARD TO AVOID HAVING TO RELIVE THE LOSS IN *THE METEOR*. HE'S DEFINITELY ON OUR SUSPECT LIST.
LESS TALK, MORE FINDING, FINDER. ALSO, DON'T BOTHER ADDING ME TO THAT LIST. I'VE HAD STUART BY MY SIDE RIGHT HERE ALL AFTERNOON.
We left the newsroom — and Courtney's prying eyes — to look for Ethan at basketball practice.
MINOTAURS! MINOTAURS!
HAVE YOU READ THE METEOR THIS WEEK?
BAKE SALE
I DON'T TRUST COURTNEY. IF SHE'S SO CONCERNED ABOUT THE PAPER, WHY'S SHE WATCHING US INSTEAD OF LOOKING FOR THE PHOTOS?
SHE'S JEALOUS OF YOU, ALISON. SHE SAYS YOU GET TOO MUCH CREDIT FOR HOW THE PAPER TURNS OUT. SHE COULD'VE STOLEN YOUR SHOTS TO GET YOU OUT OF HER WAY.

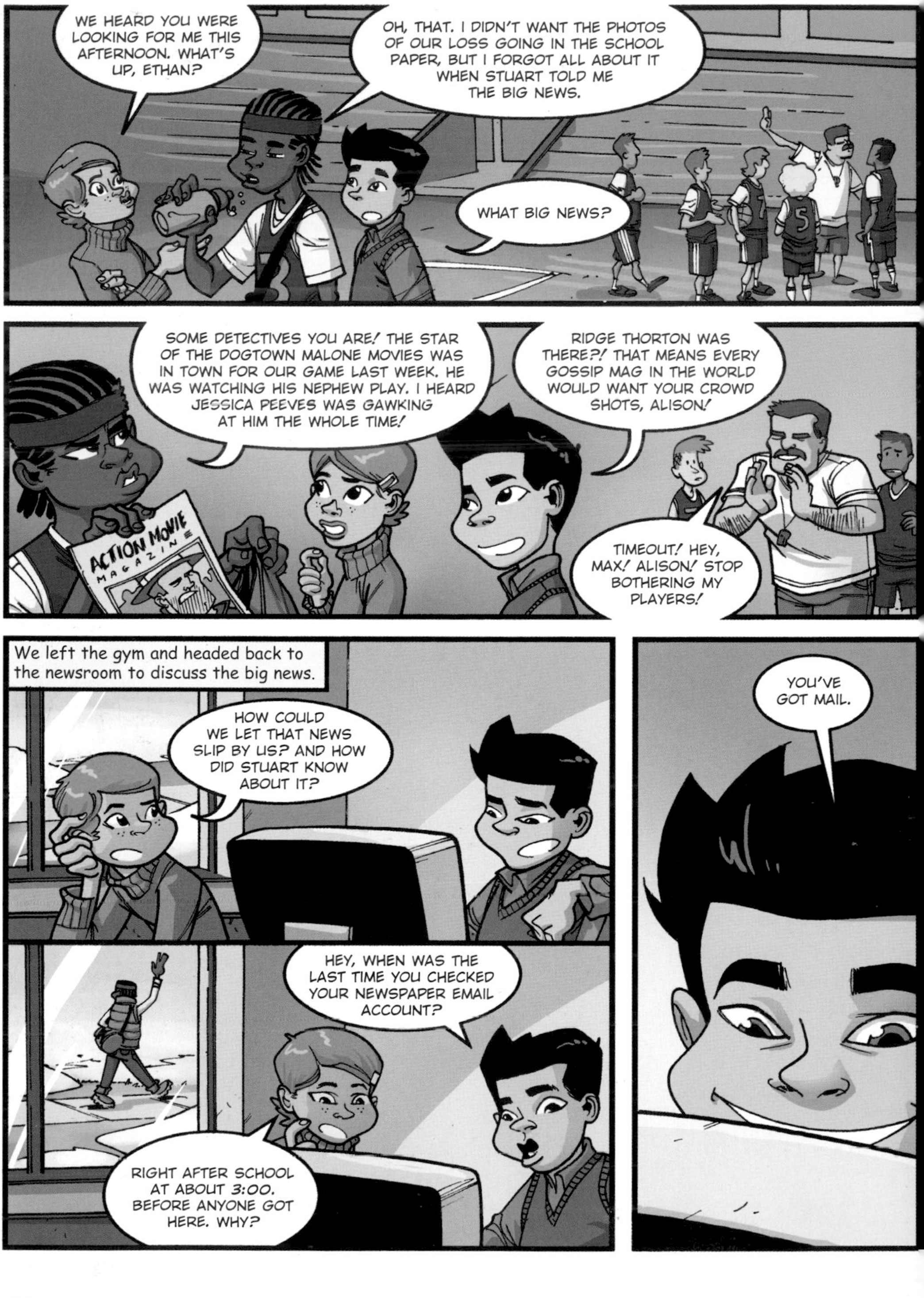

WE HEARD YOU WERE LOOKING FOR ME THIS AFTERNOON. WHAT'S UP, ETHAN?
OH, THAT. I DIDN'T WANT THE PHOTOS OF OUR LOSS GOING IN THE SCHOOL PAPER, BUT I FORGOT ALL ABOUT IT WHEN STUART TOLD ME THE BIG NEWS.
WHAT BIG NEWS?
SOME DETECTIVES YOU ARE! THE STAR OF THE DOGTOWN MALONE MOVIES WAS IN TOWN FOR OUR GAME LAST WEEK. HE WAS WATCHING HIS NEPHEW PLAY. I HEARD JESSICA PEEVES WAS GAWKING AT HIM THE WHOLE TIME!
ACTION MOVIE MAGAZINE
RIDGE THORTON WAS THERE?! THAT MEANS EVERY GOSSIP MAG IN THE WORLD WOULD WANT YOUR CROWD SHOTS, ALISON!
TIMEOUT! HEY, MAX! ALISON! STOP BOTHERING MY PLAYERS!
We left the gym and headed back to the newsroom to discuss the big news.
HOW COULD WE LET THAT NEWS SLIP BY US? AND HOW DID STUART KNOW ABOUT IT?
HEY, WHEN WAS THE LAST TIME YOU CHECKED YOUR NEWSPAPER EMAIL ACCOUNT?
RIGHT AFTER SCHOOL AT ABOUT 3:00. BEFORE ANYONE GOT HERE. WHY?
YOU'VE GOT MAIL.

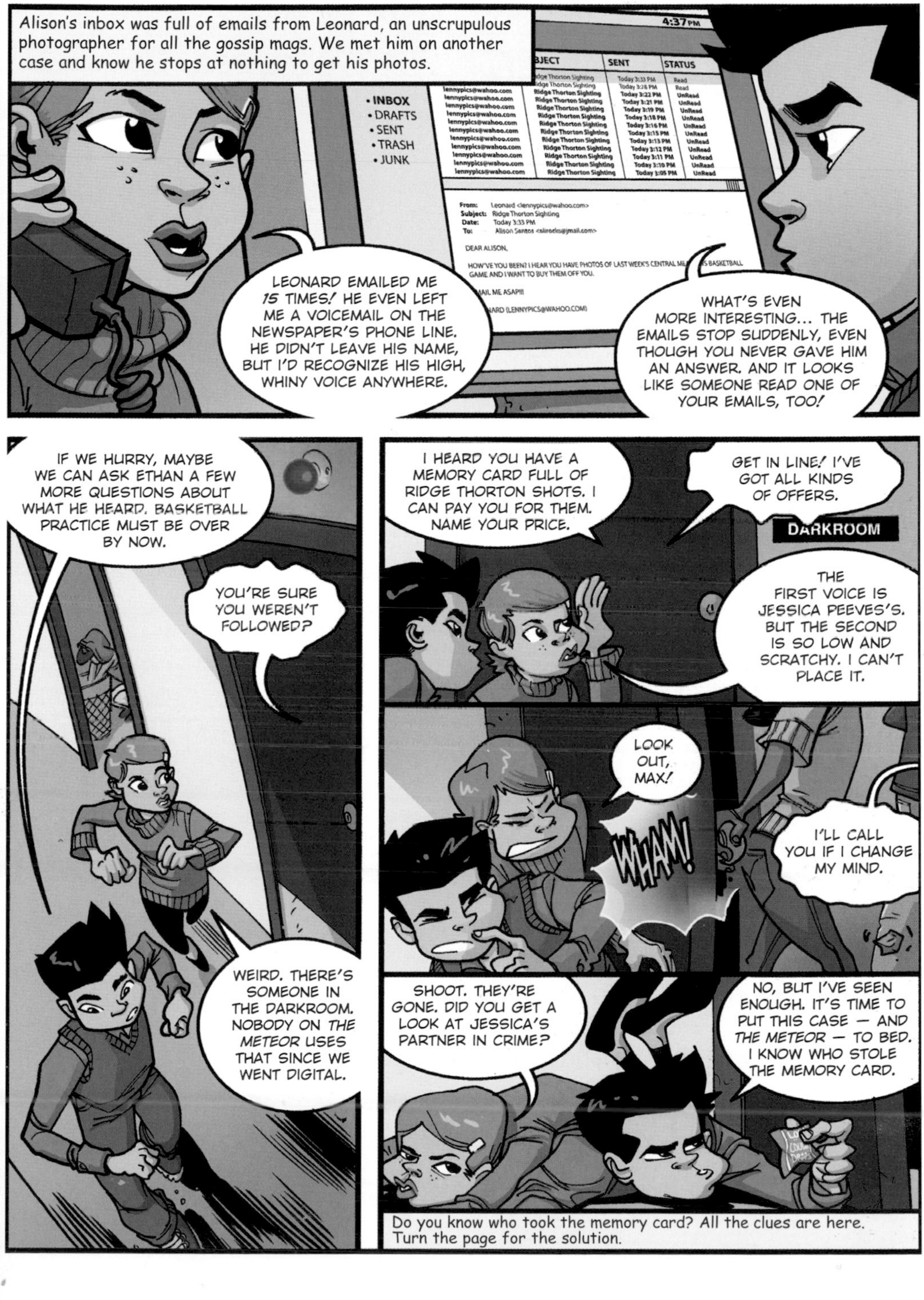

Alison's inbox was full of emails from Leonard, an unscrupulous photographer for all the gossip mags. We met him on another case and know he stops at nothing to get his photos.
4:37 PM
• INBOX
• DRAFTS
• SENT
• TRASH
• JUNK
LEONARD EMAILED ME 15 TIMES! HE EVEN LEFT ME A VOICEMAIL ON THE NEWSPAPER'S PHONE LINE. HE DIDN'T LEAVE HIS NAME, BUT I'D RECOGNIZE HIS HIGH, WHINY VOICE ANYWHERE.
WHAT'S EVEN MORE INTERESTING... THE EMAILS STOP SUDDENLY, EVEN THOUGH YOU NEVER GAVE HIM AN ANSWER. AND IT LOOKS LIKE SOMEONE READ ONE OF YOUR EMAILS, TOO!
IF WE HURRY, MAYBE WE CAN ASK ETHAN A FEW MORE QUESTIONS ABOUT WHAT HE HEARD. BASKETBALL PRACTICE MUST BE OVER BY NOW.
YOU'RE SURE YOU WEREN'T FOLLOWED?
WEIRD. THERE'S SOMEONE IN THE DARKROOM. NOBODY ON THE METEOR USES THAT SINCE WE WENT DIGITAL.
I HEARD YOU HAVE A MEMORY CARD FULL OF RIDGE THORTON SHOTS. I CAN PAY YOU FOR THEM. NAME YOUR PRICE.
GET IN LINE! I'VE GOT ALL KINDS OF OFFERS.
DARKROOM
THE FIRST VOICE IS JESSICA PEEVES'S. BUT THE SECOND IS SO LOW AND SCRATCHY. I CAN'T PLACE IT.
LOOK OUT, MAX!
WHAM!
I'LL CALL YOU IF I CHANGE MY MIND.
SHOOT. THEY'RE GONE. DID YOU GET A LOOK AT JESSICA'S PARTNER IN CRIME?
NO, BUT I'VE SEEN ENOUGH. IT'S TIME TO PUT THIS CASE — AND THE METEOR — TO BED. I KNOW WHO STOLE THE MEMORY CARD.
Do you know who took the memory card? All the clues are here. Turn the page for the solution.

Solution: The Case of the...
Stopped Presses

Who stole Alison's memory card? Stuart DeSilva. He knew he could make money off her photos, so he took the card and offered it up to the highest bidder.

Clues

* Courtney said Stuart was in the newsroom all afternoon. That means he was lying about running errands all over the school. It also means he had lots of time to read Leonard's email to Alison while she was away from her desk.

* Alison was first to arrive at the newsroom, yet Stuart's copy editing sheet was under her camera bag. That proves Stuart was meddling with the bag after she arrived.

* Max noticed a pack of green cough drops in Stuart's back pocket. When Max found the cough drop wrapper in the hallway, he knew Stuart was the unknown person with the low and scratchy voice.

* Alison couldn't recognize Stuart's voice because he had run out of cough drops to clear his throat.

* The voice in the darkroom couldn't have been Leonard's. Alison called it "high and whiny"—not low and scratchy.

* The voice couldn't have been Courtney's or Ethan's either. Ethan walked by the newsroom window on his way home while the detectives checked Alison's email and Courtney was searching her trash for the memory card when they rushed into the hallway.

Conclusion

Stuart confessed to the crime. Courtney suspended him from the newspaper staff and apologized to Alison. Everyone pitched in and put together the most popular issue of *The Meteor* in the history of Central Meadows Junior High—complete with shots of everybody's favorite action star, Ridge Thorton.

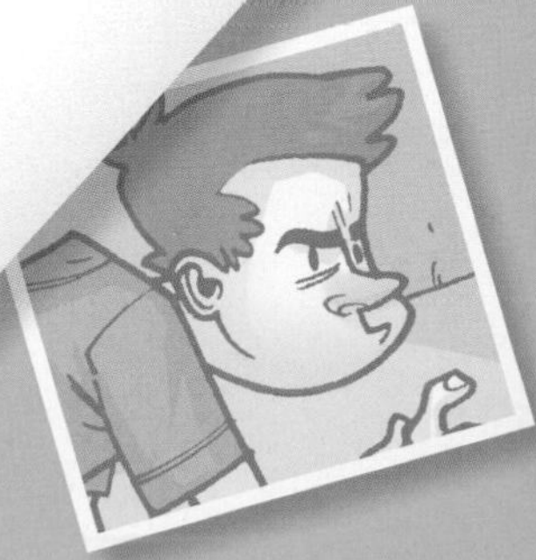

From the desk of Max Finder

The Case of the...

Graffiti Goon

W
T
MENU
DISP
HOME

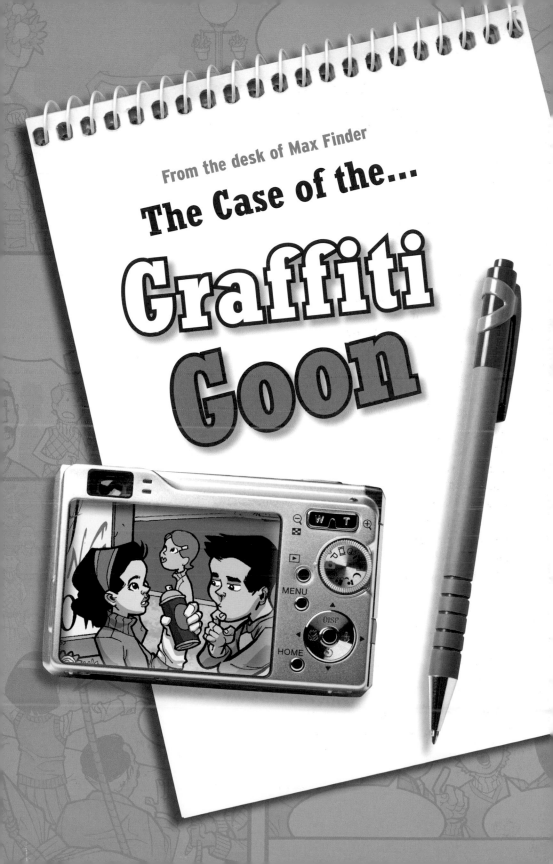

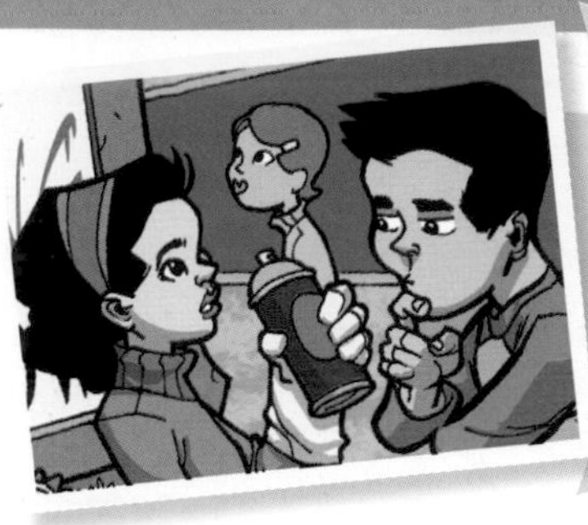

The Case of the... Graffiti Goon

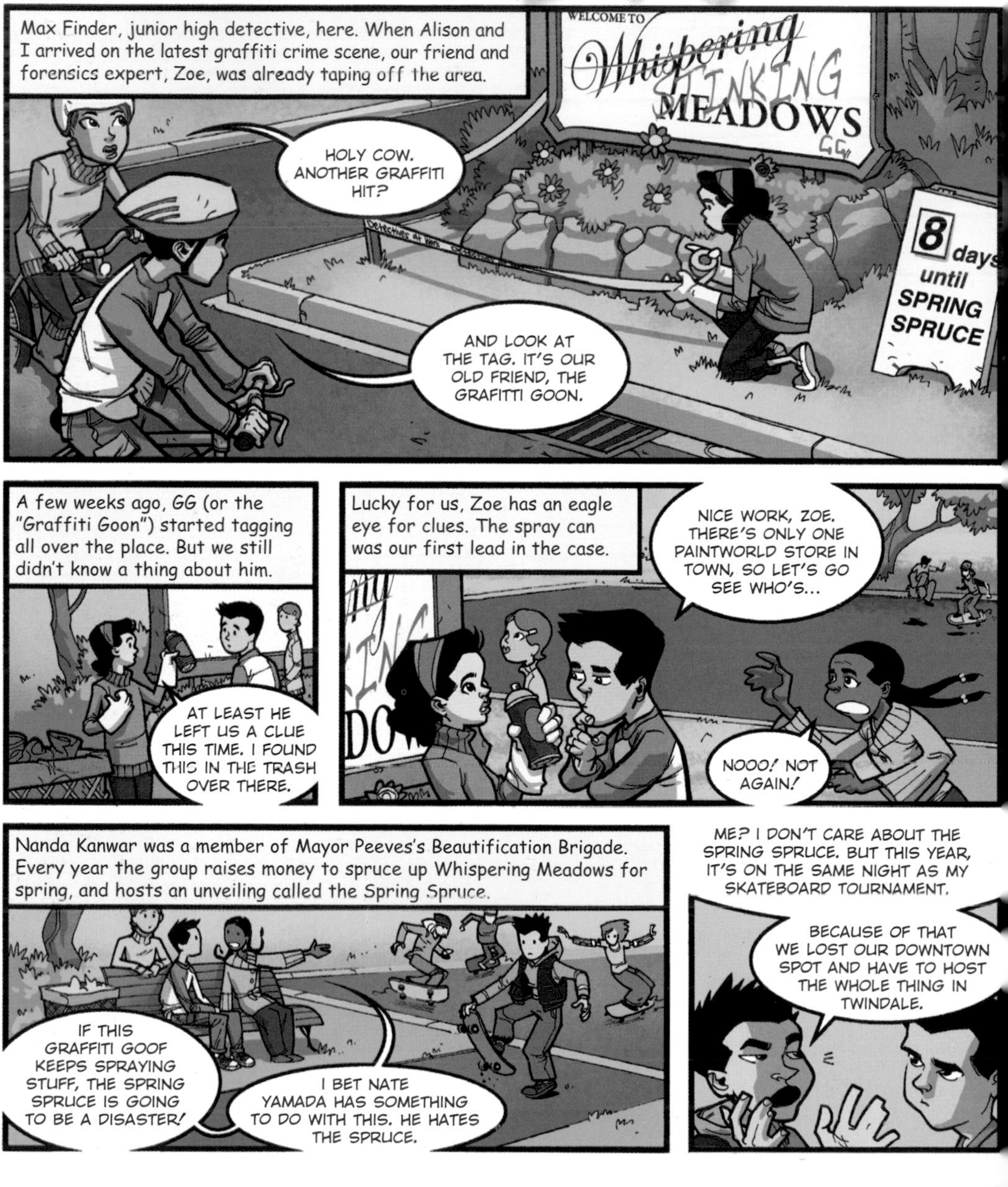

WELCOME TO Whispering STINKING MEADOWS
GG
Max Finder, junior high detective, here. When Alison and I arrived on the latest graffiti crime scene, our friend and forensics expert, Zoe, was already taping off the area.
HOLY COW. ANOTHER GRAFFITI HIT?
AND LOOK AT THE TAG. IT'S OUR OLD FRIEND, THE GRAFITTI GOON.
8 days until SPRING SPRUCE
A few weeks ago, GG (or the "Graffiti Goon") started tagging all over the place. But we still didn't know a thing about him.
AT LEAST HE LEFT US A CLUE THIS TIME. I FOUND THIS IN THE TRASH OVER THERE.
Lucky for us, Zoe has an eagle eye for clues. The spray can was our first lead in the case.
NICE WORK, ZOE. THERE'S ONLY ONE PAINTWORLD STORE IN TOWN, SO LET'S GO SEE WHO'S...
NOOO! NOT AGAIN!
Nanda Kanwar was a member of Mayor Peeves's Beautification Brigade. Every year the group raises money to spruce up Whispering Meadows for spring, and hosts an unveiling called the Spring Spruce.
IF THIS GRAFFITI GOOF KEEPS SPRAYING STUFF, THE SPRING SPRUCE IS GOING TO BE A DISASTER!
I BET NATE YAMADA HAS SOMETHING TO DO WITH THIS. HE HATES THE SPRUCE.
ME? I DON'T CARE ABOUT THE SPRING SPRUCE. BUT THIS YEAR, IT'S ON THE SAME NIGHT AS MY SKATEBOARD TOURNAMENT.
BECAUSE OF THAT WE LOST OUR DOWNTOWN SPOT AND HAVE TO HOST THE WHOLE THING IN TWINDALE.

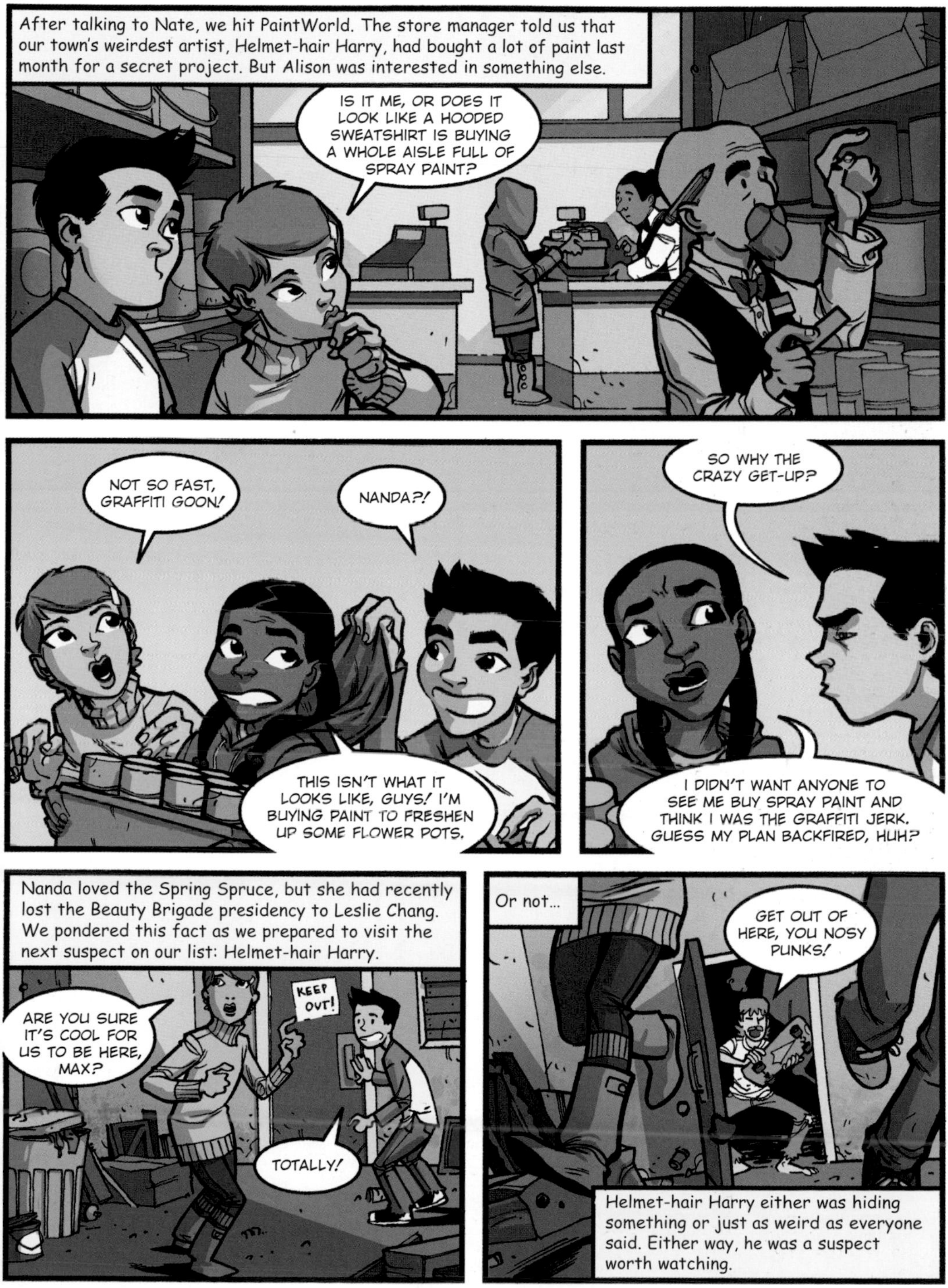
After talking to Nate, we hit PaintWorld. The store manager told us that our town's weirdest artist, Helmet-hair Harry, had bought a lot of paint last month for a secret project. But Alison was interested in something else.
IS IT ME, OR DOES IT LOOK LIKE A HOODED SWEATSHIRT IS BUYING A WHOLE AISLE FULL OF SPRAY PAINT?
NOT SO FAST, GRAFFITI GOON!
NANDA?!
THIS ISN'T WHAT IT LOOKS LIKE, GUYS! I'M BUYING PAINT TO FRESHEN UP SOME FLOWER POTS.
SO WHY THE CRAZY GET-UP?
I DIDN'T WANT ANYONE TO SEE ME BUY SPRAY PAINT AND THINK I WAS THE GRAFFITI JERK. GUESS MY PLAN BACKFIRED, HUH?
Nanda loved the Spring Spruce, but she had recently lost the Beauty Brigade presidency to Leslie Chang. We pondered this fact as we prepared to visit the next suspect on our list: Helmet-hair Harry.
ARE YOU SURE IT'S COOL FOR US TO BE HERE, MAX?
KEEP OUT!
TOTALLY!
Or not...
GET OUT OF HERE, YOU NOSY PUNKS!
Helmet-hair Harry either was hiding something or just as weird as everyone said. Either way, he was a suspect worth watching.

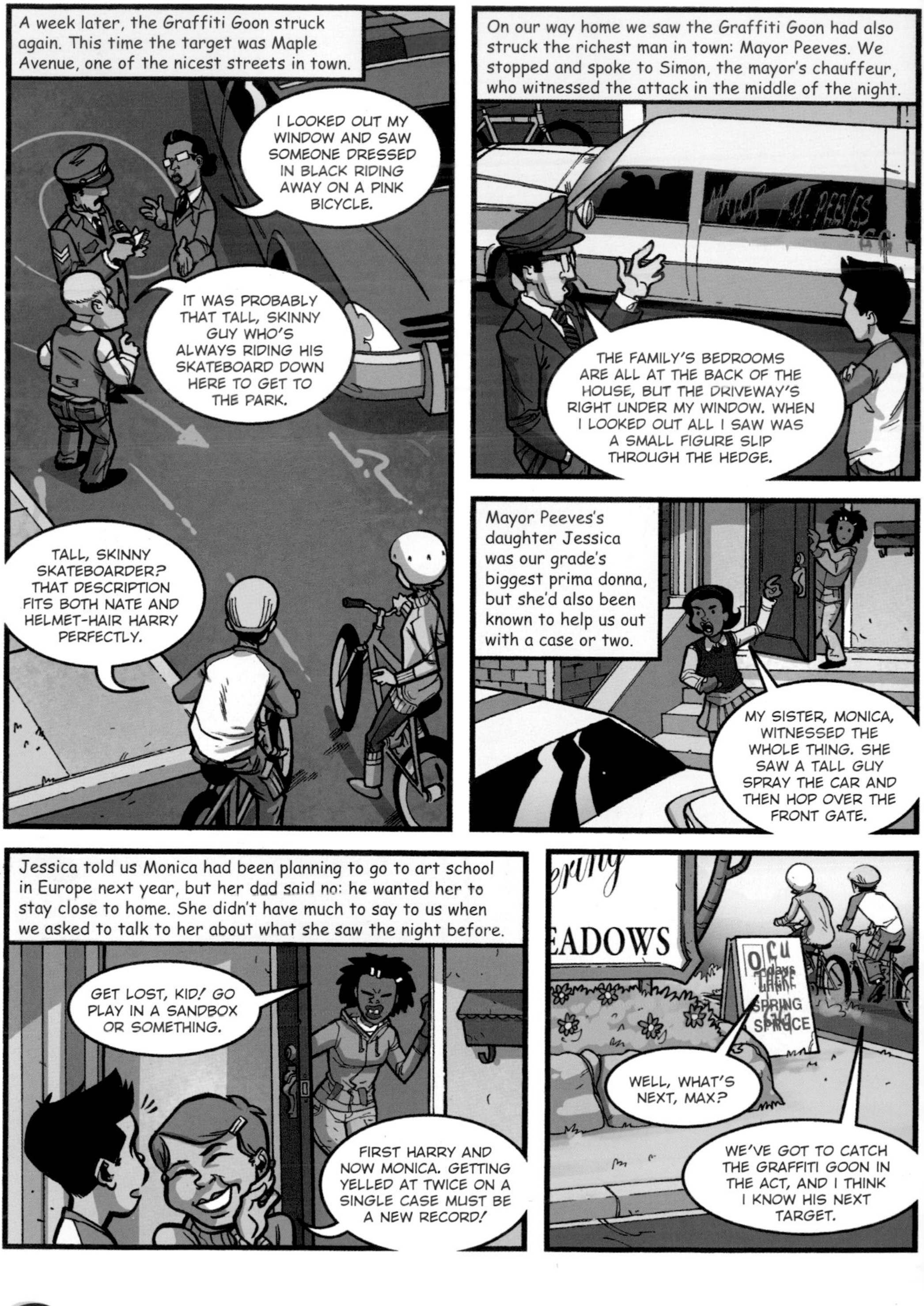

A week later, the Graffiti Goon struck again. This time the target was Maple Avenue, one of the nicest streets in town.
I LOOKED OUT MY WINDOW AND SAW SOMEONE DRESSED IN BLACK RIDING AWAY ON A PINK BICYCLE.
IT WAS PROBABLY THAT TALL, SKINNY GUY WHO'S ALWAYS RIDING HIS SKATEBOARD DOWN HERE TO GET TO THE PARK.
TALL, SKINNY SKATEBOARDER? THAT DESCRIPTION FITS BOTH NATE AND HELMET-HAIR HARRY PERFECTLY.
On our way home we saw the Graffiti Goon had also struck the richest man in town: Mayor Peeves. We stopped and spoke to Simon, the mayor's chauffeur, who witnessed the attack in the middle of the night.
THE FAMILY'S BEDROOMS ARE ALL AT THE BACK OF THE HOUSE, BUT THE DRIVEWAY'S RIGHT UNDER MY WINDOW. WHEN I LOOKED OUT ALL I SAW WAS A SMALL FIGURE SLIP THROUGH THE HEDGE.
Mayor Peeves's daughter Jessica was our grade's biggest prima donna, but she'd also been known to help us out with a case or two.
MY SISTER, MONICA, WITNESSED THE WHOLE THING. SHE SAW A TALL GUY SPRAY THE CAR AND THEN HOP OVER THE FRONT GATE.
Jessica told us Monica had been planning to go to art school in Europe next year, but her dad said no: he wanted her to stay close to home. She didn't have much to say to us when we asked to talk to her about what she saw the night before.
GET LOST, KID! GO PLAY IN A SANDBOX OR SOMETHING.
FIRST HARRY AND NOW MONICA. GETTING YELLED AT TWICE ON A SINGLE CASE MUST BE A NEW RECORD!
WELL, WHAT'S NEXT, MAX?
WE'VE GOT TO CATCH THE GRAFFITI GOON IN THE ACT, AND I THINK I KNOW HIS NEXT TARGET.

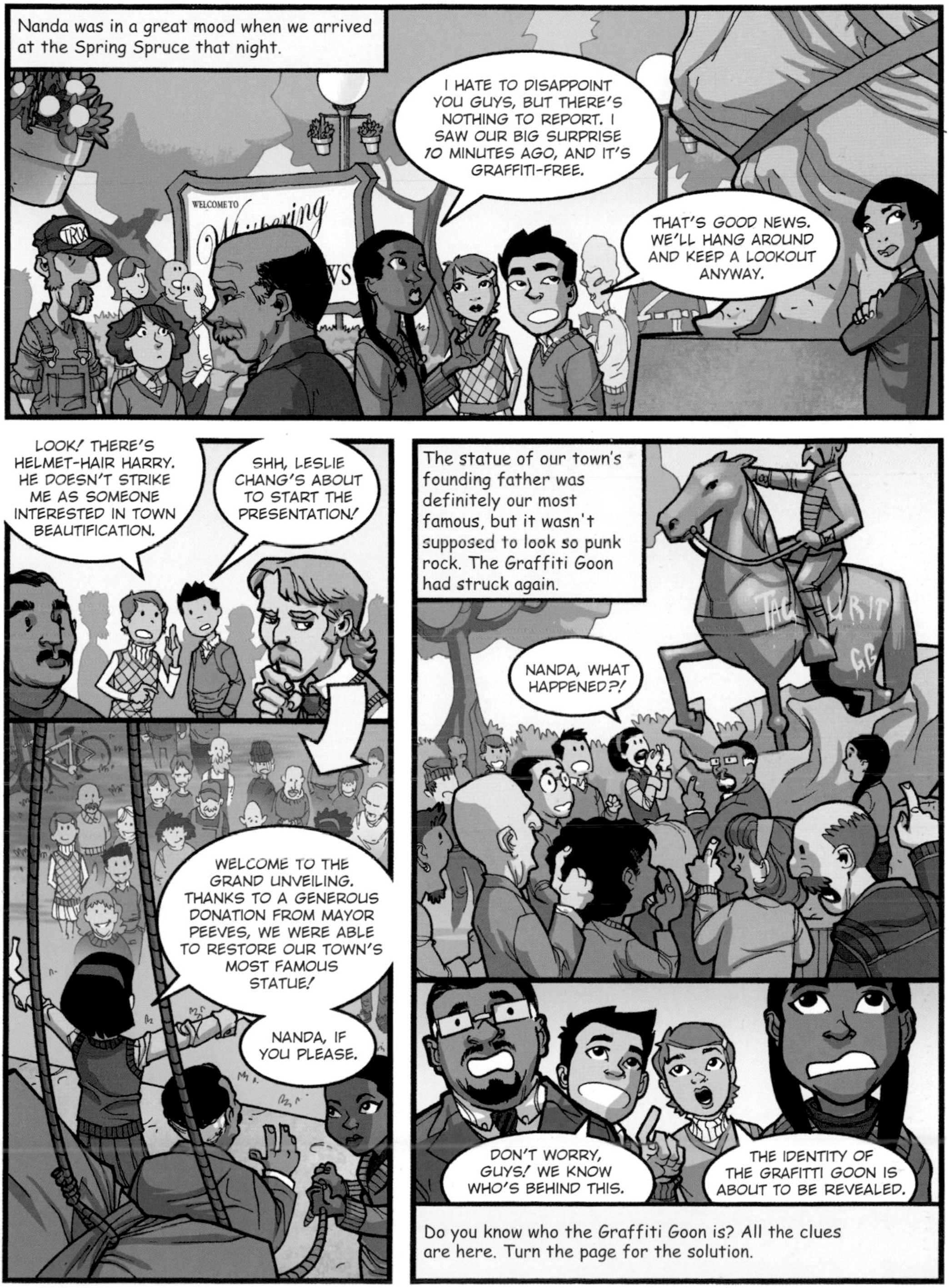
Nanda was in a great mood when we arrived at the Spring Spruce that night.
WELCOME TO Whispering ...WS
I HATE TO DISAPPOINT YOU GUYS, BUT THERE'S NOTHING TO REPORT. I SAW OUR BIG SURPRISE 10 MINUTES AGO, AND IT'S GRAFFITI-FREE.
THAT'S GOOD NEWS. WE'LL HANG AROUND AND KEEP A LOOKOUT ANYWAY.
LOOK! THERE'S HELMET-HAIR HARRY. HE DOESN'T STRIKE ME AS SOMEONE INTERESTED IN TOWN BEAUTIFICATION.
SHH, LESLIE CHANG'S ABOUT TO START THE PRESENTATION!
WELCOME TO THE GRAND UNVEILING. THANKS TO A GENEROUS DONATION FROM MAYOR PEEVES, WE WERE ABLE TO RESTORE OUR TOWN'S MOST FAMOUS STATUE!
NANDA, IF YOU PLEASE.
The statue of our town's founding father was definitely our most famous, but it wasn't supposed to look so punk rock. The Graffiti Goon had struck again.
GG
NANDA, WHAT HAPPENED?!
DON'T WORRY, GUYS! WE KNOW WHO'S BEHIND THIS.
THE IDENTITY OF THE GRAFITTI GOON IS ABOUT TO BE REVEALED.
Do you know who the Graffiti Goon is? All the clues are here. Turn the page for the solution.

Solution: The Case of the...
Graffiti Goon

Who is GG?
Monica Peeves. She was angry at her dad for asking her to go to school closer to home, so she sprayed graffiti all over town to get back at him.

Clues
* The woman on Maple Avenue said she saw someone riding away from the crime scene on a pink bicycle. Max and Alison noticed a pink bicycle at Mayor Peeves's house and at the unveiling of the spray-painted statue. It was Monica's.
* The chauffeur said the family bedrooms were at the back of the house. That means Monica couldn't have seen the crime like she said she did. She lied to draw suspicion away from herself.
* Nanda, on the other hand, wasn't lying when she said she was buying spray paint to paint flower pots. Max noticed the gold and silver pots hanging from lamps at the time of the unveiling.
* Nate Yamada may ride his skateboard down Maple Avenue every night, but he didn't tag the statue. His skateboard tournament was the night of the Spring Spruce, so he would've been in Twindale when the statue was sprayed.
* Helmet-hair Harry scared Max and Alison away from his workshop because he was secretly restoring the statue. In fact, the statue was inside the doorway of his workshop when he chased them away.

Conclusion
When Max and Alison presented their evidence, Monica came out of hiding and confessed. She agreed to spend her own money to restore the statue (again!), and spent several hours beautifying other parts of town as well. When Max and Alison asked her what "GG" stood for, she said it was simple: Graffiti Girl!

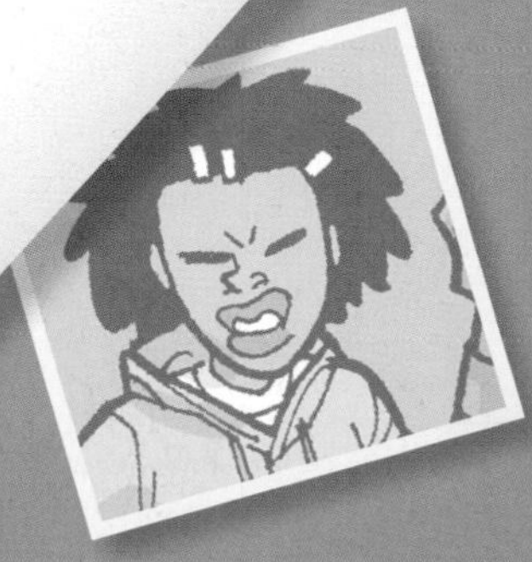

From the desk of Max Finder

From the Case of the...

The Case of the... Messed-Up Magic Show

W
T
MENU
DISP
HOME

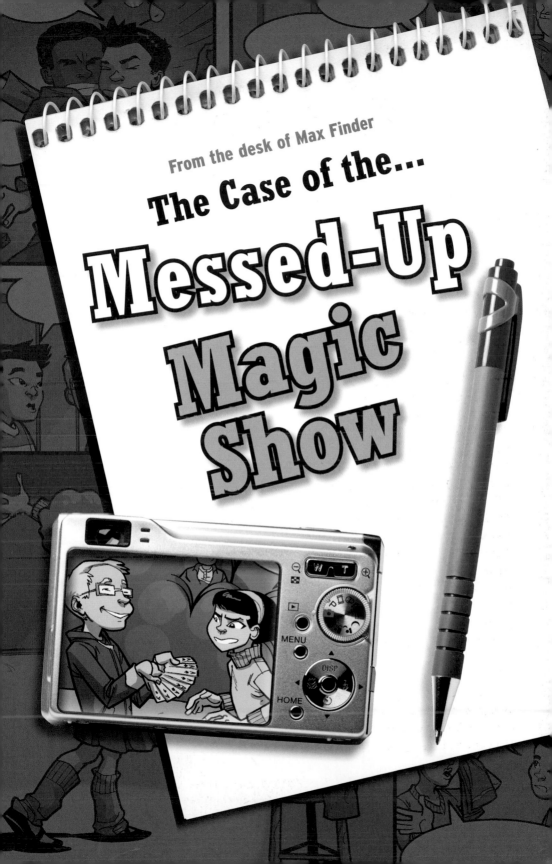

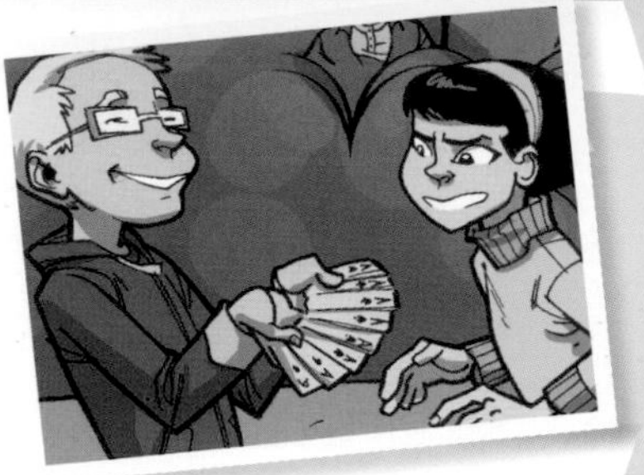

The Case of the... Messed-Up Magic Show

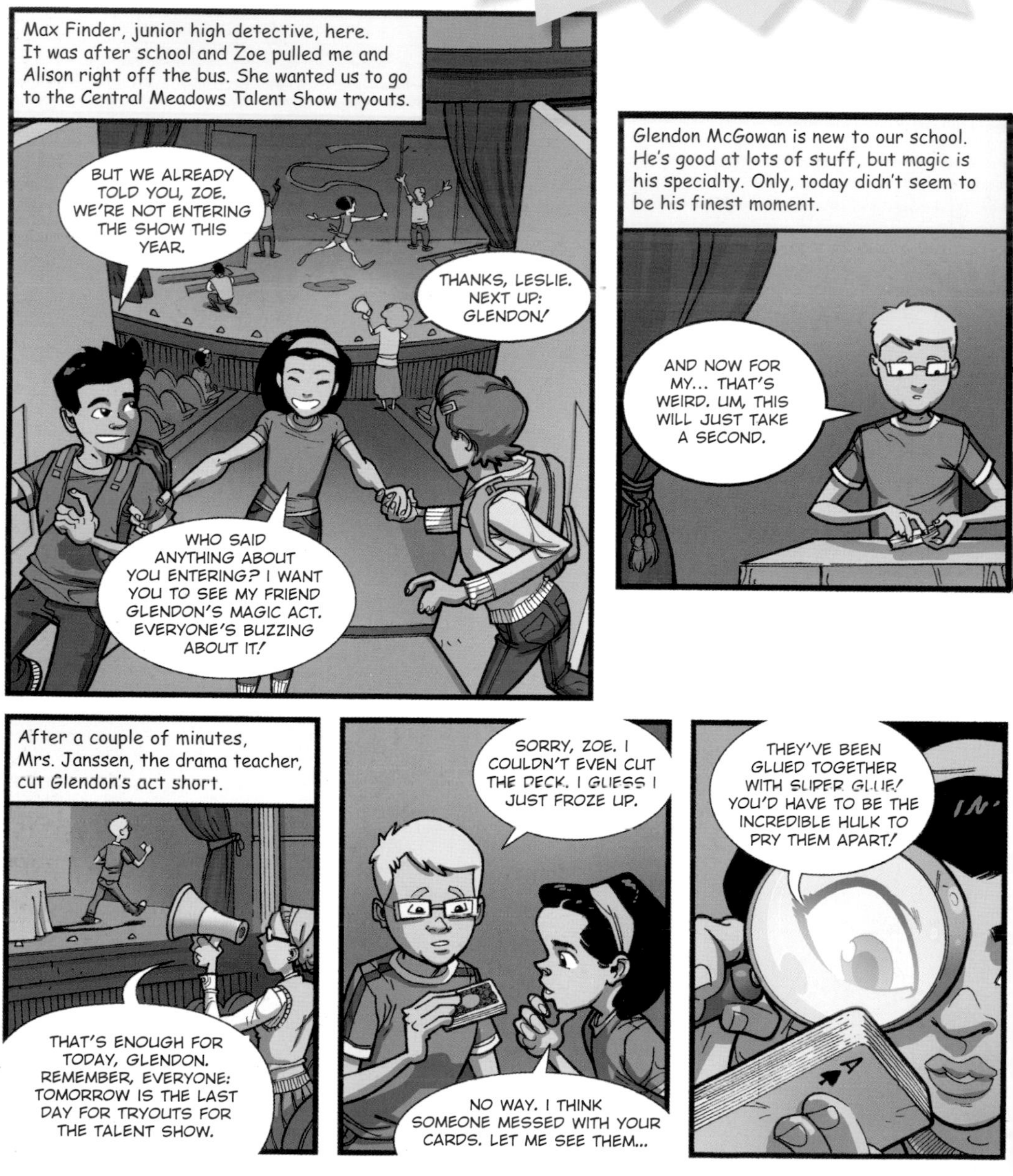

Max Finder, junior high detective, here. It was after school and Zoe pulled me and Alison right off the bus. She wanted us to go to the Central Meadows Talent Show tryouts.
BUT WE ALREADY TOLD YOU, ZOE. WE'RE NOT ENTERING THE SHOW THIS YEAR.
THANKS, LESLIE. NEXT UP: GLENDON!
WHO SAID ANYTHING ABOUT YOU ENTERING? I WANT YOU TO SEE MY FRIEND GLENDON'S MAGIC ACT. EVERYONE'S BUZZING ABOUT IT!
Glendon McGowan is new to our school. He's good at lots of stuff, but magic is his specialty. Only, today didn't seem to be his finest moment.
AND NOW FOR MY... THAT'S WEIRD. UM, THIS WILL JUST TAKE A SECOND.
After a couple of minutes, Mrs. Janssen, the drama teacher, cut Glendon's act short.
THAT'S ENOUGH FOR TODAY, GLENDON. REMEMBER, EVERYONE: TOMORROW IS THE LAST DAY FOR TRYOUTS FOR THE TALENT SHOW.
SORRY, ZOE. I COULDN'T EVEN CUT THE DECK. I GUESS I JUST FROZE UP.
NO WAY. I THINK SOMEONE MESSED WITH YOUR CARDS. LET ME SEE THEM...
THEY'VE BEEN GLUED TOGETHER WITH SUPER GLUE! YOU'D HAVE TO BE THE INCREDIBLE HULK TO PRY THEM APART!

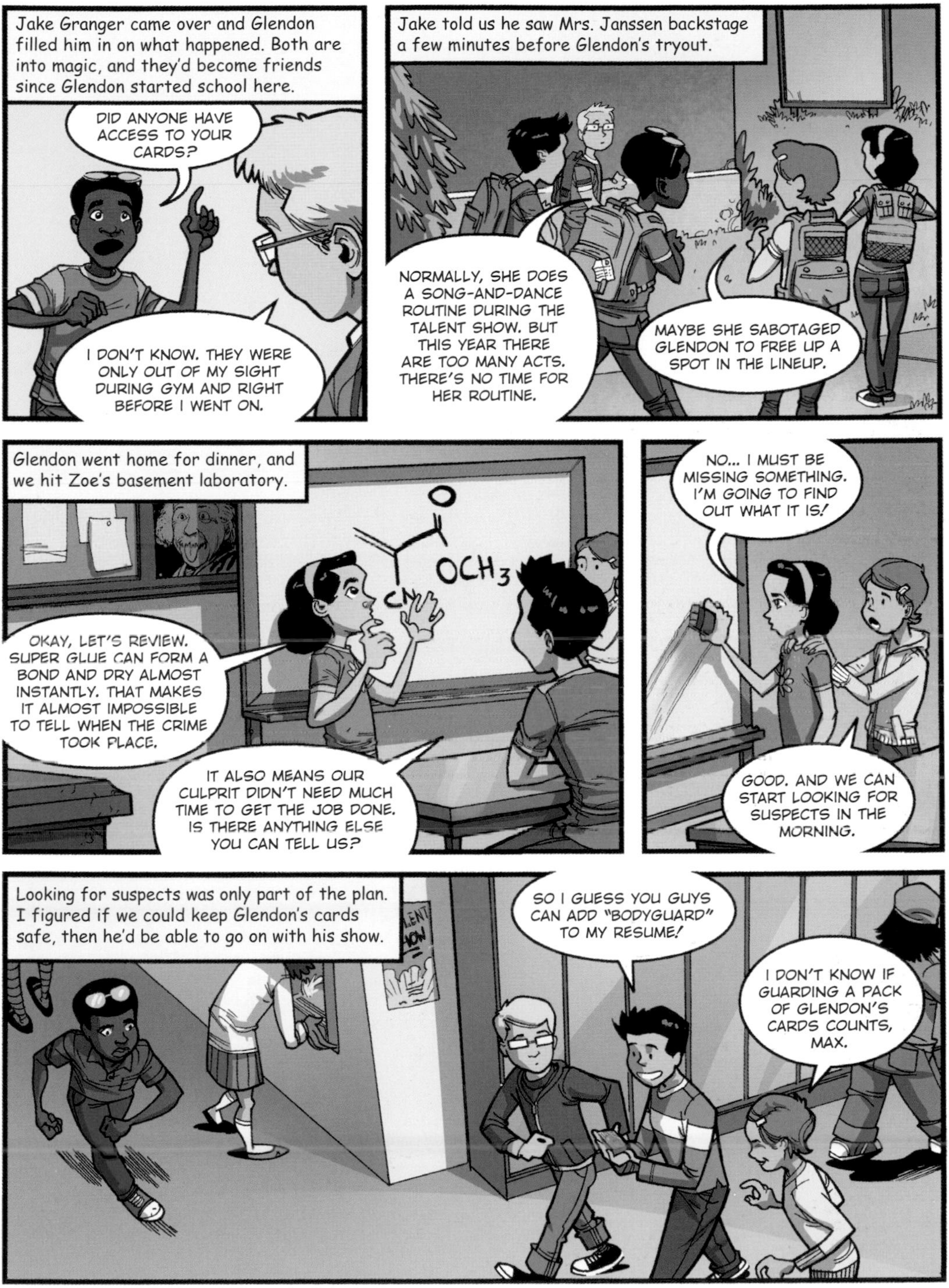

Jake Granger came over and Glendon filled him in on what happened. Both are into magic, and they'd become friends since Glendon started school here.
DID ANYONE HAVE ACCESS TO YOUR CARDS?
I DON'T KNOW. THEY WERE ONLY OUT OF MY SIGHT DURING GYM AND RIGHT BEFORE I WENT ON.
Jake told us he saw Mrs. Janssen backstage a few minutes before Glendon's tryout.
NORMALLY, SHE DOES A SONG-AND-DANCE ROUTINE DURING THE TALENT SHOW. BUT THIS YEAR THERE ARE TOO MANY ACTS. THERE'S NO TIME FOR HER ROUTINE.
MAYBE SHE SABOTAGED GLENDON TO FREE UP A SPOT IN THE LINEUP.
Glendon went home for dinner, and we hit Zoe's basement laboratory.
OCH3
CN
OKAY, LET'S REVIEW. SUPER GLUE CAN FORM A BOND AND DRY ALMOST INSTANTLY. THAT MAKES IT ALMOST IMPOSSIBLE TO TELL WHEN THE CRIME TOOK PLACE.
IT ALSO MEANS OUR CULPRIT DIDN'T NEED MUCH TIME TO GET THE JOB DONE. IS THERE ANYTHING ELSE YOU CAN TELL US?
NO... I MUST BE MISSING SOMETHING. I'M GOING TO FIND OUT WHAT IT IS!
GOOD. AND WE CAN START LOOKING FOR SUSPECTS IN THE MORNING.
Looking for suspects was only part of the plan. I figured if we could keep Glendon's cards safe, then he'd be able to go on with his show.
SO I GUESS YOU GUYS CAN ADD "BODYGUARD" TO MY RESUME!
I DON'T KNOW IF GUARDING A PACK OF GLENDON'S CARDS COUNTS, MAX.

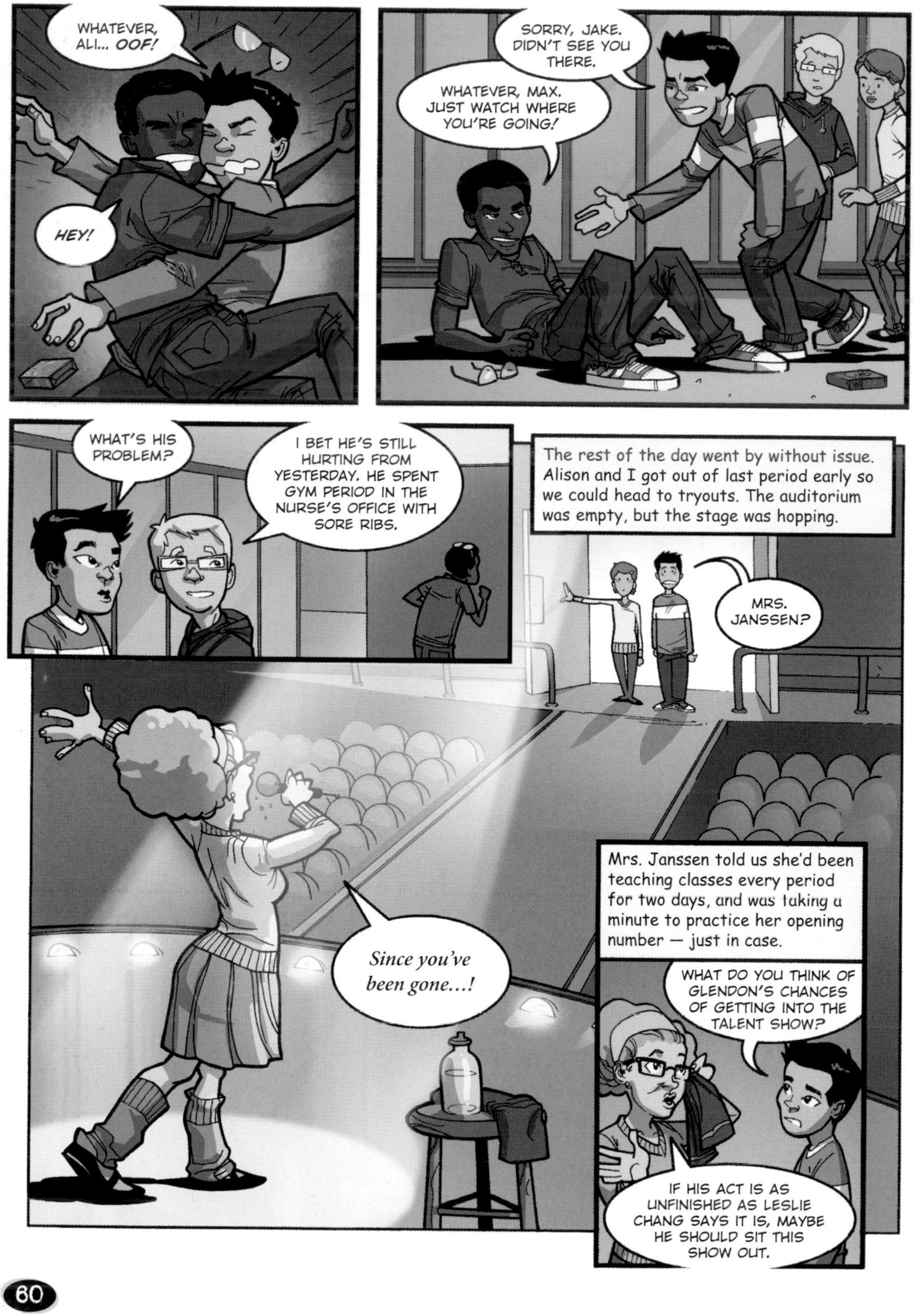
WHATEVER, ALI... OOF!
HEY!
SORRY, JAKE. DIDN'T SEE YOU THERE.
WHATEVER, MAX. JUST WATCH WHERE YOU'RE GOING!
WHAT'S HIS PROBLEM?
I BET HE'S STILL HURTING FROM YESTERDAY. HE SPENT GYM PERIOD IN THE NURSE'S OFFICE WITH SORE RIBS.
The rest of the day went by without issue. Alison and I got out of last period early so we could head to tryouts. The auditorium was empty, but the stage was hopping.
MRS. JANSSEN?
Since you've been gone...!
Mrs. Janssen told us she'd been teaching classes every period for two days, and was taking a minute to practice her opening number — just in case.
WHAT DO YOU THINK OF GLENDON'S CHANCES OF GETTING INTO THE TALENT SHOW?
IF HIS ACT IS AS UNFINISHED AS LESLIE CHANG SAYS IT IS, MAYBE HE SHOULD SIT THIS SHOW OUT.

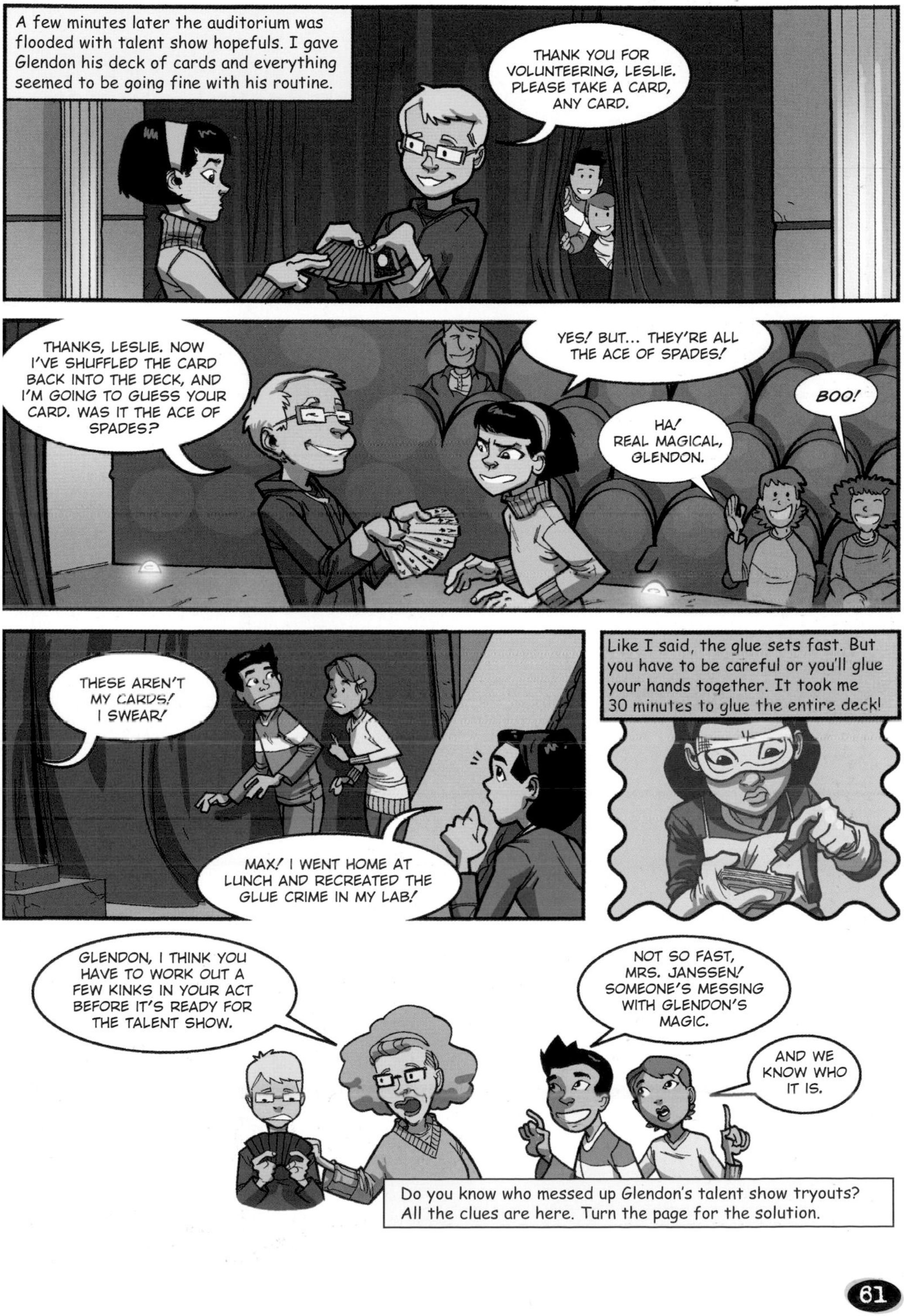
A few minutes later the auditorium was flooded with talent show hopefuls. I gave Glendon his deck of cards and everything seemed to be going fine with his routine.
THANK YOU FOR VOLUNTEERING, LESLIE. PLEASE TAKE A CARD, ANY CARD.
THANKS, LESLIE. NOW I'VE SHUFFLED THE CARD BACK INTO THE DECK, AND I'M GOING TO GUESS YOUR CARD. WAS IT THE ACE OF SPADES?
YES! BUT... THEY'RE ALL THE ACE OF SPADES!
HA! REAL MAGICAL, GLENDON.
BOO!
THESE AREN'T MY CARDS! I SWEAR!
MAX! I WENT HOME AT LUNCH AND RECREATED THE GLUE CRIME IN MY LAB!
Like I said, the glue sets fast. But you have to be careful or you'll glue your hands together. It took me 30 minutes to glue the entire deck!
GLENDON, I THINK YOU HAVE TO WORK OUT A FEW KINKS IN YOUR ACT BEFORE IT'S READY FOR THE TALENT SHOW.
NOT SO FAST, MRS. JANSSEN! SOMEONE'S MESSING WITH GLENDON'S MAGIC.
AND WE KNOW WHO IT IS.
Do you know who messed up Glendon's talent show tryouts? All the clues are here. Turn the page for the solution.

Solution: The Case of the...

Messed-Up Magic Show

Who messed up Glendon's magic act?

Jake Granger. He wanted to be the only magic act in the show and worried Glendon would upstage him.

Clues

* Glendon said Jake missed gym class with sore ribs, but he looked more annoyed than sore. Max suspected that Jake used the excuse to get out of gym and glue Glendon's cards together.

* Max dropped Glendon's second deck of cards in the hallway when Jake bumped into him. This is an old magician's trick called a "bumper." Jake did it on purpose to distract Max so he could switch the decks. Max didn't notice it at the time, but the deck of cards left beside him on the ground was a different color.

* Zoe said you have to be careful when using super glue or you could glue your hands together. Jake didn't do that, but he did glue his homework to the back of his backpack.

* Leslie Chang was jealous of Glendon—that's why she bad-mouthed him to Mrs. Janssen. But the only time she could've glued Glendon's cards together was backstage right before his first tryout. According to Zoe, that wasn't enough time to complete the task.

* Mrs. Janssen said she'd been teaching classes every period for two days straight. That means she couldn't have grabbed Glendon's cards while he was distracted in gym.

Conclusion

When Max, Alison, and Zoe presented their evidence, Jake confessed to the crime and gave Glendon back his deck of cards. Mrs. Janssen disqualified Jake from the talent show and gave Glendon his spot. On the night of the show, Glendon wowed everyone with his act and earned a standing ovation from all—including Leslie and Mrs. Janssen.

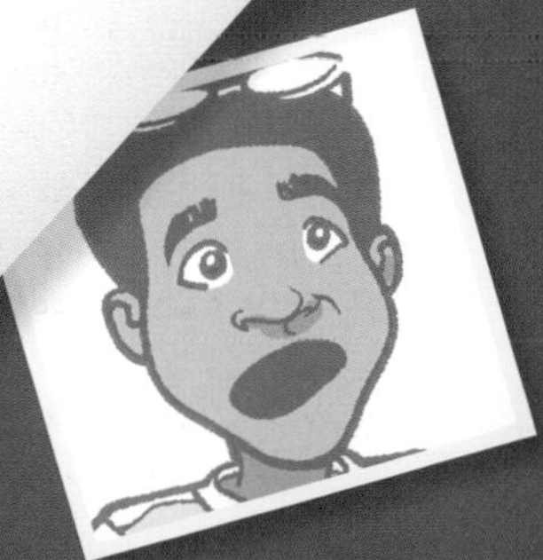

The Case of the...

Cheerleader Cheat

As told by Alison Santos

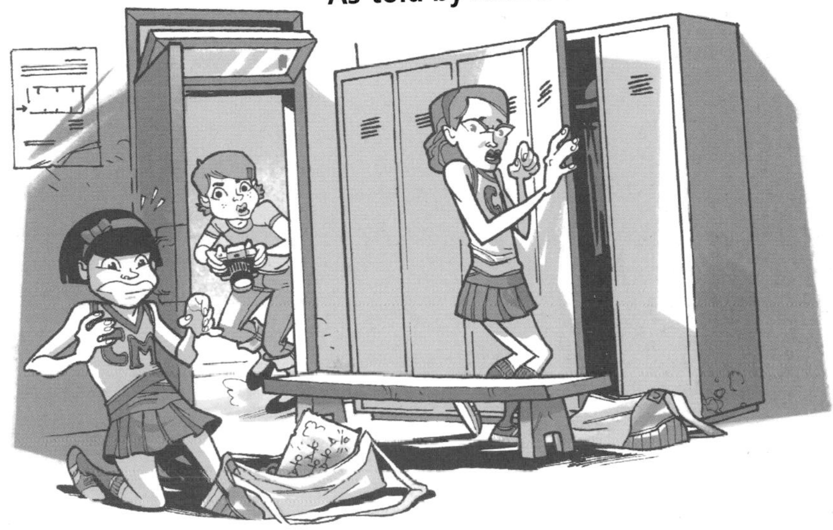

The room stank of sweat and cheers. Excited parents, exhausted teachers, and energized kids all packed into the Central Meadows Junior High gym after school to watch the City Cheerleading Finals. And I was in the middle, taking photos for the school paper.

On stage, the Twindale cheer team built themselves into an impressive pyramid. High at the top, a tiny blond girl teetered dangerously. One slip and she'd be a gym-floor pancake. I could barely look through my camera as I snapped off a few shots. The music got louder. The girl jumped and fell in a graceful arc into the waiting arms of two of her teammates.

The crowd went wild. Cheers and whistles echoed through the gym. I pushed my way to the back to get a better shot. I found some space by the door to the girls' change room and lined myself up. That's when I heard the scream. Sharp and scared.

It came from inside the girls' change room but no one else heard it over the clapping. My detective instinct kicked in. I went into the girls' change room.

Inside, Leslie Chang looked terrified. Sasha Price, captain of the school cheer team, and three other girls from the team were at her side. They all stared into Leslie's gym bag. No one said a word.

Inside Leslie's gym bag was a piece of yellow construction paper. Painted on the paper in red paint was a bunch of stick figure cheerleaders. They were balancing in an impressive pyramid all except one unlucky cheerleader who had fallen to the ground. Above the fallen cheerleader, written in messy letters was one word: LESLIE.

A thick arrow pointed to the cheerleader on the ground.

"I'm not competing!" Leslie collapsed onto a bench in front of a row of lockers. The other team members rushed to her side. "This is a warning. Something bad will happen if I go out there today."

Sasha spotted me at the door and came over.

"Someone has it in for Leslie." Sasha shook her head. "She's our new flyer and she's really nervous. Some jerk with a paintbrush thinks it's funny to scare her."

"Flyer?" I asked.

"Take it slow with Alison. She's not much of a cheer fan." Nanda Kanwar came through the door to the change room. Her dark curly braids swung back and forth as she hobbled to us. Her left foot was wrapped in a plastic walking cast. "The flyer is the toughest position on a cheer team."

"The flyer gets thrown into the air, stands on top of the pyramid, and all that fun stuff," Sasha added.

"I was the flyer for Central Meadows," Nanda gingerly lifted her left foot, wrapped in a cast covered in stickers and a big smiley face in wet red paint. "Until this happened."

"Ouch. Crash landing during practice?" I asked.

"More like crash landing during babysitting," Nanda growled. "I was looking after my little cousin Taijah and slipped on one of her toy trucks. Didn't fall far, but managed to break my ankle."

"Luckily, Leslie stepped in at the last minute to be our flyer for this competition," Sasha said. "Nanda has been teaching her the basics."

"She's good, too," Nanda said with a smile. "She's already learned a lot of the harder throws."

"If Leslie doesn't compete today, we'll be disqualified." Sasha paled. "And we are on next."

"If I can find out who's behind the threats, do you think Leslie will compete?"

Sasha shrugged. "Who knows? She's been so nervous about competing, maybe she put the note in her bag to give her a way to back out without looking bad."

I wished Max was here with his notebook. He was probably at

home stuck in some video game. There was no time to call him and get help with the case.

"Face it. We've lost," Nanda sighed. "Leslie is a mess. It's over."

Sasha glared at her. "Go away and bother someone else, Nanda."

"That was harsh," I whispered after Nanda had hobbled over to check on Leslie.

Sasha dismissed it with a wave of her hand. "Nanda wanted the whole team to drop out of the competition when she hurt her ankle."

"But Leslie stepped up to the challenge of being flyer?"

Sasha nodded. "Nanda's been a great coach, but she got grouchier every day as the finals got closer. Today, she's super grouchy because she's stuck babysitting Taijah."

"Her little cousin who caused her accident?"

Sasha nodded again. "She dropped her in the daycare down the hall. The kid still feels so bad about causing the accident, she's been doing everything Nanda asks her to do. She even has the same hairstyle as Nanda. It's really cute."

I picked up the painting. It was done on heavy construction paper, the kind you used for art in school. Same for the paint. It was totally taken from some teacher's art cupboard.

"I've got to talk to Mrs. Janssen." Sasha chewed her lip. "She's running the competition. Maybe she'll let us go last today."

"That will buy me some time to find out who is the artist behind the paintings."

Sasha left to find Mrs. Janssen. There was only one entrance into the girls' change room. Whoever planted the note was able to get in and out without looking suspicious.

I caught up with Sasha as she was making her way through the crowd in the gym toward the stage.

"Yo, Price!" A deep voice called from behind us. "Heard you lost another flyer. You've got to learn to keep your team happy!"

Three cheerleaders leaned against the wall smirking at us. Each wore blue and yellow cheer uniforms with the word 'Twindale' across the front. They were still breathing heavily from their performance.

"If Leslie doesn't compete today, we'll be **disqualified**." Sasha paled. "And we are on next."

Twindale Junior High was our biggest rival. we go head-to-head in everything from football to fund-raising.

Sasha sent the three a withering look. "whatever, Duncan. Twindale should spend more time practicing its toe touches instead of listening to rumors."

Duncan looked like he took competition way too seriously. How did he know about the painting so quickly? Either he had good gossip sources or he knew more than he was letting on. Sasha turned with a final sniff at Duncan and continued to the stage. I added him to my suspect list and I hurried to catch up with her.

Sasha blended in with the crowd and I lost her. Then, through a cluster of excited parents, I saw a flash of red. I reached out and grabbed it.

"Slow down, Sasha!" I hissed.

"Better get your eyes checked, Alison." Tony DeMatteo stared at my hand gripping his red Central Meadows cheer shirt.

I quickly let go of his shirt. "I never figured you for a cheerleader, Tony. You're normally the one getting the cheers. Shouldn't you be at basketball practice?"

"You sound like Coach Sweeny," Tony sighed. "He's pretty steamed I've been missing so many practices because of the cheer team. He won't be happy if we win today."

"Because you'll move on to the regional finals next week?" I asked.

Tony nodded. "And I'll miss our big basketball game against Twindale. He's here today, sneaking around and acting all weird."

Coach Sweeny sneaking around his own gym? That was weird. And suspicious. Could he be scaring Leslie just to get his star player back?

"why aren't you with the cheer team?" I asked. "where have you been?"

Tony smiled. "Taking my little brother to the daycare. It's his first time. He was so scared I painted some pictures with him to make him feel better."

Sasha had bought me the time I needed. And that's when I saw it: **another painting.**

Tony headed to the boys' change room to finish getting ready. That's when I noticed the smear of red paint on my right hand. The same hand I used to grab Tony's shirt. It matched the paint on Leslie's picture. What was Tony doing with red paint on his cheer uniform? Was he trying to end the cheer team's season early to have more time to play basketball?

Backstage, a sympathetic Mrs. Janssen consoled Sasha. The cheer team from Eastview Heights was going on stage. Sasha had bought me the time I needed. And that's when I saw it: another painting.

It was taped to the curtain at the side of the stage where the teams waited before going on to perform. It was made with the same sloppy red paint and showed a stick-figure cheerleader flying out of control through the air. It would have been the last thing Leslie would see before going on to do her routine. A red streak dribbled down the yellow paper. It dripped onto the footprint of a sneaker poking from underneath the curtain.

I gently pulled the curtain aside.

A line of kid-sized footprints made their jagged way through the backstage door. I followed them down the crowded hallway, around the corner, and right into a noisy room filled with little kids playing, building, and painting.

Sasha came around the corner. "What are you looking at?"

"The person scaring Leslie." I turned to her and smiled. "And I know who made it happen."

Do you know who is scaring Leslie?
Turn the page for the solution.

Solution: The Case of the...
Cheerleader Cheat

Who is scaring Leslie? Nanda Kanwar and her cousin, Taijah.

Clues
* Nanda's little cousin, Taijah, was staying at the daycare. The paintings were made with school materials from the daycare.
* Alison knew the culprit was a girl, so they could get into the girls' change room. That meant it couldn't be Tony's little brother.
* Nanda had a smiley face in red paint on her cast. The color of the paint matched the paint on the pictures.
* Tony also had red paint on his shirt but he was painting with his little brother in the daycare.

Conclusion
Nanda admitted to getting her little cousin to help scare Leslie into not competing. Nanda was afraid that if Central Meadows won the competition, she would be replaced as flyer on the cheer team. She convinced Taijah to draw the pictures and sneak into the change room and backstage to place them where Leslie would see them.

Nanda apologized and was dropped from the team. With the mystery solved, Leslie competed and the cheer team won the competition. Alison's photos of the team in action made the front page of the school paper.

From the desk of Max Finder

The Case of the...

Absent Answer Key

IN THE MEADOWS
DWAY COMMITTEE!!
MENU
DISP
HOME

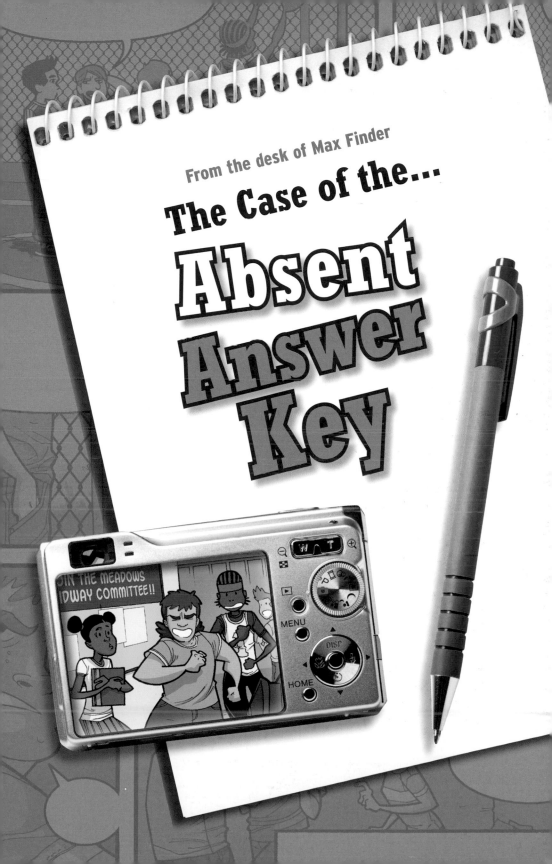

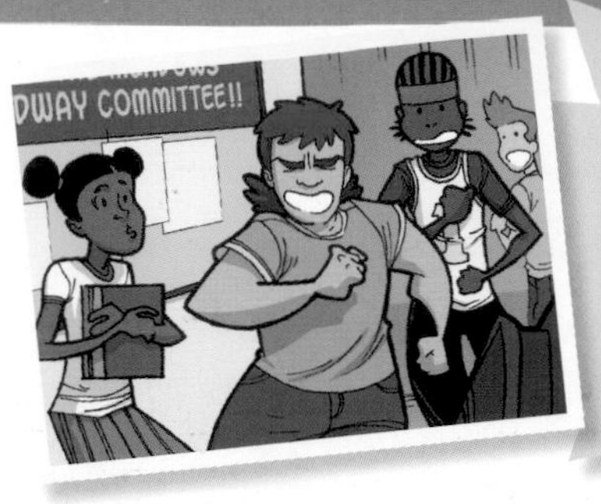

The Case of the... Absent Answer Key

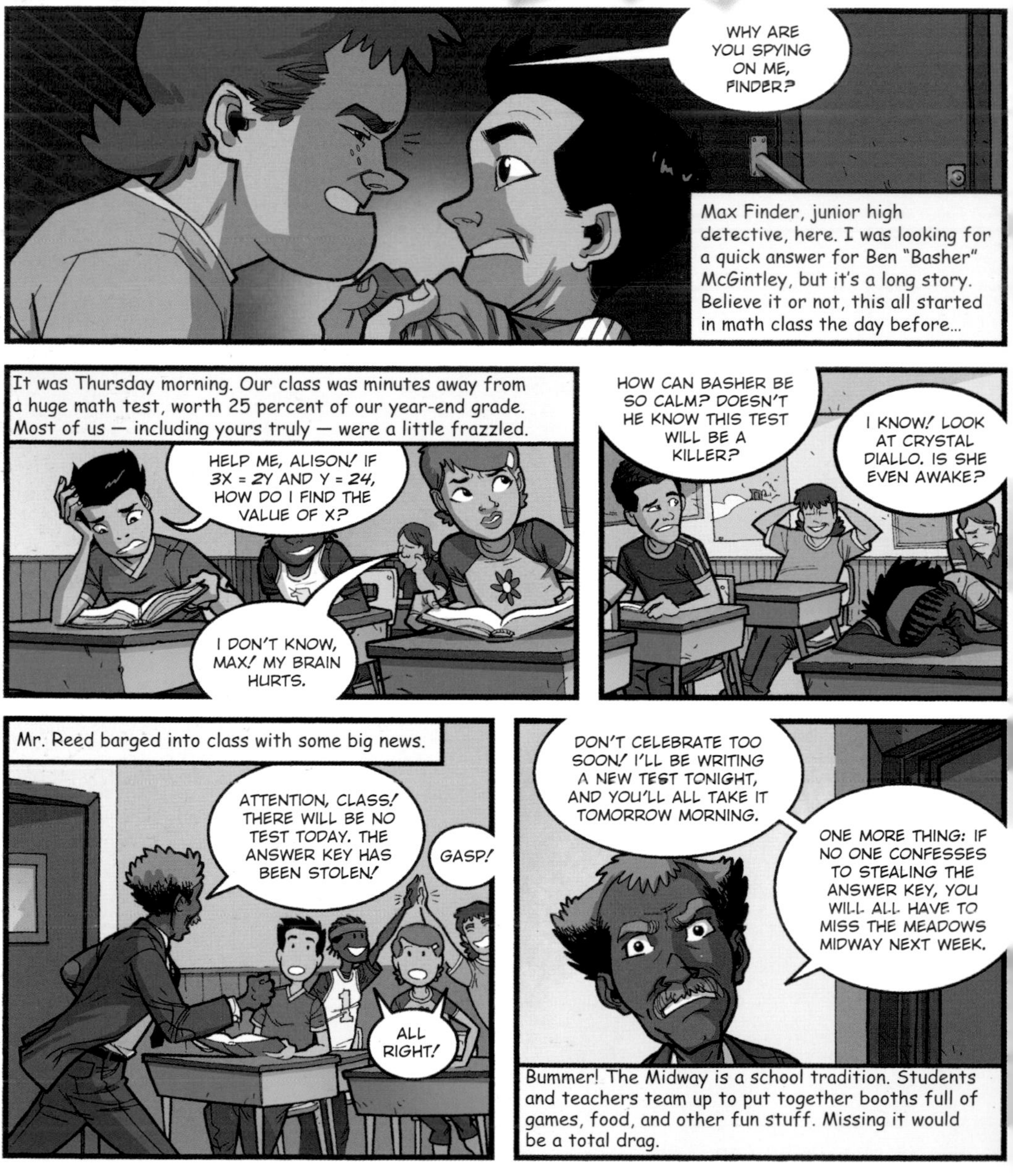
WHY ARE YOU SPYING ON ME, FINDER?
Max Finder, junior high detective, here. I was looking for a quick answer for Ben "Basher" McGintley, but it's a long story. Believe it or not, this all started in math class the day before...
It was Thursday morning. Our class was minutes away from a huge math test, worth 25 percent of our year-end grade. Most of us — including yours truly — were a little frazzled.
HELP ME, ALISON! IF 3X = 2Y AND Y = 24, HOW DO I FIND THE VALUE OF X?
I DON'T KNOW, MAX! MY BRAIN HURTS.
HOW CAN BASHER BE SO CALM? DOESN'T HE KNOW THIS TEST WILL BE A KILLER?
I KNOW! LOOK AT CRYSTAL DIALLO. IS SHE EVEN AWAKE?
Mr. Reed barged into class with some big news.
ATTENTION, CLASS! THERE WILL BE NO TEST TODAY. THE ANSWER KEY HAS BEEN STOLEN!
GASP!
ALL RIGHT!
DON'T CELEBRATE TOO SOON! I'LL BE WRITING A NEW TEST TONIGHT, AND YOU'LL ALL TAKE IT TOMORROW MORNING.
ONE MORE THING: IF NO ONE CONFESSES TO STEALING THE ANSWER KEY, YOU WILL ALL HAVE TO MISS THE MEADOWS MIDWAY NEXT WEEK.
Bummer! The Midway is a school tradition. Students and teachers team up to put together booths full of games, food, and other fun stuff. Missing it would be a total drag.

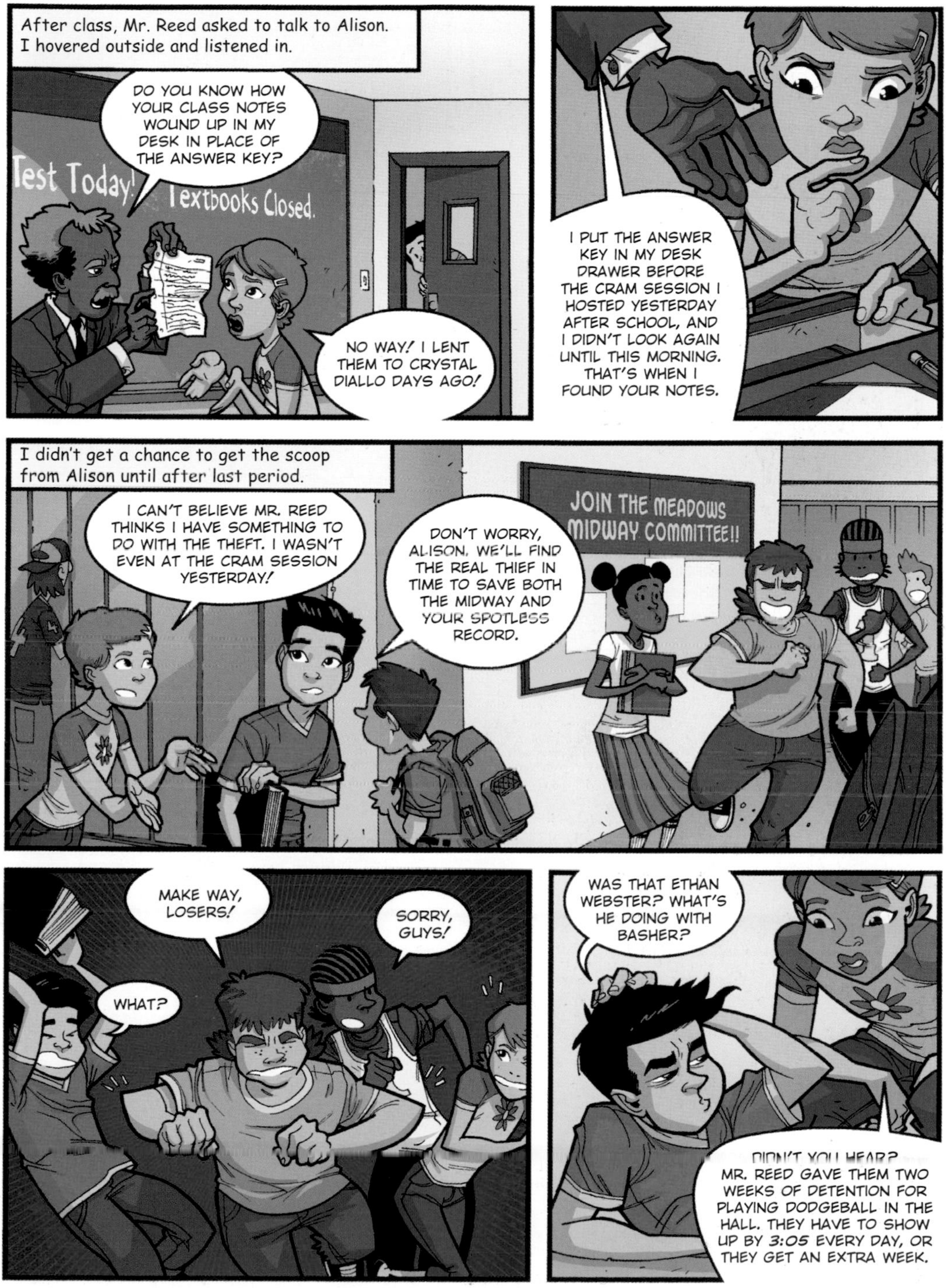
After class, Mr. Reed asked to talk to Alison. I hovered outside and listened in.
DO YOU KNOW HOW YOUR CLASS NOTES WOUND UP IN MY DESK IN PLACE OF THE ANSWER KEY?
Test Today! Textbooks Closed.
NO WAY! I LENT THEM TO CRYSTAL DIALLO DAYS AGO!
I PUT THE ANSWER KEY IN MY DESK DRAWER BEFORE THE CRAM SESSION I HOSTED YESTERDAY AFTER SCHOOL, AND I DIDN'T LOOK AGAIN UNTIL THIS MORNING. THAT'S WHEN I FOUND YOUR NOTES.
I didn't get a chance to get the scoop from Alison until after last period.
I CAN'T BELIEVE MR. REED THINKS I HAVE SOMETHING TO DO WITH THE THEFT. I WASN'T EVEN AT THE CRAM SESSION YESTERDAY!
DON'T WORRY, ALISON. WE'LL FIND THE REAL THIEF IN TIME TO SAVE BOTH THE MIDWAY AND YOUR SPOTLESS RECORD.
JOIN THE MEADOWS MIDWAY COMMITTEE!!
MAKE WAY, LOSERS!
SORRY, GUYS!
WHAT?
WAS THAT ETHAN WEBSTER? WHAT'S HE DOING WITH BASHER?
DIDN'T YOU HEAR? MR. REED GAVE THEM TWO WEEKS OF DETENTION FOR PLAYING DODGEBALL IN THE HALL. THEY HAVE TO SHOW UP BY 3:05 EVERY DAY, OR THEY GET AN EXTRA WEEK.

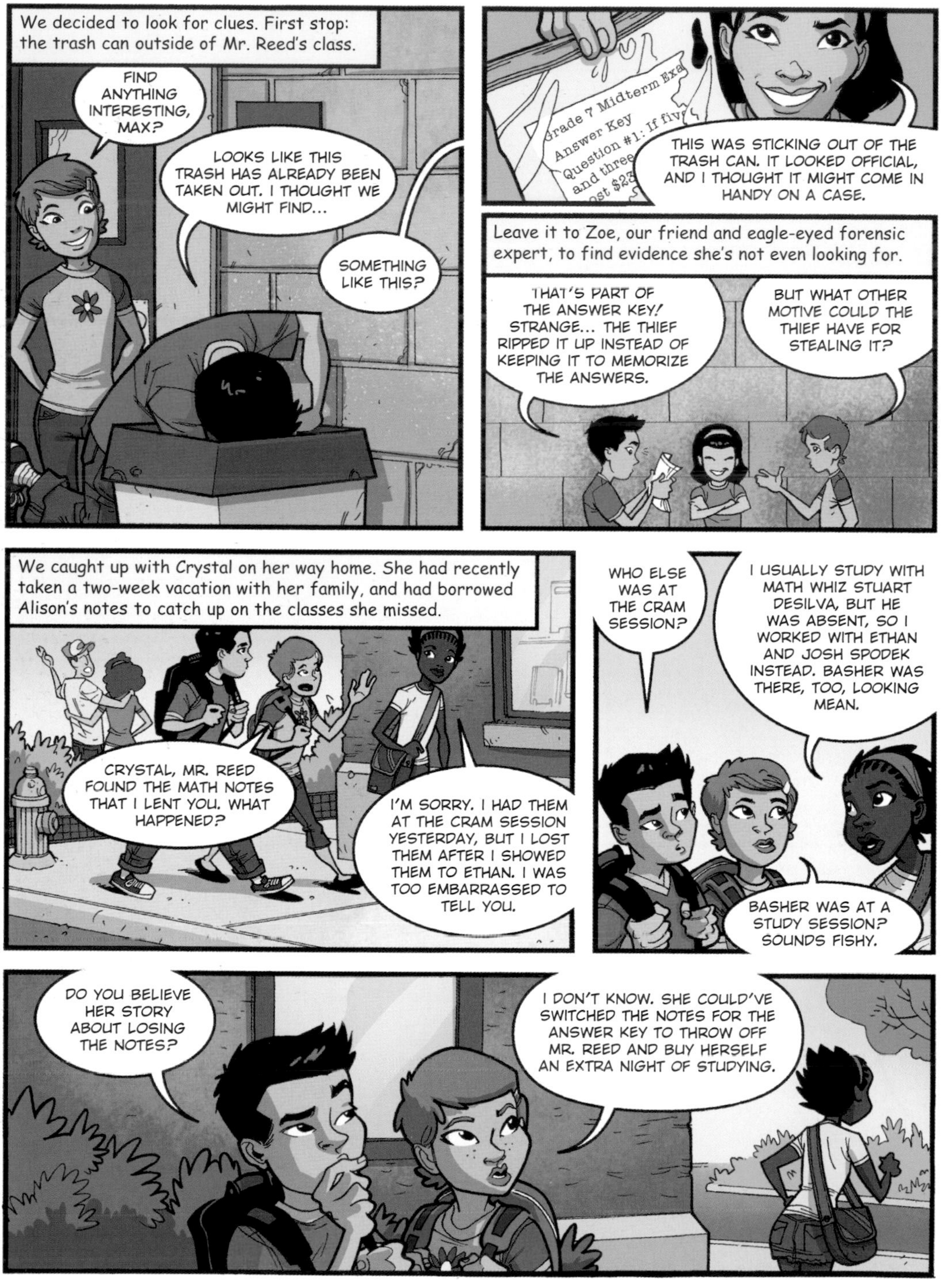
We decided to look for clues. First stop: the trash can outside of Mr. Reed's class.
FIND ANYTHING INTERESTING, MAX?
LOOKS LIKE THIS TRASH HAS ALREADY BEEN TAKEN OUT. I THOUGHT WE MIGHT FIND...
SOMETHING LIKE THIS?
Grade 7 Midterm Exa
Answer Key
Question #1: If fiv
THIS WAS STICKING OUT OF THE TRASH CAN. IT LOOKED OFFICIAL, AND I THOUGHT IT MIGHT COME IN HANDY ON A CASE.
Leave it to Zoe, our friend and eagle-eyed forensic expert, to find evidence she's not even looking for.
THAT'S PART OF THE ANSWER KEY! STRANGE... THE THIEF RIPPED IT UP INSTEAD OF KEEPING IT TO MEMORIZE THE ANSWERS.
BUT WHAT OTHER MOTIVE COULD THE THIEF HAVE FOR STEALING IT?
We caught up with Crystal on her way home. She had recently taken a two-week vacation with her family, and had borrowed Alison's notes to catch up on the classes she missed.
CRYSTAL, MR. REED FOUND THE MATH NOTES THAT I LENT YOU. WHAT HAPPENED?
I'M SORRY. I HAD THEM AT THE CRAM SESSION YESTERDAY, BUT I LOST THEM AFTER I SHOWED THEM TO ETHAN. I WAS TOO EMBARRASSED TO TELL YOU.
WHO ELSE WAS AT THE CRAM SESSION?
I USUALLY STUDY WITH MATH WHIZ STUART DESILVA, BUT HE WAS ABSENT, SO I WORKED WITH ETHAN AND JOSH SPODEK INSTEAD. BASHER WAS THERE, TOO, LOOKING MEAN.
BASHER WAS AT A STUDY SESSION? SOUNDS FISHY.
DO YOU BELIEVE HER STORY ABOUT LOSING THE NOTES?
I DON'T KNOW. SHE COULD'VE SWITCHED THE NOTES FOR THE ANSWER KEY TO THROW OFF MR. REED AND BUY HERSELF AN EXTRA NIGHT OF STUDYING.

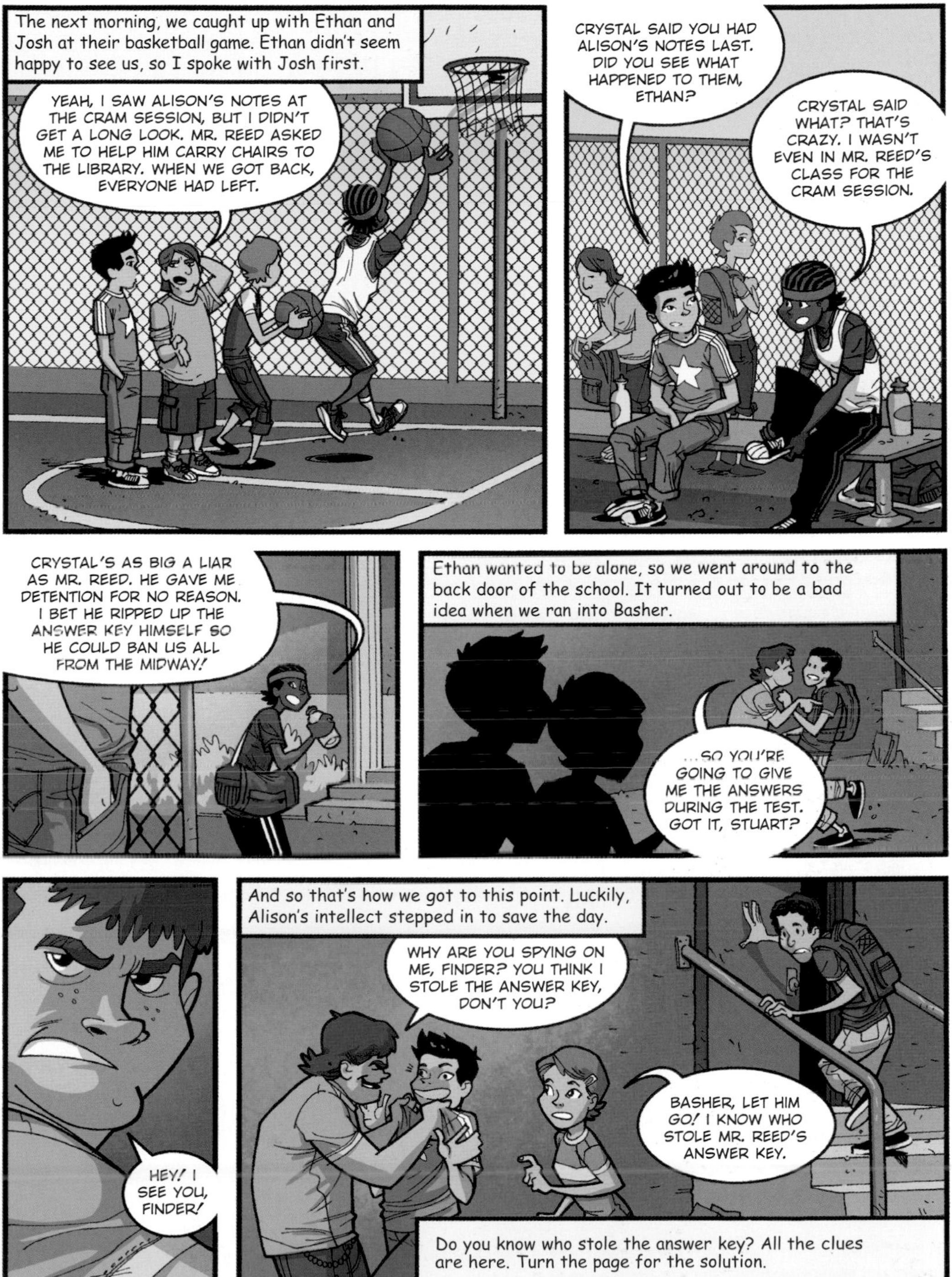
The next morning, we caught up with Ethan and Josh at their basketball game. Ethan didn't seem happy to see us, so I spoke with Josh first.
YEAH, I SAW ALISON'S NOTES AT THE CRAM SESSION, BUT I DIDN'T GET A LONG LOOK. MR. REED ASKED ME TO HELP HIM CARRY CHAIRS TO THE LIBRARY. WHEN WE GOT BACK, EVERYONE HAD LEFT.
CRYSTAL SAID YOU HAD ALISON'S NOTES LAST. DID YOU SEE WHAT HAPPENED TO THEM, ETHAN?
CRYSTAL SAID WHAT? THAT'S CRAZY. I WASN'T EVEN IN MR. REED'S CLASS FOR THE CRAM SESSION.
CRYSTAL'S AS BIG A LIAR AS MR. REED. HE GAVE ME DETENTION FOR NO REASON. I BET HE RIPPED UP THE ANSWER KEY HIMSELF SO HE COULD BAN US ALL FROM THE MIDWAY!
Ethan wanted to be alone, so we went around to the back door of the school. It turned out to be a bad idea when we ran into Basher.
...SO YOU'RE GOING TO GIVE ME THE ANSWERS DURING THE TEST. GOT IT, STUART?
HEY! I SEE YOU, FINDER!
And so that's how we got to this point. Luckily, Alison's intellect stepped in to save the day.
WHY ARE YOU SPYING ON ME, FINDER? YOU THINK I STOLE THE ANSWER KEY, DON'T YOU?
BASHER, LET HIM GO! I KNOW WHO STOLE MR. REED'S ANSWER KEY.
Do you know who stole the answer key? All the clues are here. Turn the page for the solution.

Solution: The Case of the...

Absent Answer Key

Who stole the answer key from Mr. Reed's desk?

Ethan Webster. He wanted to get back at Mr. Reed for giving him detention.

Clues

* Ethan said he wasn't in Mr. Reed's class after school, but he was lying. He had detention with Basher and would have been there to avoid getting an extra week added to his punishment.
* Alison said Ethan and Basher had been in detention for days. That means both would know that Mr. Reed had been working on the test—and that he kept his work in his bottom desk drawer.
* Crystal was in class at the time of the theft, but she wouldn't have known where to look for the test. She had her head on her desk before the test because she was nervous about failing.
* Basher wanted to cheat to do well on the test—that's why he was threatening math whiz Stuart DeSilva behind the school. If he had stolen the answer key, he would've kept it in hopes that Mr. Reed would use the same or similar questions. In this case, his sinister motives actually cleared him of a crime!
* Ethan knew the answer key was ripped up, but Max didn't tell him it was. Ethan knew because he was the one who did the ripping.

Conclusion

When Max and Alison presented their evidence, Ethan confessed to stealing the answer key. He got two more weeks of detention added on to his sentence, and in that time he and Mr. Reed finally shook hands and made up. Basher, meanwhile, got two more weeks of detention as well—he got caught trying to cheat off Stuart during the test!

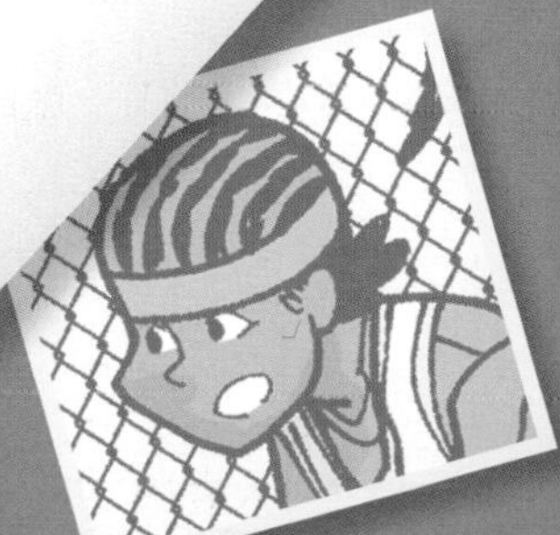

From the desk of Max Finder

The Case of the... Mad Money

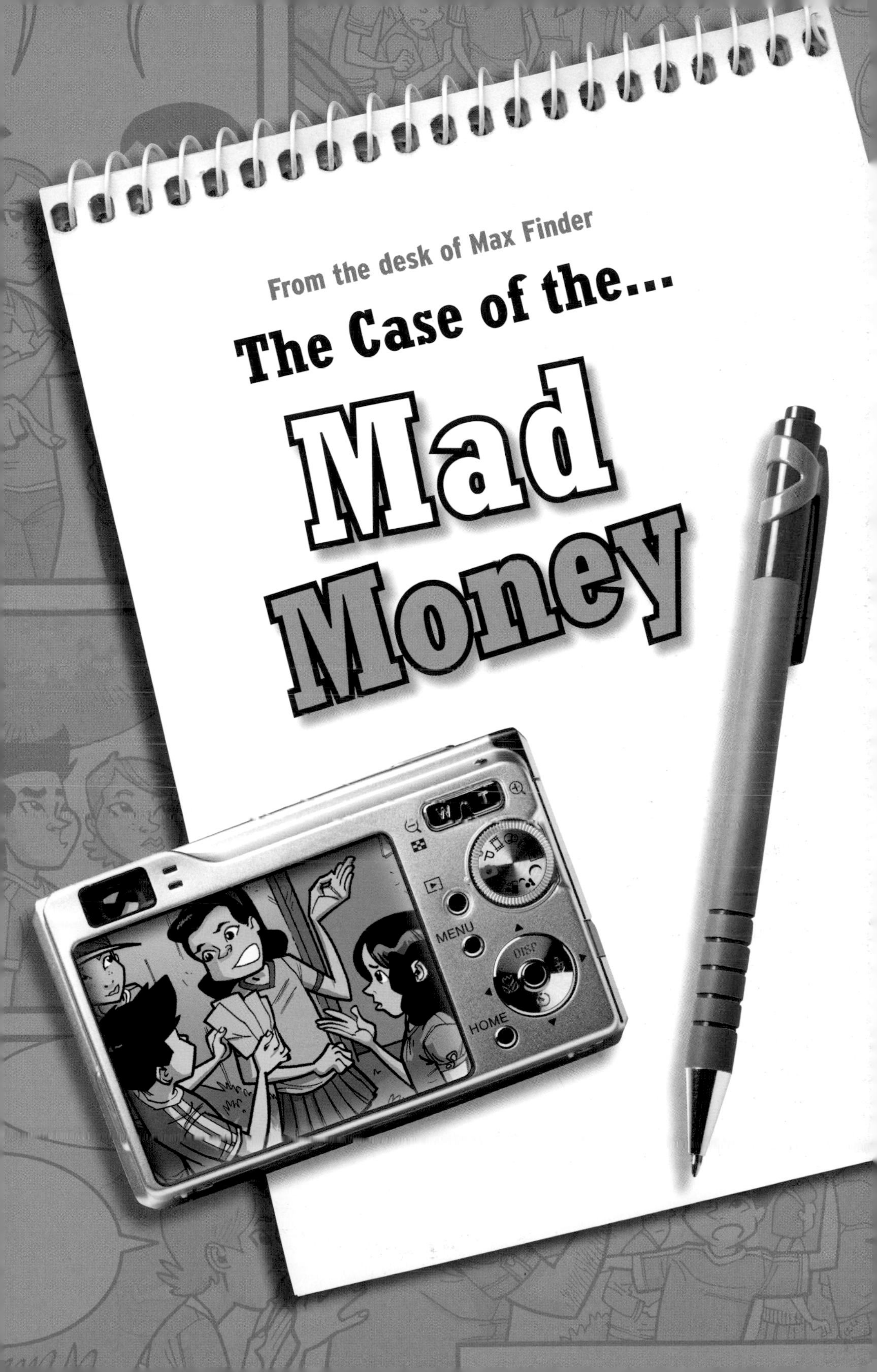
MENU
HOME

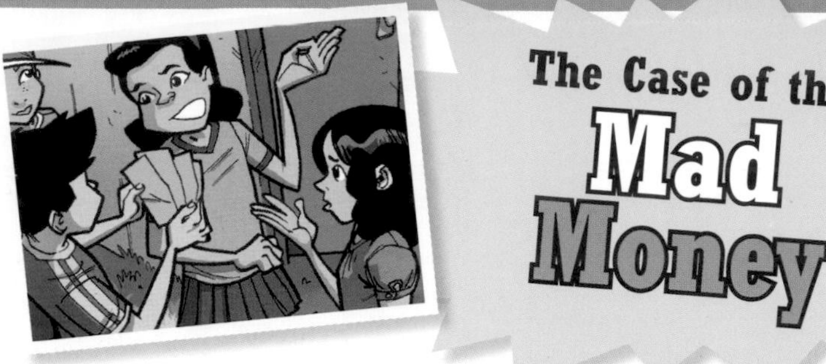

The Case of the... Mad Money

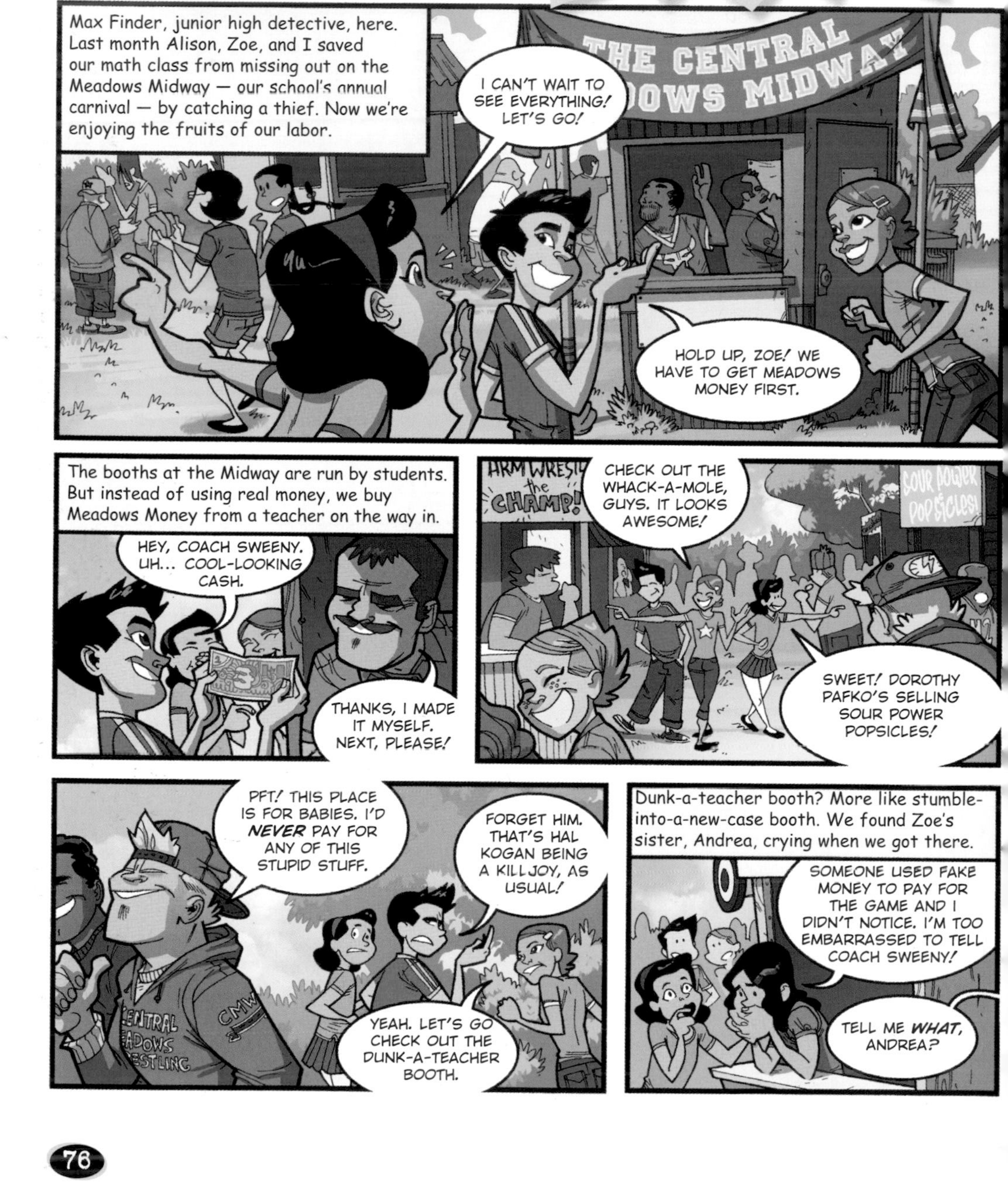

Max Finder, junior high detective, here. Last month Alison, Zoe, and I saved our math class from missing out on the Meadows Midway — our school's annual carnival — by catching a thief. Now we're enjoying the fruits of our labor.
THE CENTRAL MEADOWS MIDWAY
I CAN'T WAIT TO SEE EVERYTHING! LET'S GO!
HOLD UP, ZOE! WE HAVE TO GET MEADOWS MONEY FIRST.
The booths at the Midway are run by students. But instead of using real money, we buy Meadows Money from a teacher on the way in.
HEY, COACH SWEENY. UH... COOL-LOOKING CASH.
THANKS, I MADE IT MYSELF. NEXT, PLEASE!
ARM WRESTLE the CHAMP!
SOUR POWER POPSICLES!
CHECK OUT THE WHACK-A-MOLE, GUYS. IT LOOKS AWESOME!
SWEET! DOROTHY PAFKO'S SELLING SOUR POWER POPSICLES!
PFT! THIS PLACE IS FOR BABIES. I'D *NEVER* PAY FOR ANY OF THIS STUPID STUFF.
FORGET HIM. THAT'S HAL KOGAN BEING A KILLJOY, AS USUAL!
YEAH. LET'S GO CHECK OUT THE DUNK-A-TEACHER BOOTH.
CENTRAL MEADOWS WRESTLING
CMW
Dunk-a-teacher booth? More like stumble-into-a-new-case booth. We found Zoe's sister, Andrea, crying when we got there.
SOMEONE USED FAKE MONEY TO PAY FOR THE GAME AND I DIDN'T NOTICE. I'M TOO EMBARRASSED TO TELL COACH SWEENY!
TELL ME *WHAT*, ANDREA?

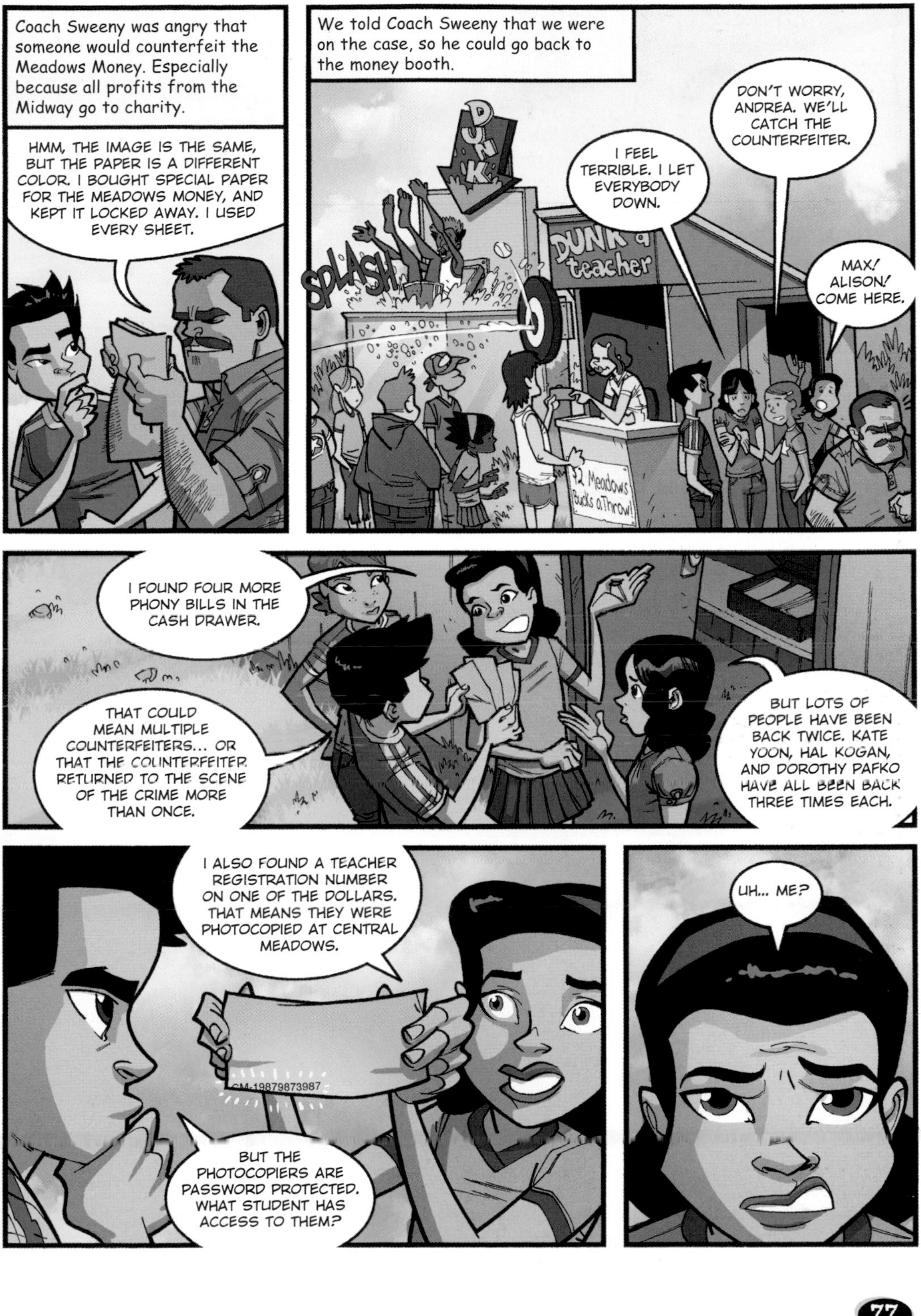
Coach Sweeny was angry that someone would counterfeit the Meadows Money. Especially because all profits from the Midway go to charity.
HMM, THE IMAGE IS THE SAME, BUT THE PAPER IS A DIFFERENT COLOR. I BOUGHT SPECIAL PAPER FOR THE MEADOWS MONEY, AND KEPT IT LOCKED AWAY. I USED EVERY SHEET.
We told Coach Sweeny that we were on the case, so he could go back to the money booth.
DUNK
SPLASH
DUNK a teacher
$2 Meadows Bucks a Throw!
I FEEL TERRIBLE. I LET EVERYBODY DOWN.
DON'T WORRY, ANDREA. WE'LL CATCH THE COUNTERFEITER.
MAX! ALISON! COME HERE.
I FOUND FOUR MORE PHONY BILLS IN THE CASH DRAWER.
THAT COULD MEAN MULTIPLE COUNTERFEITERS... OR THAT THE COUNTERFEITER RETURNED TO THE SCENE OF THE CRIME MORE THAN ONCE.
BUT LOTS OF PEOPLE HAVE BEEN BACK TWICE. KATE YOON, HAL KOGAN, AND DOROTHY PAFKO HAVE ALL BEEN BACK THREE TIMES EACH.
I ALSO FOUND A TEACHER REGISTRATION NUMBER ON ONE OF THE DOLLARS. THAT MEANS THEY WERE PHOTOCOPIED AT CENTRAL MEADOWS.
CM-19879873987
BUT THE PHOTOCOPIERS ARE PASSWORD PROTECTED. WHAT STUDENT HAS ACCESS TO THEM?
UH... ME?

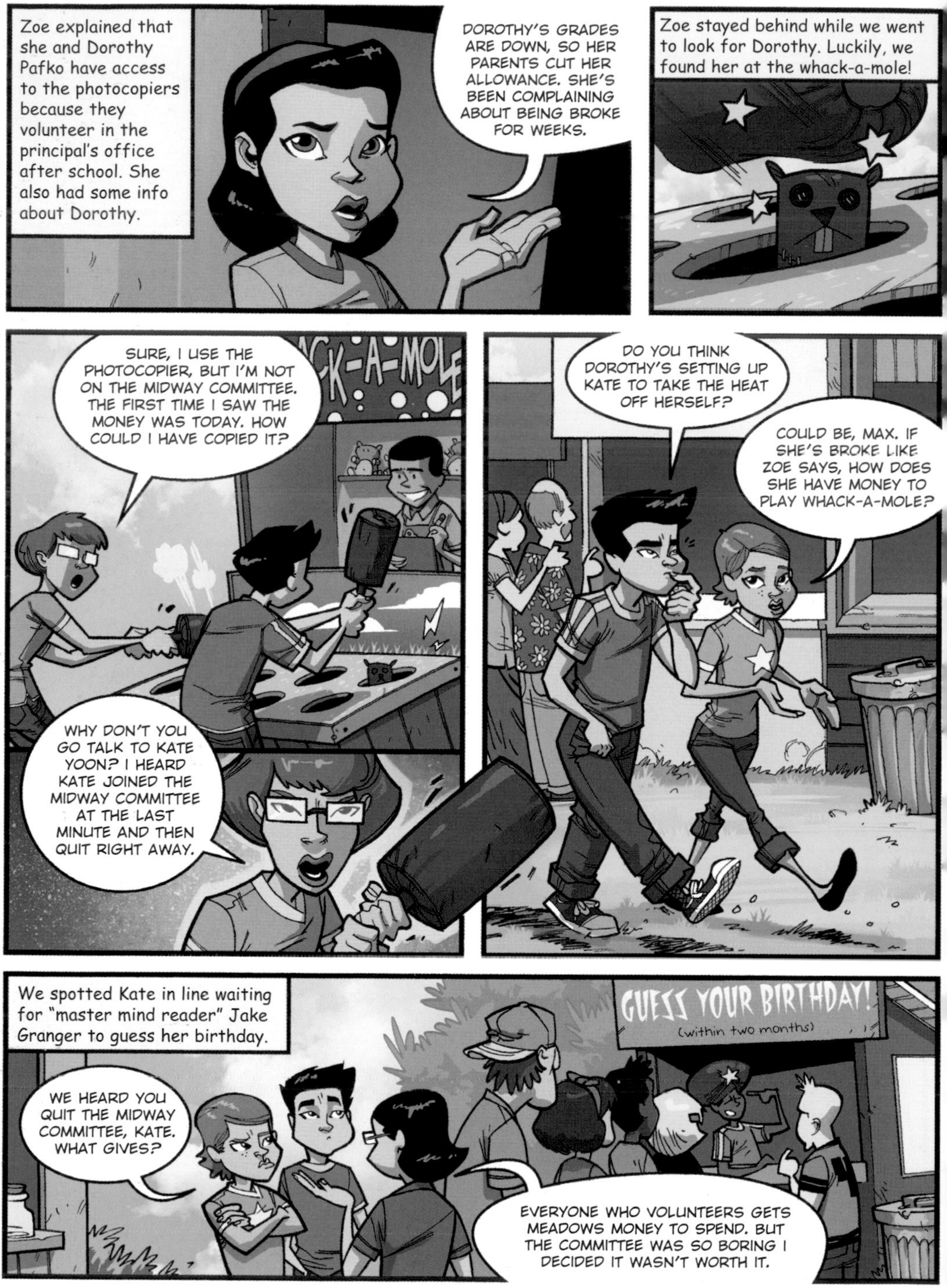
Zoe explained that she and Dorothy Pafko have access to the photocopiers because they volunteer in the principal's office after school. She also had some info about Dorothy.
DOROTHY'S GRADES ARE DOWN, SO HER PARENTS CUT HER ALLOWANCE. SHE'S BEEN COMPLAINING ABOUT BEING BROKE FOR WEEKS.
Zoe stayed behind while we went to look for Dorothy. Luckily, we found her at the whack-a-mole!
SURE, I USE THE PHOTOCOPIER, BUT I'M NOT ON THE MIDWAY COMMITTEE. THE FIRST TIME I SAW THE MONEY WAS TODAY. HOW COULD I HAVE COPIED IT?
WHY DON'T YOU GO TALK TO KATE YOON? I HEARD KATE JOINED THE MIDWAY COMMITTEE AT THE LAST MINUTE AND THEN QUIT RIGHT AWAY.
DO YOU THINK DOROTHY'S SETTING UP KATE TO TAKE THE HEAT OFF HERSELF?
COULD BE, MAX. IF SHE'S BROKE LIKE ZOE SAYS, HOW DOES SHE HAVE MONEY TO PLAY WHACK-A-MOLE?
We spotted Kate in line waiting for "master mind reader" Jake Granger to guess her birthday.
GUESS YOUR BIRTHDAY!
(within two months)
WE HEARD YOU QUIT THE MIDWAY COMMITTEE, KATE. WHAT GIVES?
EVERYONE WHO VOLUNTEERS GETS MEADOWS MONEY TO SPEND. BUT THE COMMITTEE WAS SO BORING I DECIDED IT WASN'T WORTH IT.

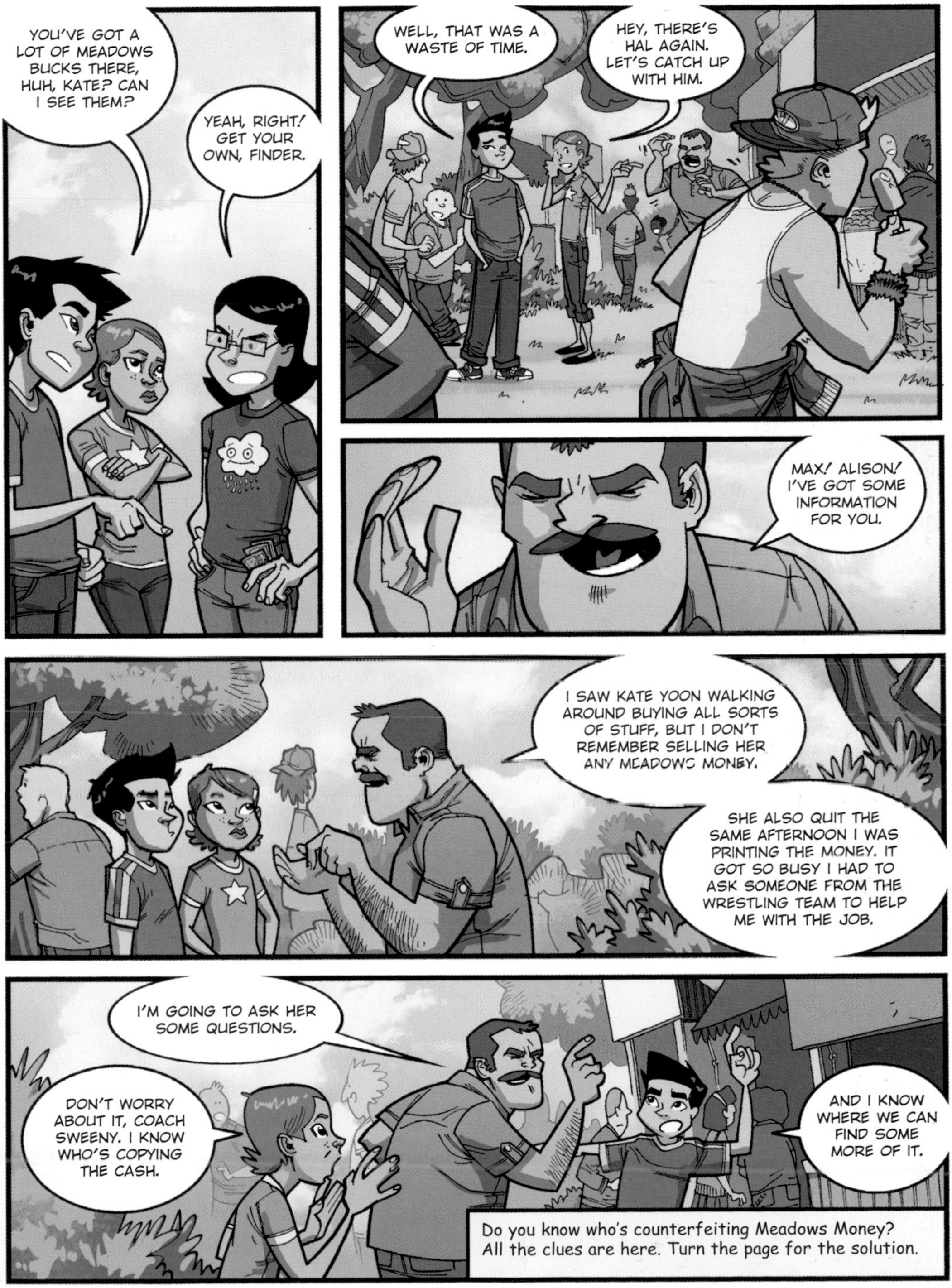
YOU'VE GOT A LOT OF MEADOWS BUCKS THERE, HUH, KATE? CAN I SEE THEM?
YEAH, RIGHT! GET YOUR OWN, FINDER.
WELL, THAT WAS A WASTE OF TIME.
HEY, THERE'S HAL AGAIN. LET'S CATCH UP WITH HIM.
MAX! ALISON! I'VE GOT SOME INFORMATION FOR YOU.
I SAW KATE YOON WALKING AROUND BUYING ALL SORTS OF STUFF, BUT I DON'T REMEMBER SELLING HER ANY MEADOWS MONEY.
SHE ALSO QUIT THE SAME AFTERNOON I WAS PRINTING THE MONEY. IT GOT SO BUSY I HAD TO ASK SOMEONE FROM THE WRESTLING TEAM TO HELP ME WITH THE JOB.
I'M GOING TO ASK HER SOME QUESTIONS.
DON'T WORRY ABOUT IT, COACH SWEENY. I KNOW WHO'S COPYING THE CASH.
AND I KNOW WHERE WE CAN FIND SOME MORE OF IT.
Do you know who's counterfeiting Meadows Money?
All the clues are here. Turn the page for the solution.

Solution: The Case of the... Mad Money

Who counterfeited the Meadows Money?
Hal Kogan. He copied lots of money on different paper for himself when he helped Coach Sweeny make the real Meadows Money.

Clues

* Andrea found two fake bills in the dunk-a-teacher booth cash box, and Zoe found four more. Since it costs two Meadows dollars to dunk a teacher, that means the counterfeiter paid three separate times. According to Andrea, only Hal, Kate, and Dorothy paid three times.
* Hal told everyone who'd listen that he would never pay for anything at the Midway. Yet he paid three times to dunk a teacher. Max and Alison also spotted him with a Sour Power Popsicle that could be bought only with Meadows Money. He used counterfeit money to buy everything.
* Coach Sweeny said someone from the wrestling team helped him copy the Meadows Money. Max noticed Hal was wearing a Central Meadows wrestling team hooded sweatshirt when he first saw him in the Midway.
* Coach Sweeny doesn't remember Kate Yoon buying Meadows Money because he was turned around when she did it. Max, Alison, and Zoe were right behind her when she made her purchase. All her dollars were real.
* Dorothy Pafko may have had her allowance cut off, but she didn't need any cash to buy Meadows dollars. Kate Yoon reminded Max and Alison that anyone who volunteered for the Midway got paid for his or her time in Meadows Money.

Conclusion

When Max and Alison presented their evidence—including two more counterfeit dollars Max found at Dorothy's popsicle booth—Hal confessed. He paid for the things he'd bought with his counterfeit money, and received a hefty detention sentence on top.

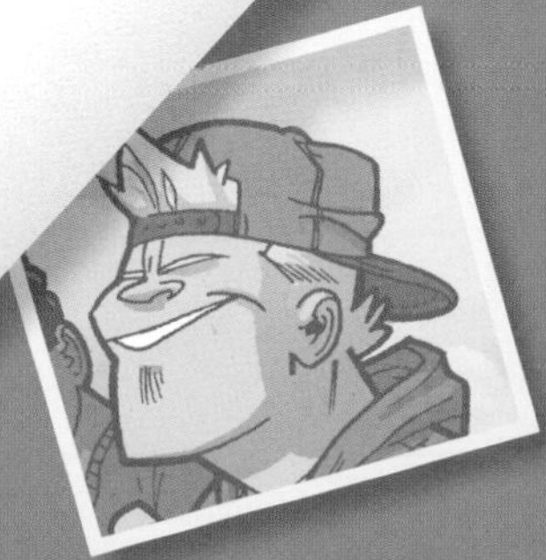

From the desk of Max Finder

The Case of the... Campsite Crime Spree

SWIM SAFE!
ONLY YOU CAN PREVENT FOREST FIRES!
If you SEE something, SAY something!
MENU
DISP
HOME

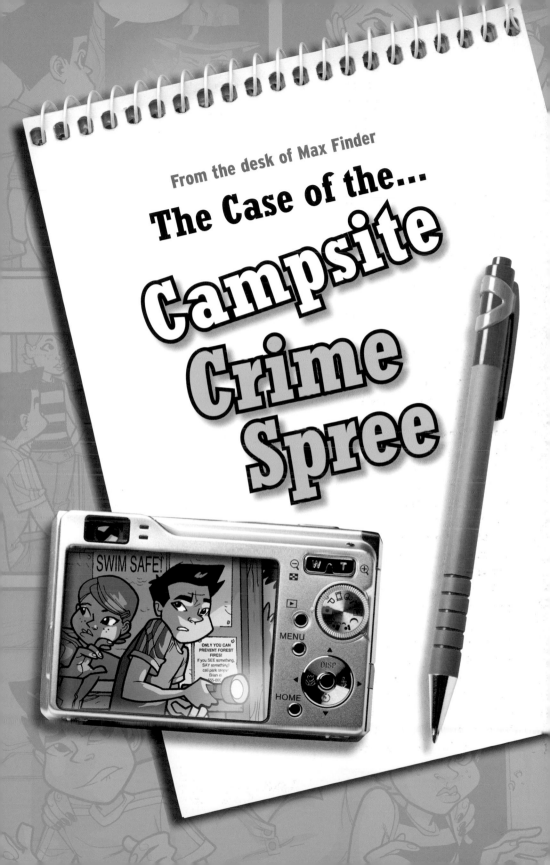

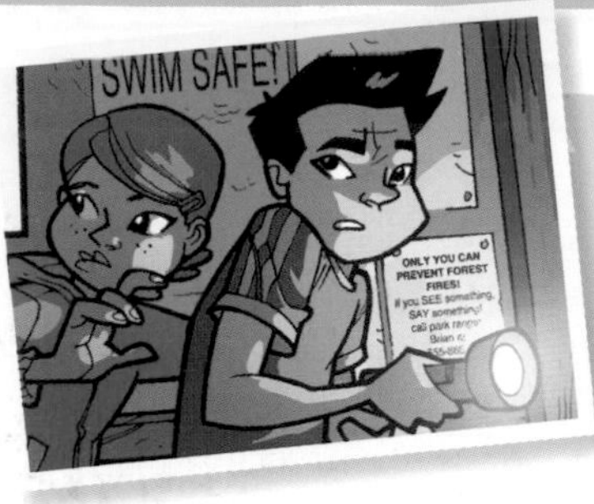
SWIM SAFE!
ONLY YOU CAN PREVENT FOREST FIRES!

The Case of the... Campsite Crime Spree

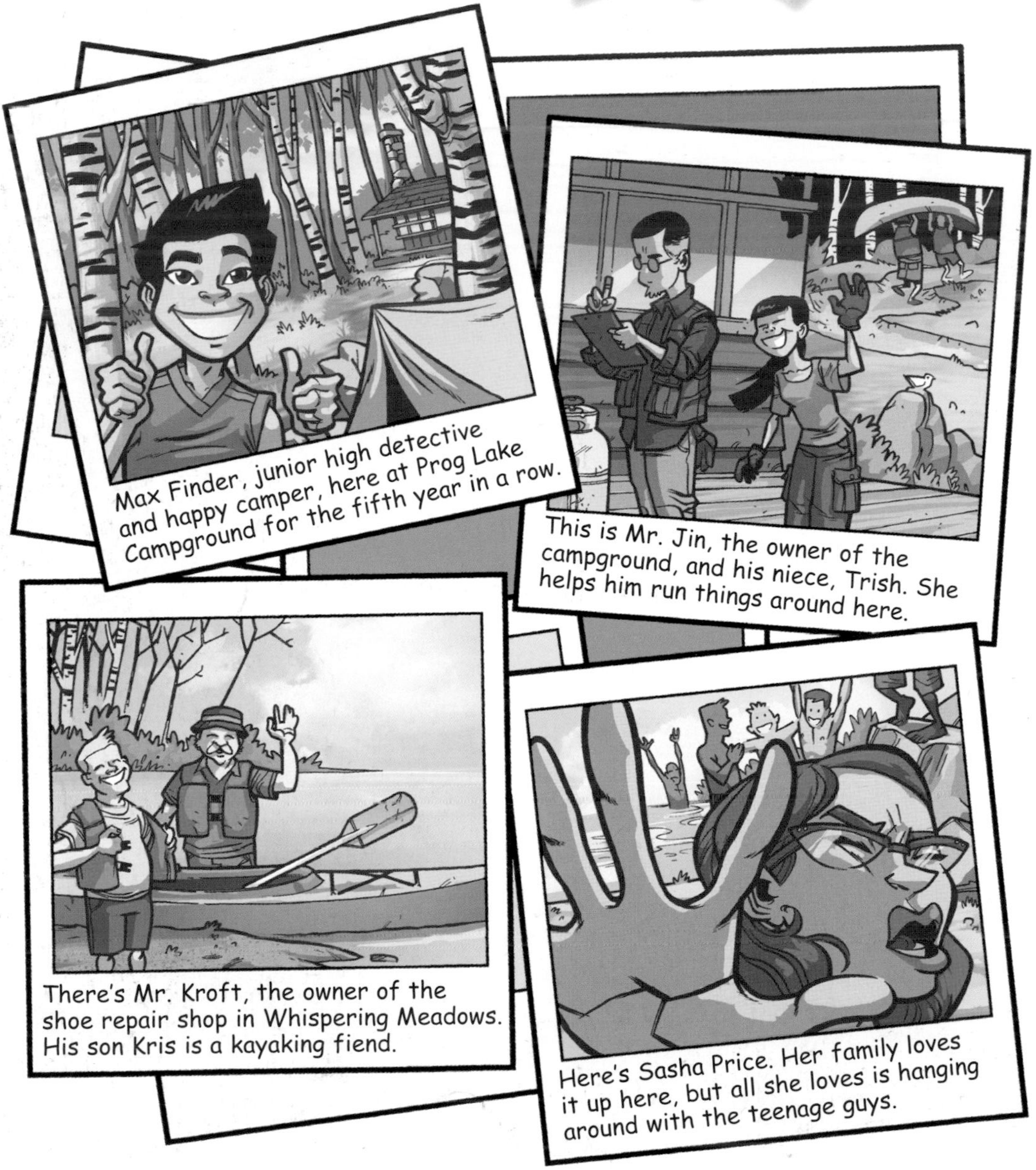
Max Finder, junior high detective and happy camper, here at Prog Lake Campground for the fifth year in a row.
This is Mr. Jin, the owner of the campground, and his niece, Trish. She helps him run things around here.
There's Mr. Kroft, the owner of the shoe repair shop in Whispering Meadows. His son Kris is a kayaking fiend.
Here's Sasha Price. Her family loves it up here, but all she loves is hanging around with the teenage guys.

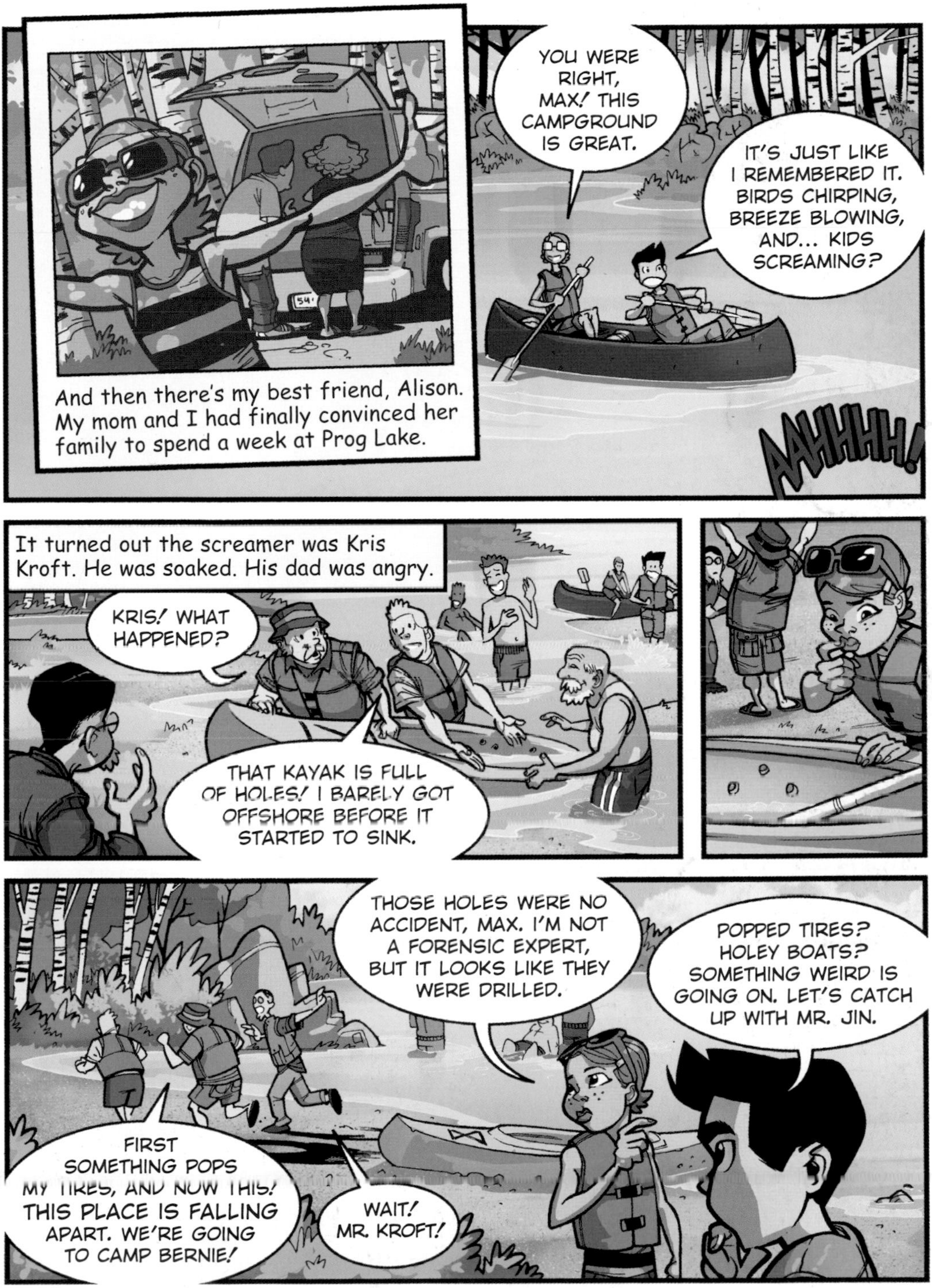
And then there's my best friend, Alison. My mom and I had finally convinced her family to spend a week at Prog Lake.
YOU WERE RIGHT, MAX! THIS CAMPGROUND IS GREAT.
IT'S JUST LIKE I REMEMBERED IT. BIRDS CHIRPING, BREEZE BLOWING, AND... KIDS SCREAMING?
AAHHHH!
It turned out the screamer was Kris Kroft. He was soaked. His dad was angry.
KRIS! WHAT HAPPENED?
THAT KAYAK IS FULL OF HOLES! I BARELY GOT OFFSHORE BEFORE IT STARTED TO SINK.
FIRST SOMETHING POPS MY TIRES, AND NOW THIS! THIS PLACE IS FALLING APART. WE'RE GOING TO CAMP BERNIE!
WAIT! MR. KROFT!
THOSE HOLES WERE NO ACCIDENT, MAX. I'M NOT A FORENSIC EXPERT, BUT IT LOOKS LIKE THEY WERE DRILLED.
POPPED TIRES? HOLEY BOATS? SOMETHING WEIRD IS GOING ON. LET'S CATCH UP WITH MR. JIN.

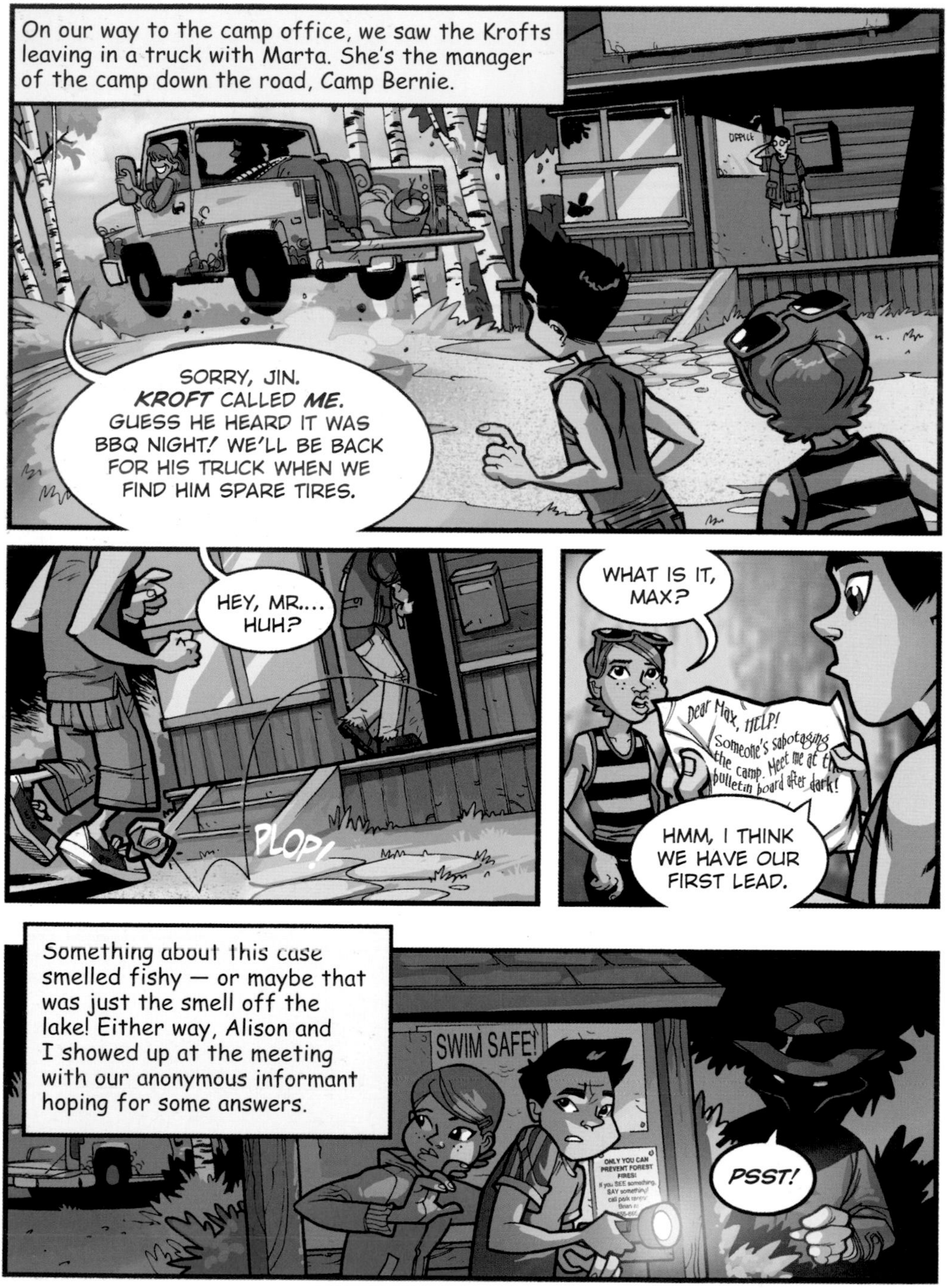
On our way to the camp office, we saw the Krofts leaving in a truck with Marta. She's the manager of the camp down the road, Camp Bernie.
SORRY, JIN. *KROFT* CALLED *ME*. GUESS HE HEARD IT WAS BBQ NIGHT! WE'LL BE BACK FOR HIS TRUCK WHEN WE FIND HIM SPARE TIRES.
HEY, MR.... HUH?
PLOP!
WHAT IS IT, MAX?
Dear Max, HELP! Someone's sabotaging the camp. Meet me at the bulletin board after dark!
HMM, I THINK WE HAVE OUR FIRST LEAD.
Something about this case smelled fishy — or maybe that was just the smell off the lake! Either way, Alison and I showed up at the meeting with our anonymous informant hoping for some answers.
SWIM SAFE!
ONLY YOU CAN PREVENT FOREST FIRES!
PSST!

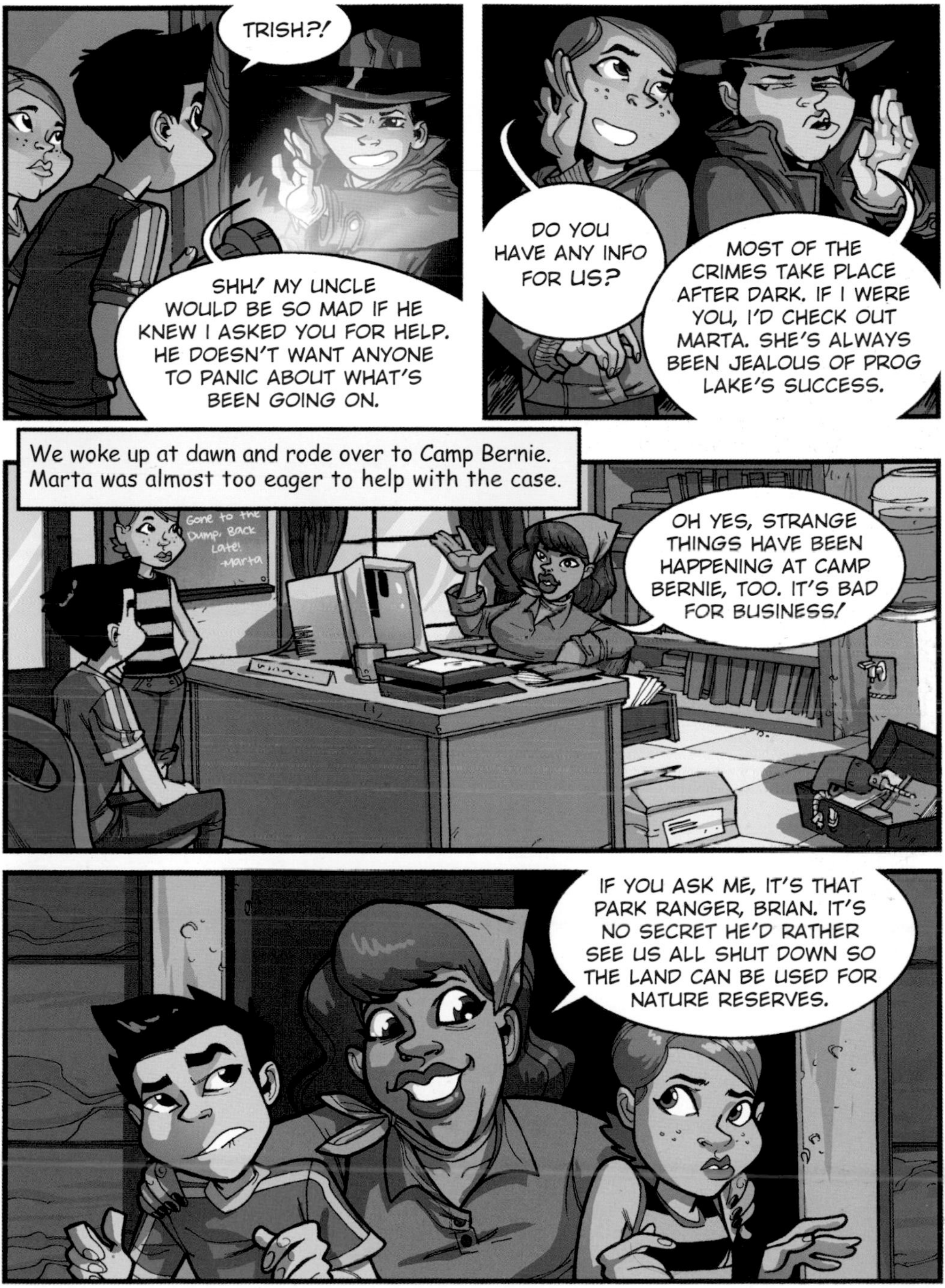
TRISH?!
SHH! MY UNCLE WOULD BE SO MAD IF HE KNEW I ASKED YOU FOR HELP. HE DOESN'T WANT ANYONE TO PANIC ABOUT WHAT'S BEEN GOING ON.
DO YOU HAVE ANY INFO FOR US?
MOST OF THE CRIMES TAKE PLACE AFTER DARK. IF I WERE YOU, I'D CHECK OUT MARTA. SHE'S ALWAYS BEEN JEALOUS OF PROG LAKE'S SUCCESS.
We woke up at dawn and rode over to Camp Bernie. Marta was almost too eager to help with the case.
Gone to the Dump, Back Late! -Marta
OH YES, STRANGE THINGS HAVE BEEN HAPPENING AT CAMP BERNIE, TOO. IT'S BAD FOR BUSINESS!
IF YOU ASK ME, IT'S THAT PARK RANGER, BRIAN. IT'S NO SECRET HE'D RATHER SEE US ALL SHUT DOWN SO THE LAND CAN BE USED FOR NATURE RESERVES.

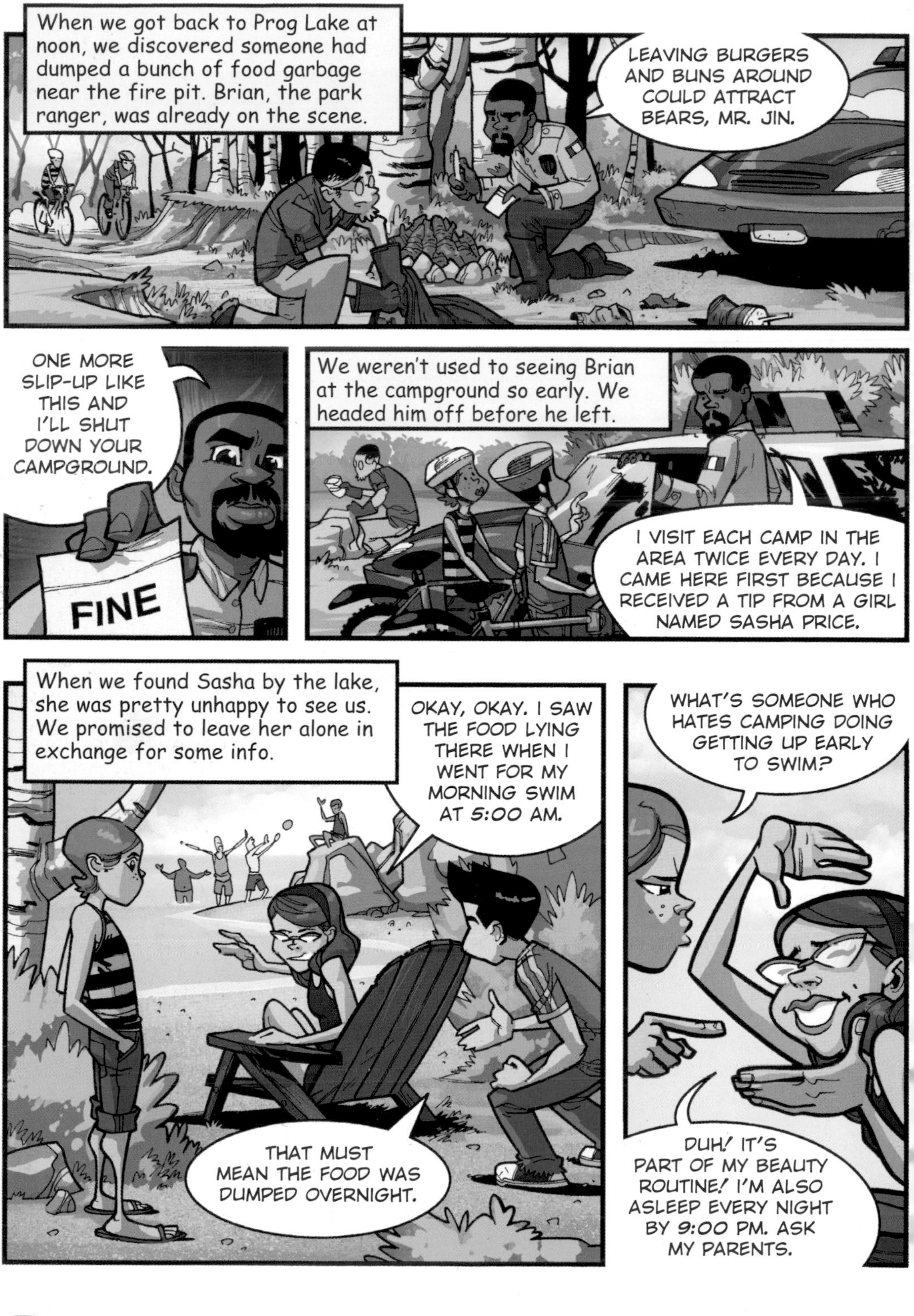
When we got back to Prog Lake at noon, we discovered someone had dumped a bunch of food garbage near the fire pit. Brian, the park ranger, was already on the scene.
LEAVING BURGERS AND BUNS AROUND COULD ATTRACT BEARS, MR. JIN.
ONE MORE SLIP-UP LIKE THIS AND I'LL SHUT DOWN YOUR CAMPGROUND.
FINE
We weren't used to seeing Brian at the campground so early. We headed him off before he left.
I VISIT EACH CAMP IN THE AREA TWICE EVERY DAY. I CAME HERE FIRST BECAUSE I RECEIVED A TIP FROM A GIRL NAMED SASHA PRICE.
When we found Sasha by the lake, she was pretty unhappy to see us. We promised to leave her alone in exchange for some info.
OKAY, OKAY. I SAW THE FOOD LYING THERE WHEN I WENT FOR MY MORNING SWIM AT 5:00 AM.
THAT MUST MEAN THE FOOD WAS DUMPED OVERNIGHT.
WHAT'S SOMEONE WHO HATES CAMPING DOING GETTING UP EARLY TO SWIM?
DUH! IT'S PART OF MY BEAUTY ROUTINE! I'M ALSO ASLEEP EVERY NIGHT BY 9:00 PM. ASK MY PARENTS.

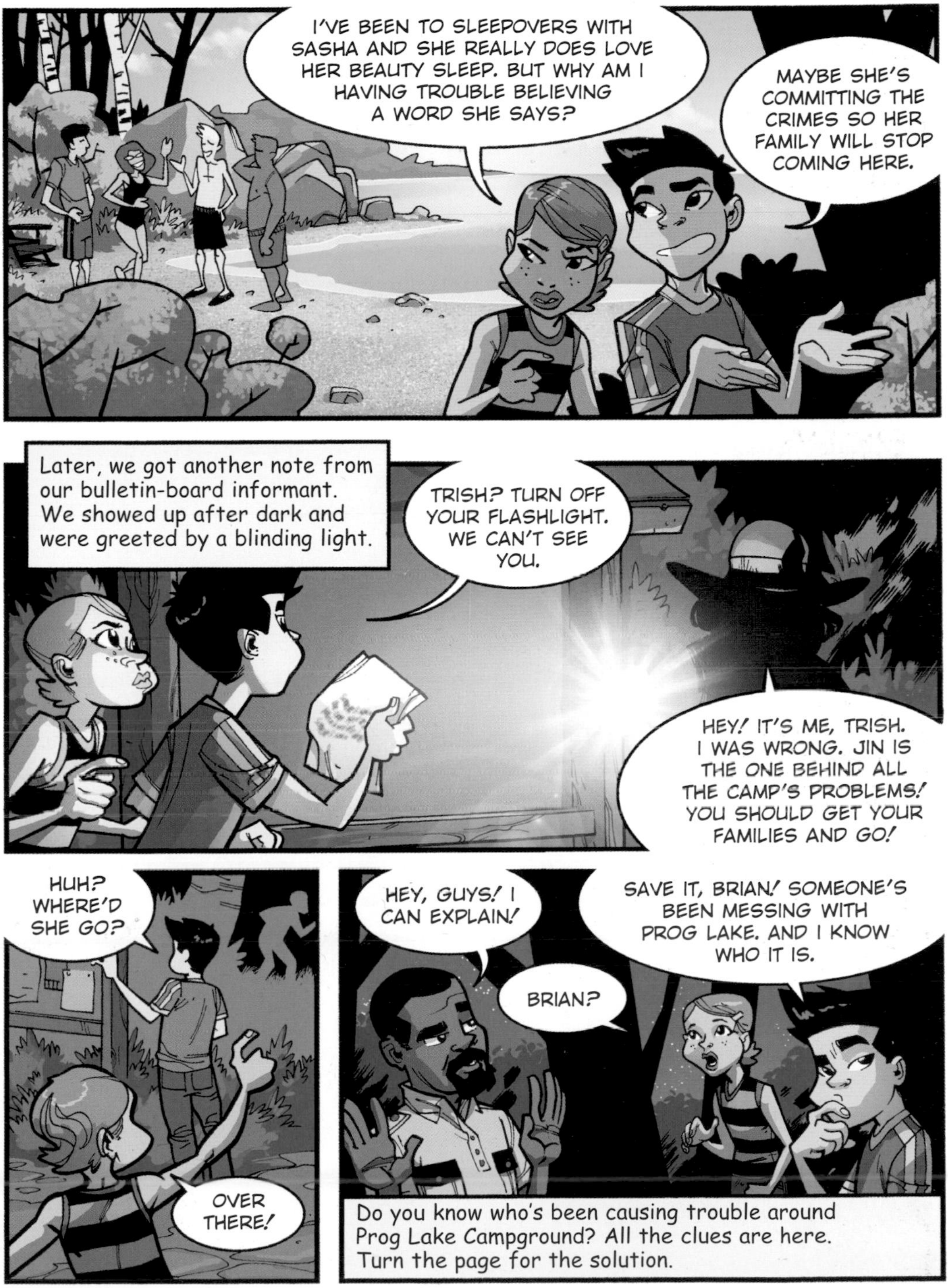
I'VE BEEN TO SLEEPOVERS WITH SASHA AND SHE REALLY DOES LOVE HER BEAUTY SLEEP. BUT WHY AM I HAVING TROUBLE BELIEVING A WORD SHE SAYS?
MAYBE SHE'S COMMITTING THE CRIMES SO HER FAMILY WILL STOP COMING HERE.
Later, we got another note from our bulletin-board informant. We showed up after dark and were greeted by a blinding light.
TRISH? TURN OFF YOUR FLASHLIGHT. WE CAN'T SEE YOU.
HEY! IT'S ME, TRISH. I WAS WRONG. JIN IS THE ONE BEHIND ALL THE CAMP'S PROBLEMS! YOU SHOULD GET YOUR FAMILIES AND GO!
HUH? WHERE'D SHE GO?
OVER THERE!
HEY, GUYS! I CAN EXPLAIN!
BRIAN?
SAVE IT, BRIAN! SOMEONE'S BEEN MESSING WITH PROG LAKE. AND I KNOW WHO IT IS.
Do you know who's been causing trouble around Prog Lake Campground? All the clues are here. Turn the page for the solution.

Solution: The Case of the...
Campsite Crime Spree

Who has been sabotaging Prog Lake Campground? Marta. She wanted to get Prog Lake shut down so she could have more customers at Camp Bernie.

Clues

* Marta told Mr. Jin it was BBQ night at Camp Bernie. The food garbage around the firepit the next morning—burgers and buns—was stuff you'd find at a BBQ. Marta dumped Camp Bernie's leftovers there to get Mr. Jin in trouble.
* When Max and Alison visited Camp Bernie, they spotted a drill that could have been used to make the holes in Kris Kroft's kayak. They also noticed a note that said Marta went to the dump after her BBQ. That gave her lots of time to drop her leftover food around the firepit—and to spy on Max and Alison talking to Trish. That's how Marta knew to pose as Trish to try to trick Max and Alison.
* When Max and Alison met Trish on the first night, she said, "My uncle," when referring to Mr. Jin. The informant on the second night called him "Jin." Marta was the only one who called him that.
* Alison said she could vouch for Sasha's early bedtimes. Because most of the campground crimes happened at night, Sasha couldn't have been the culprit.
* Brian told Max and Alison that he had to visit each campground twice a day. That's why he was hanging around Prog Lake Campground after dark.

Conclusion

After Max and Alison presented their evidence, Brian helped them look for Marta. As it was on the first night, her truck was parked near the bulletin board. Marta confessed to her crimes and apologized to Mr. Jin. Mr. Kroft and his son came back to Prog Lake, and Brian apologized to Mr. Jin. He also passed the illegal dumping fine on to Marta.

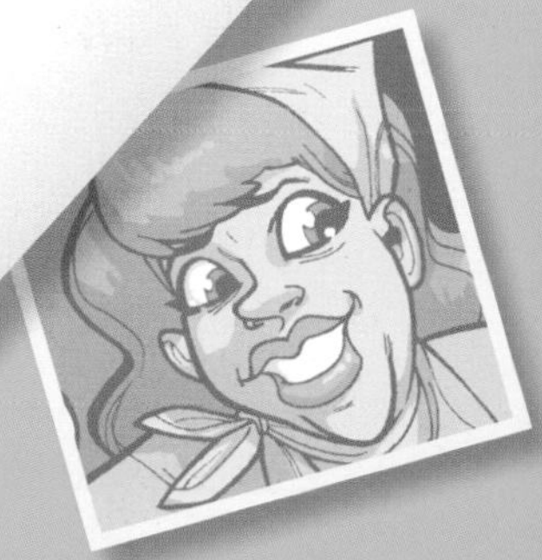

HOW to BE a Detective

Spoiler Alert!
The next few pages include actual clues from some of the cases in this book.

With Max Finder and Alison Santos!

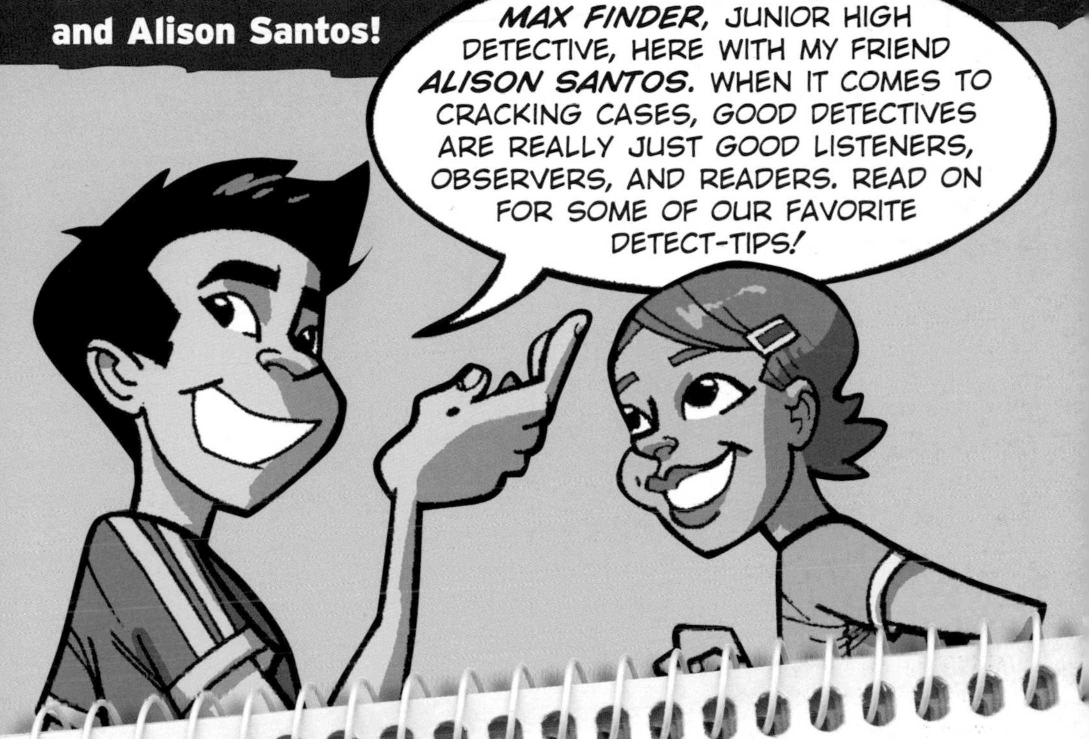
MAX FINDER, JUNIOR HIGH DETECTIVE, HERE WITH MY FRIEND ALISON SANTOS. WHEN IT COMES TO CRACKING CASES, GOOD DETECTIVES ARE REALLY JUST GOOD LISTENERS, OBSERVERS, AND READERS. READ ON FOR SOME OF OUR FAVORITE DETECT-TIPS!

CONDUCTING RESEARCH

MAX

First narrow your list of sources and potential suspects. You don't need to talk to everyone in a five-mile radius! In "The Case of the Mad Money," we knew that the culprit had access to the school's photocopier, so we started with the kids who volunteer in the principal's office after school. Before long we had our crooked counterfeiter.

ALISON

When it comes to interviews, ask probing questions: exactly where was the suspect when the crime took place? What was he or she doing? Listen closely for concrete details and alibis to figure out what to look for and who to cross off your list of suspects!

Detective Lingo!
Alibi (n.): a claim that one was elsewhere when an alleged act took place.

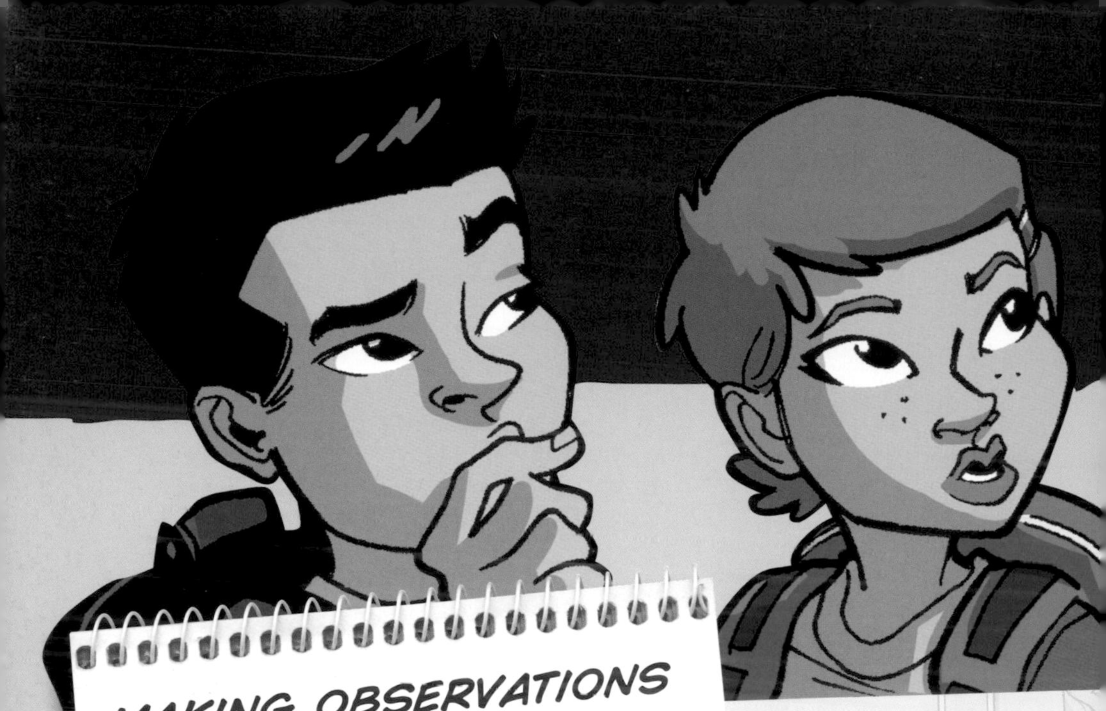

MAKING OBSERVATIONS

MAX

Not all information is spoken or written down. Small visual details matter a lot. Look for things that stand out or seem out of place, and assume that nothing is an accident. If something looks strange, it might be a red herring—but it also might be the key clue you need to crack your case.

ALISON

If you heard about a particular concrete detail from one of your sources or suspects—say someone suspicious was riding a pink bicycle, as in "The Case of the Graffiti Goon"—start looking out for it. And rack your brain to find out if you've seen that detail before.

Detective Lingo!

Red herring (n.): a misleading clue or distraction. Sometimes crafty criminals intentionally use red herrings to frame others or throw a detective off their scent.

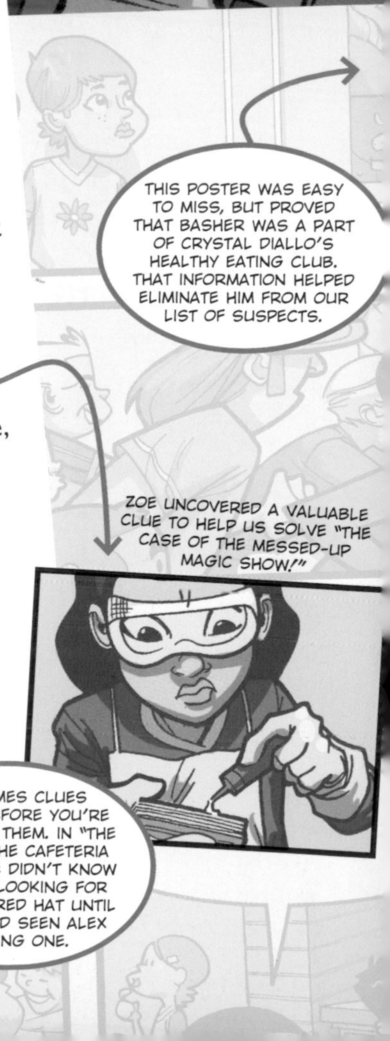
THIS POSTER WAS EASY TO MISS, BUT PROVED THAT BASHER WAS A PART OF CRYSTAL DIALLO'S HEALTHY EATING CLUB. THAT INFORMATION HELPED ELIMINATE HIM FROM OUR LIST OF SUSPECTS.
ZOE UNCOVERED A VALUABLE CLUE TO HELP US SOLVE "THE CASE OF THE MESSED-UP MAGIC SHOW!"
SOMETIMES CLUES APPEAR BEFORE YOU'RE READY FOR THEM. IN "THE CASE OF THE CAFETERIA CRISIS," WE DIDN'T KNOW WE WERE LOOKING FOR A KID IN A RED HAT UNTIL AFTER WE'D SEEN ALEX WEARING ONE.

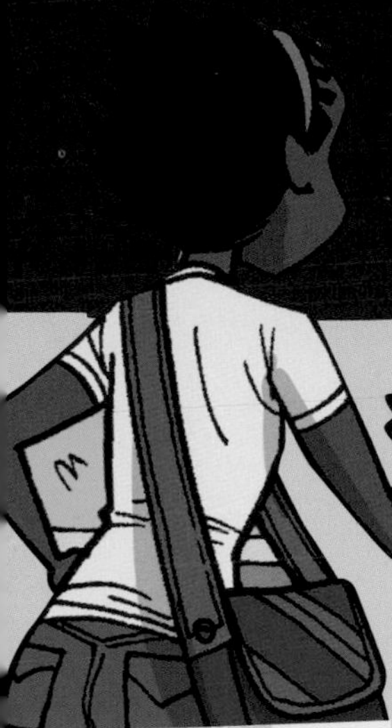

COMPLETING CASES

ALISON

Now it's time to add everything up—the info you gathered from interviews, the things you saw and overheard, and so on. What info connects with other info, and what leads you into a dead end? Whose testimony conflicts with someone else's? Make inferences about who's lying and who's telling the truth. This will help you connect the dots of the case and get you closer to a collar.

MAX

As Sir Arthur Conan Doyle—creator of Sherlock Holmes—said, "When you have eliminated the impossible, whatever remains... must be the truth." So your job is to eliminate the impossible. Ask yourself, "Who didn't do it?" as often as you ask yourself who did. The suspect you're left with after you eliminate everyone else is the criminal.

Detective Lingo!
Inference (n.): the forming of a conclusion based on new information and previous experience. This is also known as "reading between the lines."

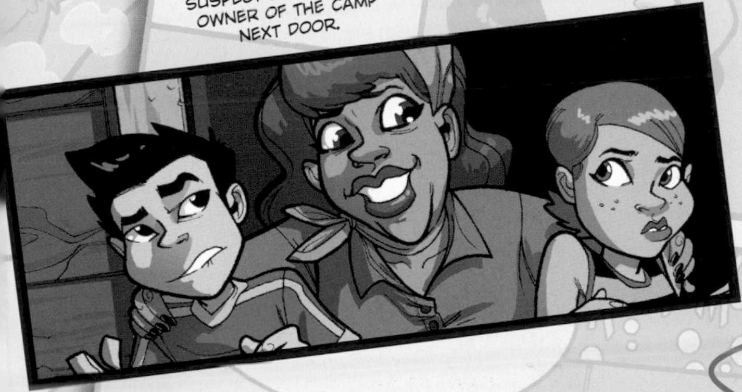
I CLOSED THIS CASE BY ELIMINATING EVERY SUSPECT BUT ONE, THE OWNER OF THE CAMP NEXT DOOR.
FOLLOW EVERY LEAD. IN "THE CASE OF THE MAD MONEY," ONE INTERVIEW LED TO ANOTHER, WHICH LED TO ANOTHER! EVENTUALLY ALL THE INTERVIEWS ADDED UP TO A COLLARED COUNTERFEITER!

Sit Down with the Creators

What's it like making the comics that make up Max Finder? We asked creator and original writer **Liam O'Donnell,** present writer **Craig Battle,** and illustrator **Ramón Pérez** some questions about their experiences and plans for the future of Max!

LIAM O'DONNELL

1 WHAT INSPIRES YOU TO COME UP WITH A STORY?

LO: Everything around me. I get mystery ideas when I'm out riding the streetcar or my bike, or even when I'm doing the dishes at home. Every story I write starts with me asking "What if..." and then the ideas bubble up from there.

CB: Everything! I look to my own experiences, the news, and sometimes even old movies. In fact, I based "The Case of the Halloween Heist" on *Clue*, a murder-mystery movie from the 1980s.

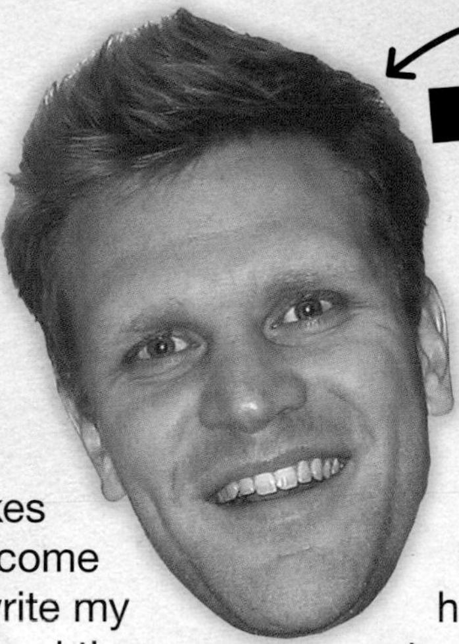

CRAIG BATTLE

2 HOW LONG DOES IT TAKE TO FINISH YOUR PART OF EACH COMIC?

LO: For me, it takes about a month to come up with an idea, write my pitch and outline, and then the final draft of the script. I'm not at my desk writing this whole time, but I'm always thinking about the plot or what clues Max and Alison and the reader need to solve the mystery.

CB: It changes from issue to issue. I start out with a pitch, which looks a lot like a two-page short story. That's where I figure out the basics of the mystery, and it takes about a day. Writing the actual comic often takes two full days or more.

RP: The comics are quite dense—image-wise and story-wise—and are quite heavy on dialogue. The most amount of time is spent on layout, making sure the images balance with the dialogue and everything that needs to be there is there. After that, things are relatively a breeze.

3 BESIDES MAX AND ALISON, WHO IS YOUR FAVORITE CHARACTER TO WORK ON AND WHY?

LO: All the characters in Whispering Meadows have a special meaning to me, because each one is inspired by a real person.

CB: Zoe is really interesting to me. She's younger than Max and Alison, so she doesn't quite have their instincts or street smarts. That said, her mom's a CSI, so solving crimes is in her blood.

RP: Basher, as bullies are fun to draw; Layne Jennings, whom I'm taking in a more punky direction than (original Max illustrator) Michael Cho did; and Zoe—she's a little younger than Max and Alison and I play that up by making her more animated.

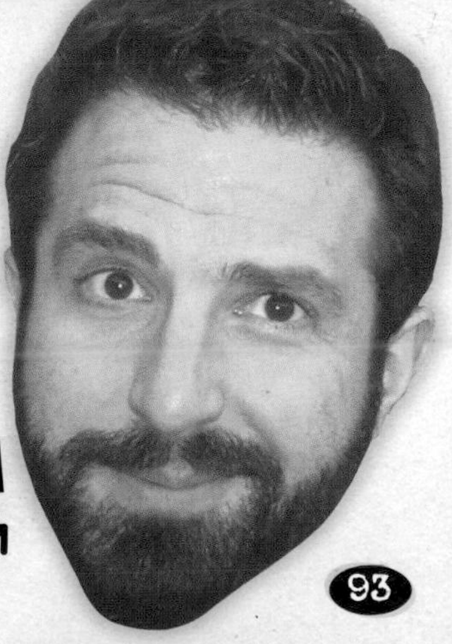

RAMÓN PÉREZ

4 WHAT IS YOUR FAVORITE PART OF WORKING ON MAX FINDER?

LO: I love thinking up new ways to hide the clues in the story. I want the clue to be just hard enough to give readers a challenge, but not so hard to find that they give up.

CB: I love writing the parts of the story where Max and Alison are just hanging out, trading good-natured barbs and stuff. They're really good friends, and I love how they interact.

RP: Tackling new characters and making them my own.

5 WHAT WOULD YOU LIKE TO SEE MAX AND ALISON DO IN THE FUTURE?

LO: I'd like to see Max and Alison crack a bigger case that has the local police stumped. I know they could do it.

CB: In the future, I want to see Max and Alison—in the future! I would love to do a flash-forward episode in which Max and Alison are adults—Max would be working as a private detective and Alison as a star journalist. That would be so cool.

RP: I would love to see a long-form mystery—perhaps a full Max Finder Mystery graphic novel. This would be a great opportunity to showcase many characters and go more in depth than we are able to do in four pages on a monthly basis.

6 WHERE DID LIAM'S IDEA FOR MAX FINDER MYSTERY COME FROM?

LO: When I was 10 years old, I loved a series of "you solve it" books called Encyclopedia Brown. He was a kid who solved mysteries in his neighborhood, but it was up to the reader to figure out the mystery. I thought it'd be fun to do the same style of story as a comic. I suggested the idea to OWL and they liked it. Even better, the readers liked it, too!

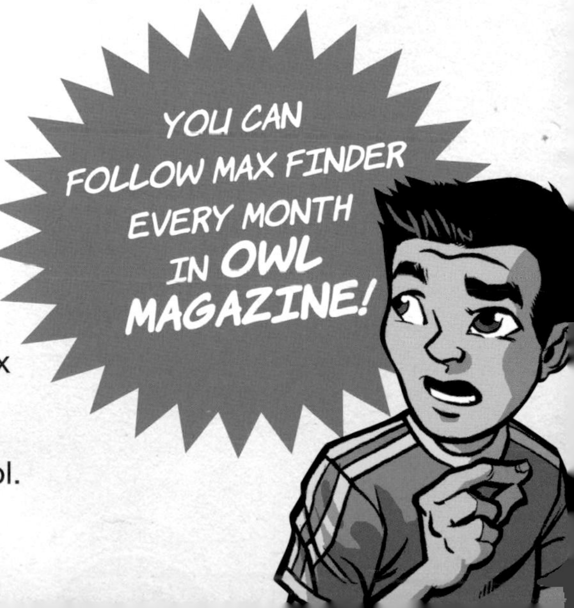
YOU CAN FOLLOW MAX FINDER EVERY MONTH IN OWL MAGAZINE!

Easy ways to use Max Finder in the classroom

Want to go beyond the mystery on the page? There are all sorts of fun challenges and ways to read Max Finder beyond just discovering a story's culprit. Every comic is loaded with lessons on character, mystery writing, graphic novel structure and more. Here are a few pointers to help get you off in the right direction.

Readers' Theater:
Assign the different characters to students in your class and have them read their parts aloud. The rest of the class can work together to solve the mystery.

Classroom connections: drama, language arts

Genre Study:
What makes a mystery? Students can work in groups to research the elements of mysteries—clues, suspects, detectives, red herrings—and present their findings to the rest of the class.

Classroom connections: language arts, media literacy

DIY Mystery:
Using the guide in Volume 3, students can write and illustrate their own mini-mystery, then trade with a partner and try to solve someone else's creation.

Classroom connections: language arts, media literacy, visual arts

Character Study:
Have students study the roles (bully, snitch, prankster) that Max Finder characters play over a number of the comics and graph the results. Is there a pattern?

Classroom connections: math, language arts, media literacy

Comic Format Study:
What makes a comic? Students can work in groups to research the conventions of comics—speech bubbles, caption boxes, paneled illustrations—and present their findings to the rest of the class.

Classroom connections: language arts, media literacy

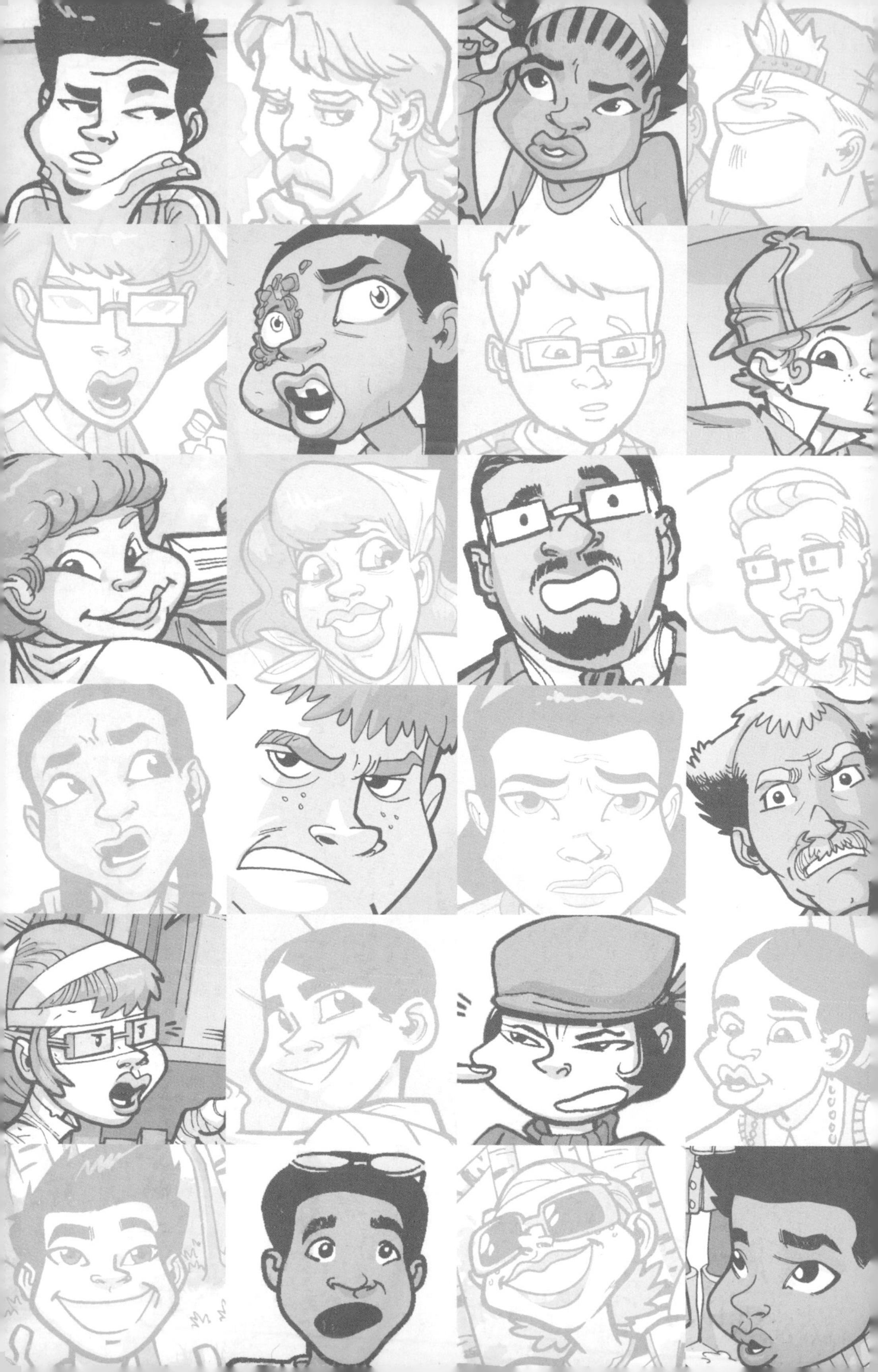